I AM A C[

German Sadulaev was born in 1973 and grew up in the village of Shali. At sixteen, before the start of the first Chechen war, he left to study law in St Petersburg. He lives there now and is the author of five books. Sadulaev's work has unleashed heated debate in Russia.

GERMAN SADULAEV

I am a Chechen!

TRANSLATED FROM THE RUSSIAN BY
Anna Gunin

VINTAGE BOOKS
London

Published by Vintage 2011

2 4 6 8 10 9 7 5 3 1

Copyright © German Sadulaev and Ultra Kultura 2006
English translation copyright © Anna Gunin, 2010

German Sadulaev has asserted his right under the Copyright,
Designs and Patents Act 1988 to be identified as the author
of this work

This book is sold subject to the condition that it shall not,
by way of trade or otherwise, be lent, resold, hired out,
or otherwise circulated without the publisher's prior
consent in any form of binding or cover other than that
in which it is published and without a similar condition,
including this condition, being imposed
on the subsequent purchaser

First published in Russian as *Ya – chechenets!*
by Ultra Kultura in 2006

First published in Great Britain in 2010 by
Harvill Secker

Vintage
Random House, 20 Vauxhall Bridge Road,
London SW1V 2SA

www.vintage-books.co.uk

Addresses for companies within The Random House Group Limited
can be found at: www.randomhouse.co.uk/offices.htm

The Random House Group Limited Reg. No. 954009

A CIP catalogue record for this book
is available from the British Library

ISBN 9780099532354

The Random House Group Limited supports the Forest
Stewardship Council® (FSC®), the leading international forest
certification organisation. All our titles that are printed on
Greenpeace approved FSC® certified paper carry the FSC® logo.
Our paper procurement policy can be found at
www.randomhouse.co.uk/environment

Typeset in Quadraat by Palimpsest Book Production Limited,
Falkirk, Stirlingshire
Printed and bound by CPI Group
(UK) Ltd, Croydon, CR0 4YY

Dedicated to the fond memory of
my mama, Vera Pavlovna Sadulaeva

One Swallow Doesn't Make a Summer

A Tale in Fragments

1

I could probably carry on living like this. In the morning turn off the alarm ringing on my mobile phone, brush my teeth, shave, run a bath and lie in the warm water for half an hour, dissolving the night's dreams. In the daytime walk or drive, shuffle papers, exercise my face muscles and vocal cords, do all those things known as 'work' and for which I'll be paid money. In the evening read books. One could live that way for ever. As though there were nothing else. As though nothing else had been.

And if there are dreams, then they are only dreams, they will dissolve in the morning, in the warm water.

And if there is memory, that too is dreams, it will dissolve in the stream of the street.

And if there are thoughts, they are of the dreams and of

the past; but the dreams have gone, and the past is also a dream.

And if my heart . . .

If my heart does not stop.

One day it will stop.

And I will tell you of my love, my fear, my loneliness, my grief and delight, my guilt towards you, Mama.

Can you forgive me? Remember when I walked along your meadows, sat by your brooks, embraced your trees, you purred to me as a cat on my lap, you sang as the swallows, you shone for me as the sapphire stars. I was your youngest, and you loved me, I know you loved me more than the others. Perhaps because I was sickly, weak and timid. A mother always loves most the one she pities. The others were proud, strong and independent, but I would come to you and lay my head on the flowers and the grasses, and you'd caress me. And my words took the form of verse, I sang you songs and read you poems in the tall thickets, the burdock standing high. And you smiled at me, yes, but you didn't laugh. You enveloped me in willow branches and hid me from others: let nobody see, let nobody say that my boy is feeble and crazy, for all my soul is in him.

And I loved you as no one else loved you. When you moaned from pain during gruelling nights and you cried, I sat with you on our old sofa, I stroked your legs all bumpy from your gout, and that terrible word 'blood-clot' – I burnt it with the fierce ray of my eyes, I dissolved it in my tears. And during the day I drowsed in class, stood silent at the blackboard, didn't answer the teachers, just collected my book and sat down. I couldn't say: My mama is ill. For the third night, my mama's pain won't let up.

And then I left you. It became stifling, terrifying, unbearable. I ran away. An enormous spider, here he comes, crawling across his delicate web – I'm terrified, terrified, Mama! I close my eyes. And suddenly the spider's gone. This is my nightmare, but I'll run away; I'll close my eyes and it will disappear.

2

I had wanted to run away for a long time. Because I knew that you had to die, and that you would die slowly, in agony. I couldn't watch it. Fear dwelled in me, Mama, fear!

You turned green with the fresh grass of the glades, you adorned yourself with chamomiles and dandelions, and with autumnal gold of the highest purity. And I felt the gouty bumps beneath your skin, with the grape juice I drank your blood, and it was too sweet, the sugar levels were too high, so the doctor said. And the clot, I saw it moving slowly along your arteries, deep beneath the earth, closer and closer to your delicate heart.

When the excavator bucket furrowed your beloved body, on the edge of the field, beyond our house, I went down to the bottom, I pressed my cheek against your warm, aromatic flesh. It pulsated and breathed, and it was sick. Sick with premonition.

Premonitions filled my mind. On the long path between home and school I silently counted the combat units, saw the maps of operations, played through the scenes of battles fought over each of your houses, at that time still calm and untroubled. They couldn't have been my thoughts: they were your thoughts, Mama, and you thought them through me. And I was terrified.

On my eighteenth birthday, I tried to run away for the first time. I came back from St Petersburg; my school friends assembled, boys and girls. The adults left and we drank sweet, scorching vodka. I was unused to drink, the alcohol robbed me of my outer senses; I got up and left the house as if bewitched. In the distance I saw the mountains, it was a clear day, and I saw the faraway blue mountains. And I headed for them. The others seized me, dragged me back. I tried to break away, shouting: 'I need to go, I must leave for the mountains, we all need to leave for the mountains otherwise it will be too late, soon it will be too late!' No one wanted to listen to me, but I knew: there was little time left.

Then I lost all strength, went limp and let them put me to bed. I awoke an hour later, almost choking on my vomit. I tried to say: Have no fear! I remember everything, I know what we must do. Hordes of nomads have come, an enormous cohort, hundreds of thousands of them, and the dust raised by the hooves of their horses is blotting out the sun. We'll take up arms on the plain and almost all of us will die. We will defend you, Mama! And you will mourn each of us with tears of bitter sap from the broken fern. And later, when too few of us remain, you'll say to us: 'Go to the mountains. Leave me here and don't grieve for me. I'll pretend to be dead, or no, I'll pretend to be alive, I'll leave my likeness here, bereft of blood, and, by night, past the guards' campfires, past the khans' tents, I'll creep after you, I'll find you in the mountains. One day you'll see my face in the mountain brook, you'll hear a maiden's laughter and realise that you never left your mother, and your mother never abandoned you. She is with you.'

And that's what we did. I left for the blue mountains; there, on the rocks, I built a tower from stone blocks and nearby, on a small plateau, I built a crypt where I lived on after death. And Mama came. At the edge of the gorge, on the narrow terraces, she pressed her warm cheek of fertile earth against me tenderly, she turned green with wheat and rye, her neat, supple, maidenly breast swelled each autumn, and I fell upon her nipples and she suckled me.

3

On the road to Vedeno, beyond Serzhen-Yurt, in the beech-forested Black Mountains, pioneer camps were held. I spent one summer there. In the mornings we had assembly, drill and breakfast. In the evenings there were dances in the asphalt square. And at night we broke out of the accommodation blocks, climbed over the tall fence and went to the Black Mountains. We knew the location of a slagheap where we could get white slate. We needed the slate to make towers.

Every Chechen must know how to build towers. We made our towers from the white slate, a truncated pyramid with battlements on the roof. We polished the slate with an aluminium spoon secretly smuggled out of the dining room, then dried it in the sun. Each child brought a tower home from the pioneer camp. A man must know how to make towers because the time will come when we'll leave for the mountains. And we'll build towers in order to survive.

My tower was in the library. One day, while dusting the bookcase, my sister brushed against it and the tower fell and smashed. My sister became serious, picked up all the pieces, stuck them together again, and, to hide the cracks, coated the tower in scarlet nail polish. Now my tower was blood red.

In fourteen years' time, my sister will fall in the village square, flattened by the blast wave of a surface-to-surface missile launched from a submarine or distant missile site. I'll fly to Narzan, walk into the hospital ward, gather her in my arms and carry her to an aeroplane. We'll set off for St Petersburg, and for one and a half years, doctors will pick up the pieces and stick her body together again.

4

Three hundred years passed; the nomads slew one another and scattered across the steppe, and the dust clouds raised by the hooves of their cavalry settled. Then I returned. I remember touching your breast – sunken, pummelled by the hooves of the military camps – with the wooden plough. And it was dry, barren of milk. I fell upon the ground, I embraced you and cried, Mama. Then we held rites. In the summer we caught snakes and hung them on trees. We plundered crows' nests. We ploughed up the bed of the dried river in both directions. And we looked towards the mountains. And you returned to us, Mama. The next spring you shyly bared your shoulder, the black earth was tilled, and once more the milk flowed for us.

No need to fear the moment when death comes; we'll leave for the mountains and build towers there.

5

But I did not leave for the mountains. I boarded a train and returned to the northern city. And I was not there with you. Can you forgive me, Mama?

I was not with you when the first heavy bombs fell, when you had nothing to cover your body with, when your dress ripped, the crater wounds turned your womanly flesh inside out, and even the cruel, shameless sky shut his eyes. I should have cleaved to your wounds, I should have shielded you from at least one shrapnel fragment, washed your body with my blood, pressed my face to you and absorbed your pain, but I was not there with you.

You hurried to the bomb shelter, already half blind, with pain in your legs, linking arms with your friend and neighbour, a Russian nurse whom the whole neighbourhood loved. She was known as Aunty Dasha – everyone remembers her, lame from birth – and a pilot fired at you with his machine gun just for fun and you started crying and sat down at the roadside. Because you couldn't go any faster on your tired legs, deformed by your gouty joints and varicose veins, and Aunty Dasha sat down with you and cried too. The pilot's ammunition ran out and he flew off. You lifted your white hand, stretched it upwards, looked to the sky with eyes that could now barely see, and said, 'Damn you!'

You had no Stinger rockets, no anti-aircraft guns, no surface-to-air missiles or air defence radars. Only your curse, addressed to the sky with its host of powerless angels and to the pilot at the controls of the fighter. Dark clouds cloaked the sky, and it rained for three days. The pilot was brought down by a single shot from a Kalashnikov; they found him on the ground, tangled in the cords of his parachute, and cut his throat.

But I – I was not there with you.

And when the heavy tank tracks crushed you, when the attacks persisted for days on end, when you bled, your houses falling, demolished by vacuum bombs, when you quietly moaned in pain in the far room of our house, when you stopped covering the shrapnel marks on the walls and gave up reglazing the windows, I was not there.

I was afraid to see you when I came back. I was afraid to look into your eyes. I returned and realised that I needn't have feared finding reproach in your eyes. When I returned and saw your eyes, there was none in them. They were blind. And the house was blind, with empty eye sockets for windows.

But you took my hand in yours and said, 'Hello, son! It's good you're home.'

6

It's hard to be a Chechen. If you're a Chechen, you must feed and shelter your enemy when he comes knocking as a guest; you must give up your life for a girl's honour without a second thought; you must kill your blood foe by plunging a dagger into his chest, because you can never shoot anyone in the back; you must offer your last piece of bread to your friend; you must get out from your car to stand and greet an elderly man passing on foot; you must never run away, even if your enemy are a thousand strong and you stand no chance of victory, you must take up the fight all the same. And you can never cry, no matter what happens. Your beloved women may leave you, poverty may lay waste to your home, your comrades may lie bleeding in your arms, but you may never cry if you are a Chechen. If you are a man. Only once, once in a lifetime, may you cry: when your mother dies.

At the very beginning of the war, my elder sister asked our parents to join her in Novorossiysk. Mama and Papa didn't want to, they still believed that the war would be short, that it was all a terrible mistake, a misunderstanding, and would be over soon; they didn't want to abandon their native soil. They went to visit my sister, watched television, believed it again when military operations were said to be at an end, and returned home despite their daughter's pleas. This happened many times over, until finally our parents decided to stay with her. So they moved, leaving our second sister, Zarema, behind in Shali. Zarema had married and flatly refused to leave.

After a long, difficult life, after a terrible war, Mother and Father spent three years in Novorossiysk, their happiest years. Until then something or other had always got in the way, stopping them from simply being together. First there was work, Father's drinking with colleagues, guests, quarrels with relatives. Then prison. And the war. But all that had passed. Mama was already blind, severely ill, how could they have been happy? Yet they were. All day long Father was with Mama. They chatted, they no longer hurried anywhere. Every evening he took her arm and they would go out for long walks, especially during the summer when the south makes you drunk with its scents and dizzy with its warmth. All the neighbours looked at them in fond envy, the couple in love, together for more than thirty years.

When Zarema was wounded, Mama's condition began to deteriorate alarmingly. That surface-to-surface missile brought death nearer, cost my father and mother several years, several years of true happiness.

Within a year Zarema was much better, she was almost cured, but Mama... Our elder sister called, and we flew from St Petersburg that very day. When we reached the apartment, Mama was still alive, or... I'm not sure. Could she hear us, did she realise that we were near her? Could she feel me holding her hand? Mama was in a coma all night. She passed away in the morning.

In the house the mirrors were covered, so I didn't see myself. My sister looked at me and said, 'Your temples are grey.' I'd turned grey overnight.

And I cried out my tears. Just once in a lifetime a man may cry, and at that time he cries out all his tears, a whole lifetime's worth, for all that has been and all that is yet to come.

In the morning I went outside and looked at the world. Feeling a light, ringing hollowness. There was no more fear. That morning I stopped being afraid. Nothing bad can happen now. It has all happened already. There will be no more tears. I shall never cry again.

7

Death no longer terrifies me. See, death is no longer a parting: death is a meeting with you, Mama.

And I plead for your forgiveness. I kiss your hands, your flowers, your grasses, I smooth your hair and embrace your earth. For my unvoiced love, for unspent tenderness, for not being with you for so many years, forgive me, Mama! Can you forgive me?

Can your mountains forgive me, the blue distant ones, seen only in clear weather, and the black close ones, visible always; can your gardens forgive me, your golden fields, your scarlet roses along the roadside, the lilac and the acacia, your spring breezes and autumn rains, your clouds and stars?

Can your swallows forgive me?

8

Let me tell you about the swallows.

Spring in the Caucasus starts early. In February the snows disappear, in March the lilac is already in bloom. The lilac lilac – for what else can we call this colour, if it's the colour of lilac – and the white. I remember on 8 March[1] the lilac is already in bloom, and we go to school to congratulate our teachers, all carrying armfuls of lilac. It's planted along the roadside and in the central square, and in people's gardens lilac grows too.

Lilac tells you the grades you'll get that term. Most of the flower heads have three or four tiny flowers, but sometimes you get heads with five.[2] We pull them apart, a twig at a time, looking for our grades of excellence.

And in April the orchards are already in flower: the apple orchards are in blossom, the pear and cherry trees blossom, and the peach trees blossom in tender pink flowers. In May the first cherries ripen.

But only when the swallows arrive does it become quite clear that tomorrow will be summer.

Each year they fly here on a different date. I don't know who supplies them with such accurate weather forecasts, but they always arrive a day ahead of summer. Nobody supplies the trees with such forecasts. The trees hurry into flower, and it may happen that a late cold spell will dash the flowers to the frosty ground. But the swallows always arrive on time.

We all wait, we search the sky, and everyone wants to be the first to spot them. At last the day arrives, and some lucky soul hurries home, overjoyed as if a miracle had occurred: I saw the swallows, they've come.

It's always as if we're unsure, we are never quite certain they'll come back. They flew here last year, and the year before, but maybe they won't come this year, and then – then what will we do? How will we live if the swallows fail to return?

I don't know where they fly to, perhaps it's worth asking the ornithologists, although it would be better to ask the children. Every child knows where the swallows fly away to at the onset of autumn: of course, they fly to the warm fairytale land where the summer spends the winter months. And they fly back, carrying summer on their elegant wings, slicing through the warming air. But no, summer comes the day after, perhaps the swallows are the vanguard or the reconnaissance squad, they fly ahead and inform the summer by Morse code, in whistles and chirps: 'All clear! You can come now.' And summer comes, summer occupies our villages, but this is an army of liberation, and the earth greets the summer with ripening fruits and brilliant flowers in the green meadows.

Perhaps, the ornithologists will say, they winter in Syria or in Africa. But do the ornithologists know why they fly back? For four brief months, from a faraway warm land, to rear their young hurriedly then fly off again: why don't they stay in the never-ending summer, what lures them from their climatic migration? They are simply flying home; in this there is no logic other than the logic of love. So each year we wonder: when will the swallows arrive? Or perhaps they won't come?

If there's no love left in the world, if the motherland is wherever you feel warmest, then they won't return. That means we too need not live here; it means everyone should find the place that's warmest for him.

9

And here they are, but that's not all. On the first day, flocks of swallows swirl among the houses over streets stationary in anticipation. The swallows choose sites for their nests. And in secret jealousy neighbours eye those beneath whose roofs birds already cheep, and again, each thinks: Will no swallows build their nests and rear their chicks over my threshold this year? Could my house have been cursed?

At long last, early in the morning, as they're leaving the house, they notice with relief: Here they are, already fussing and fitting their bits of clay and straw, building their nests on to the wall. That means all is well, all will be well, my house will remain standing, my family will survive. And if two pairs of swallows begin building nests on opposite sides of the house, it's doubly good: This year my son will bring home a bride and I'll have grandchildren.

The swallow is a totem, a sacred bird, to kill a swallow is a grave sin. Nobody kills swallows. We are cruel children, we practise our marksmanship by hitting sparrows with catapults, we set traps for pigeons. Sometimes we kill pigeons just for fun, sometimes we light a campfire in the field and roast their tender meat on the flames, but we never shoot at swallows. I suppose we were told from an early age never to do that, or perhaps not, I don't actually remember anyone telling us not to, it's just that we never shot at swallows.

And even the cats. Our cat, a glorious specimen of an ancient genus, a breed mixed in the extreme – with kittens as black as coal, blue as topaz, cinnamon-coloured – is the fourth generation to bear the name Pushka. Pushka the Fourth, that's what I call her. Her distant ancestor was given to my grandmother as a little fluffy ball; at first everyone thought it was a tomcat and they chose the name Pushok.[3] But Pushok turned out to be a girl. Rather than giving her a new name, they simply adapted her old one. Thus, Pushka[4] the First, then Pushka the Second, the Third and Fourth. Cat ancestry passes down the female line – just you go and try finding the father of a kitten among the neighbourhood's tailed Don Juans.

Pushka the Fourth is not just a huntress: she's a dedicated worker. She regularly flattens rats and mice but she never eats them. She understands that this is her duty, what she is expected to do. One evening, when the family was gathered in front of the television, Father complained about the hamsters gnawing at the roots of the pumpkins in the kitchen garden; the cat sat nearby and listened attentively. The next morning a row of nine crushed hamsters lay on the doorstep in the yard, the entire guilty clan. The cat sat nearby, waiting for praise and recognition of her service. And, of course, she ate not one of them.

Our cat preferred bird's meat.

One warm summer day, Mama was busy about the yard, Pushka was basking in the sunshine, the swallow chicks were attempting their first clumsy flights. Out of habit the cat coiled herself into a spring, following their moves attentively. Mama grabbed hold of her broom and with surprising steel in her voice addressed the cat: 'Just you dare!' That's what Mama told her.

Our cat never did hunt swallows. And after that she didn't even eye them, and when the chicks ran about the yard, she deliberately looked the other way, her entire appearance announcing: Oh no, they're not of the slightest interest to me, those swallows of yours.

10

I suppose the swallows die. The bulk of them must die during the migration. If, out of two generations that take to the wing over a summer, just one bird remains alive, it will instinctively return to the house where it hatched and repair its nest, or sometimes build it anew.

But we don't see the dead swallows. For us, swallows are immortal. And the swallow who flies back this spring is the same swallow who flew back last spring, the same swallow who has always flown back.

Swallows are the souls of our ancestors. My mama will never die, she will become a swallow, she'll fly to me from a faraway land, across the seas and mountains, she'll be an angel, watching me from the skies, but from low skies, very low, no higher than the eaves above my door. What can angels see from so far away, from beyond the clouds?

And when young children die, they turn straight into swallows.

11

I was already fairly big when I found out that I had actually had three sisters. Mama had named the very first Tanya. She died in infancy. At that time Mother and Father lived high up in the old house, with Father's brothers. Our village, Shali, is divided into the upper and lower parts, along the course of the river.

She was buried in the cemetery but without funeral rites. Children don't need rites. They are innocent, they need no purification, no priests or prayers; children become angels immediately, but if they love us dearly then they don't fly high above the feathery clouds, they become swallows and live with us.

The following year Mama and Papa moved to a new house in the lower part of the village. Their very own home, beautiful, spacious, and free from the uncomfortable proximity of large numbers of neighbouring relatives. Yet a house is nothing but empty walls until love dwells there.

So, Mama awaited her first spring in the new place with trepidation. And look, all the neighbours have swallows building nests in their houses of course, they are the fledglings from last year, they remember their homes, whereas our new house stands soulless and empty. How her mother-in-law had wished that Papa wouldn't marry a Russian. Their first child was dead. Almost every night Mama cries quietly, burying herself in the pillow, all alone in the far room of the house. She doesn't dare say a word against her husband's parents. Could they be right? Will nothing come of it, will the beautiful love between a quarrelsome Russian girl and a fine fellow – an amateur actor and first-rate tractor driver, later the chairman of the Party Committee, later still the director of the State Farm – turn out to be a barren flower?

But the very first spring the swallows came. Mama went out with her cloth, wiped away the droppings from the freshly painted doorstep and watched the amorous pair busily weaving their nest. Once again tears filled her eyes, but these were bright, clear tears of happiness.

From that day on Mama straightened her shoulders, her voice became confident and firm. Mama put her husband's entire clan in their place. Now nobody could say a single hurtful word to her. She was a lawful wife. A mother. The mistress of the house. Swallows flew to her.

One after another, in the new house, two beautiful and clever daughters were born, and third came a son. Mama no longer went to the cemetery, to the unmarked little mound beside the fence. Only from time to time, glancing at her swallow chirping trustfully over her brood, she'd quietly murmur, 'Tanya . . .'

12

The war began in winter. The New Year blitzkrieg, the plan to take Grozny with tank forces, failed miserably. On the streets of the city Russian tanks burned; inside the tanks burned soldiers. The radio waves dripped with blood, spewing out dying men's curses and the call, reedy as a tuning fork, desperate as a newborn babe's cry: 'Request reinforcements, reinforcements, reinforcements!'

Reinforcements never came. War began – genuine, deathly slow war. Fresh combat units entered Ichkeria[5] from the north. The first tanks and armoured personnel carriers in the first villages on the invasion route were met by women bearing flowers. The flowers fell to the mud, under the wheels and the heavy tracks. The bombardments and mop-up operations began. The women went out again to meet the troops, throwing down their headscarves in front of the military vehicles.

Chechen custom decreed that even if two blood foes stood face to face with their daggers drawn, a woman could stop the fight by letting her hair down and throwing her headscarf between the men. But who knew about Chechen customs? The scarves fell to the mud, under the wheels and the heavy tracks.

Then the women went home. Out of the houses emerged children. Boys of twelve disabled tanks and infantry combat vehicles with grenades, pelted them with petrol bombs. Getting the first vehicle in the column and the last. And then from behind cover you could shoot at the whole sub-unit.

The Federal[6] units responded to this embittered resistance with carpet-bombing, with artillery, mortar and rocket shelling of the villages. House after house was reduced to rubble, interring people beneath.

13

And in the spring?

In the spring the swallows arrived. They appeared in their tailcoats, festive and happy. They whirled in flocks along the familiar streets, started searching for their nests.

Have you ever heard swallows scream? Do you think they cannot scream? Swallows chirp, peal, twitter, their high-pitched warbles modulating; how could they scream?

That spring, panic-stricken flocks of birds flew over the ruins of the houses and screamed, continually, mournfully, inconsolably.

Ornithologists will say that this is impossible, that it simply does not happen. But when the swallows saw dust and ashes where only last summer they'd left their nests, they didn't stay in their homeland. Dashing about the streets, they flew back, to the fairytale warm land where the summer spends the winter months.

Because in our land no love remains. Only death.

14

Let me tell you about the mountains.

We have lived on a plain for three hundred years but the mountains are always nearby; in the morning they are an arm's length away, and in the evening they are an arm's length away; only on summer days when the air ripples in the sultry heat do they seem far away, yet on sultry days even the water tower seems far away, though I can run to it for a bet in ten minutes.

The mountains guard us to the south. The mountains await us, that's why we live on the plain; we don't bury ourselves under the ground like hamsters, and we don't fly away into the sky like swallows: we live along the sloping banks of the muddy river. If misfortune comes, we can always flee to the mountains. There each clan has its own rock; upon the rock stands a tower, tall and impregnable; inside it are arrow slits, wide from within and narrowing towards the outer wall, so that an archer may stand in comfort. Near the tower is a vault, within it live our ancestors, we don't bury them under the ground, no, we place them on the stone slabs of the vault, and they are always near us. In the evenings we visit them to talk of our affairs and hear their mute advice. But when an enemy appears and every warrior in the clan counts, they too rise to the arrow slits. When a battle is waged, no warrior is surplus. If misfortune comes, we can flee to the mountains.

Misfortune always comes from the north.

15

In the north is the Great Steppe. On the steppe live nomadic people – a wild-spirited people. There are many of them, always so many, thousands. They sweep across the steppe on steeds as fast as hurricanes. When hurricanes blow from the north, they twist trees from the roots, rip roofs from the houses, flatten the barley and wheat to the earth.

The wind carries a cloud of dust – a storm of dust, and the arrows too fly in storms, yet we stand on the plain, shoulder to shoulder. We defend the mountains. The dust makes our eyes water, blood runs down our faces, then we fall, and whoever remains will leave for the mountains.

What is our land to these shrieking nomads? She is neither wife nor mother: she is a random girl caught in the rider's lasso. And here they hoot and guffaw, a furious glint glowing in their narrow eyes, their steeds whinnying, they seize the girl by the hair and drag her into the tent. Inside, ripping away her green clothes, they rape her. Their members bristling, their faces burning in anticipation of their pleasure, they enter her in a frenzy. But her loins stay dry, causing the rapist pain, yielding no delight. Then they kindle the lamps and see: on the carpet lies not a girl but a doll of dry clay mixed with manure, with straw on her head and crotch instead of hair. Where is the girl? How did she trick them?

Enraged, the nomads burn the forests and mountain villages; their flamethrower reaches seven hundred metres, eight hundred at most, but there are also mortars, long-range guns, multiple-launch rocket systems called 'Hail' and 'Hurricane', and in the faraway sea floats a submarine for launching surface-to-surface missiles.

After three hundred years, they depart for the Great Steppe, only to return later with new horses and new faces.

16

One day they came quietly from the Great Steppe, on downcast steeds. They had neither spears nor arrows, only a big book which decreed what people should do from dawn till dusk, for six days. And that people should do nothing on Saturday.

They said: We are poor and we've been driven out, our land has been ravaged. Take us in, allow us to live with you. We won't be a nuisance, we'll build our villages in the most distant mountains, where even the narrow terraces hold no soil. We'll adopt your tongue, learn your dances and songs. Don't drive us out!

And the mountains took them in. But the nomads didn't begin ploughing and sowing, rather they learnt that you can steal all you need from your neighbour while he sleeps. They started to trade, exchanging barley from one mountain village for wheat from another, and this trading too was akin to thievery, and the ploughmen of the two villages thought: How is it that they gather neither barley nor wheat yet enjoy the one and the other in abundance, while our granaries remain empty?

Then they set the clans one against another, and fighting broke out everywhere, and even within the clans blood flowed; whereupon they nodded their heads and spoke: 'Yes thus was it enjoined, each man for himself, thus spoke the god of the big book.' And many of the clans burnt the wooden body of Mother Tusholi[7] and went to join them and their big book, because the newcomers told them their god was the most powerful, and they believed it.

The earth alone responded to the wild-spirited people; her loins turned dry, and her eyes became moist. That was worse than the hurricane from the steppe.

17

Still further north, beyond the Great Steppe, is the Land of Snow. There live people in the skins of beasts, whose hands grip not the curved sabres of the nomads; rather, straight, long swords. In that land are cities and villages, plentiful honey and butter, the girls are lovely as the morning and bring happiness, because golden wheat grows straight from their heads.

But the wild-spirited people from the Great Steppe descend on the villages and burn them down, storm the cities, take the girls into captivity, as the sun is stolen by the night. They sell the girls, fair as the sun, overseas and receive round gold coins; they trample down the sowings, and all that is reaped they take for themselves; they slaughter cattle and feast on the meat boiled up in huge kettles.

The Land of Snow wails, it cries for its suns.

But here the brave people of the Land of Snow have assembled a retinue and set forth on a campaign to the Great Steppe. When their prince, his wife and child fell captive to the nomads, a youth from the south helped them escape and promised to shelter them in the mountains. Because we are brothers, we stand together and hold the Great Steppe: some from the north, others from the south.

18

Let me tell you more about the mountains.

The mountains come in many colours. There are the Black Mountains, and the blue mountains with white snowy caps, under a hazy veil of clouds. If you drive south from Shali the road will lead to Serzhen-Yurt and straight after Serzhen-Yurt begin the Black Mountains. They are not even mountains but foothills, a ridge of large, wooded hills. The Black Mountains are an ancient range. Once they were rocky, but time, the wind and the rivers running through them transformed these mountains into hills. Their summits and slopes became blanketed in beech forests. When summer arrives, and the trees come into leaf, the hills look dark green. In autumn they are ablaze with gold, bronze and copper. And when the leaves fall away, and the branches are left bare, the woods look black from afar, and the mountains seem black.

Further, beyond Serzhen-Yurt, lies Vedeno. There the blue

mountains begin. They are of rock; this is a young range, the backbone of the Caucasus.

Looking from Shali, the Black Mountains will always be visible, whereas the faraway mountains are often shrouded in the horizon's clouds. But on a clear, sunny day – it seems so like a miracle, dream or mirage – all of a sudden the blue mountains appear, enchanting and beckoning. We gaze at them for a long time and every detail becomes visible: the summits and slopes, the outlines of glaciers, the winding ribbons of rivers.

Then I hear my heart sing: Go! Go to the mountains. There in the mountains is your clan's rock; upon it stands the stone tower; near it lies the vault. There the sky becomes closer, there is silence and the music of pure mountain rivers, there you can wait for the end of this era, this Iron Age, in which people once more have gone mad. And long this music resounds in me.

19

I have noticed that I often confuse the four directions. The mountains have always seemed to be in the north. I remember where the sun rises: if you stand facing the mountains, the sun comes up on the left, and the fire of the sunset blazes to the right. So the mountains lie south. If you stand facing north, then the east will be to the right. That's what they taught us at school. In our geography lessons we were taught – I remember the maps – here's the Caucasian range, we live to its north, south of it is Transcaucasia. I was always a good student, I remember it all.

Why then does it seem that the mountains lie north?

Perhaps because even in summer snow rests on the summits of the faraway mountains. Snow means cold, winter, the north. Where the ice never melts, where the winter resides during summer.

Or perhaps because to the north of the Indus valley stand the Himalayas, whither, thousands of years ago, I also withdrew to die before the arrival of the Iron Age.

20

Creech-creech, squeak the wheels of the carts. The solid wooden wheels, without rims, hubs or spokes. Just a thick disc of wood. To the carts are yoked bulls; upon the carts sit women and children. Alongside the carts ride the men on horseback. Here the eldest man gives the signal to stop. It is already growing dark, we shall stop here for the night. The carts form a circle on the bank of a stream; inside the circle they kindle a fire.

The man is named Ger, because in his hands is a spear: a spear is called 'ger' in his people's tongue. They have come from afar, their journey has lasted for hundreds of years. At one time there was a host of tribes, a multitude of peoples, fair-headed, fiery-haired, tawny and black as the coal they use to caulk their barks. They left the shores of the warm sea and headed for the rising sun. They left the old wars, fought over ever-diminishing land, but found only new wars in new parts. Along the way and during the battles they died, they were burnt in communal funeral pyres, their high burial mounds strewn across the steppe. In a new land far away, where wide rivers flow, where the mountains lie to the north, they subdued the local tribes of swarthy peoples. Yet the warring did not cease, the tribes started to fight, one against the other, exterminating generation after generation. Some left for the setting sun; thus will they complete their circle, and their journey will end.

When the sun rose, Ger awoke and went to the river to wash his body. On the high bank, a family priest sat rapt, looking into the distance. The morning was clear, the clouds had dispersed, and on the horizon mountains appeared, blue ones with white peaks, which had not been visible yesterday.

The priest saw Ger, pointed with his palm to the mountains and said, 'There lies Asgard, City of the Gods.' Ger nodded and walked down to the river. Cupping the water in his palms, he washed. Swallows flew above the river. They lived here, making their nests in the tiny caves of the sheer, high bank.

Ger entered the water. The current was swift and powerful. When he had washed, Ger came out and walked to the carts. The women and children had already awoken, the children were running around, the women began preparing food. Ger watched a pair of swallows fussing near his cart, plucking out straw and carrying it to their nest.

The priest saw this too. He walked up and said, 'This is a good sign. We can stay here. There is no need to travel further. We'll take our water from the river, not far off is the forest, we'll build our houses from the thick tree trunks, and there, a little further on, in the middle of the field stands a high, woodless hill. On its summit we can kindle a holy fire and offer a sacrifice.'

I remember all this. Remember the carts and the worn-out people. Remember their bulls, their cows and horses. Remember how at the break of dawn they lit a fire on the top of the hill, fed the flame with clarified butter and chanted invocations. I still dream of it sometimes. When I close my eyes, I see it clearly. Only I see it from above – not from too high up, not from the distant heavens. I see it from the level of a bird's flight. From the level of a swallow aloft over the land in spring.

21

The war is over, the war ended long ago. They have written so in the newspapers and said so on television. In Chechnya civilian life is resuming. On the television they showed the schools opening again. On 1 September, Day of Knowledge, they hold a lesson about peace in all the schools. There is no more war. The dour generals have declared that the rebel gangs are smashed, that the separatists are no longer capable of organised resistance. Only the remnants of the gangs are sheltering in the forests and the mountains, but they will all be eliminated. Tomorrow. Or next week. After the weekend.

When spring arrives, and the forests burst into leaf, and after spring comes summer, the dour generals say: The bandits are making use of the 'growth' to evade detection, if it weren't for the 'growth' we'd have eliminated them by now. I never realised you could call it that – when spring arrives, and the forests are covered in leaves as tender as the skin of a newborn babe – 'growth'.

And when autumn arrives, and after autumn comes winter, the dour generals say: There is rain in the mountains, visibility is very poor, when the slopes freeze over and the roads turn into ice rinks it is difficult to manoeuvre our motorised units, the remaining armed gangs are making use of this to attack villages, capture them, then return to the mountains.

All year long, trucks filled with soldiers are blown up on the roads, officials serving the administration are fired at, terrorist acts are carried out in Grozny. Chechnya is at peace, Chechnya has long enjoyed stability – a stability which people in the Russian heartland could but dream of; here, jobs in law enforcement are even for life. For the full two weeks of life you'll have left.

The war has ended; perhaps soon they will even reduce the size of the limited contingent of troops based in Chechnya. Yet the artillery remains. And, in order to justify their combat pay, they fire shells.

Sometimes the soldiers tire of firing – the heavy artillery rounds make their heads ache and their ears pop. They collect the shells, carry them to the woods, bury them in the earth. A week later, they inform their mates in the infantry of the location of the buried ammunition. A special operation is mounted, then they announce on television: 'The rebels' latest cache has been discovered, along with a supply of explosives. Another terrorist act has been successfully averted.' The infantry too earn their combat pay.

But some of the shells are fired. Each night the artillery based outside Shali fires into the mountains. Officially the shelling is aimed according to bearings, according to intelligence received about clusters of combatants. But they cannot have such data every night. They are simply firing into the mountains. As if the mountains were at war with them.

Each night the heavy shells fly howling over the houses in the direction of the mountains and explode with a boom somewhere far away. The mountains shudder and moan, yet they are tremendously large. To kill the mountains you would need to fire for a tremendously long time.

That will indeed be a famous victory. When the mountains die.

When they are razed to the earth, and this proud range stands no longer. *Gordost* – pride – and *gory* – mountains: they share the same root. There'll be no more pride of the mountains, just the docility of the plains. Or the emptiness of the steppe.

No more mountains, only the Great Steppe, without end and without border.

22

They say that an ass who's experienced the shade won't work again in the blaze of the sun. We won't return to Chechnya. The Chechens of Moscow, St Petersburg, Omsk, Yaroslavl, Voronezh, Saratov, Astrakhan, Perm and God knows where else. The Russian Chechens. We have grown used to life here. Even when hounded with surveillance, rejected by employers, refused police registration, and then told by those same police to cough up for not being registered, we'll stay here all the same. And not just those on whom fate has smiled, who have become wealthy and successful in Russia. But also those who drift from rented flat to rented flat, earning each day only enough bread for the next.

We have become feminine and weak, we can no longer live under the harsh gaze of the faraway mountains. To follow our tribal laws, answer with our lives for every word, weigh each action knowing that our children will be held to account, that all will be revealed to everyone, and in a hundred years' time our descendants will be reproached for the ignominious behaviour of their ancestors. To preserve one's chastity, practise abstinence, know only one's wife. In the freedom of Russia, Chechen men follow different rules: a man has only one mother, all other women are his wives.

They bring in tanks and armoured personnel carriers, they have artillery and missiles, they have aeroplanes: fighters, assault planes and bombers. The foolish Russians. Women – that's Russia's most terrible weapon. Russian women alone can disperse and destroy the Chechen nation.

Here they are, so long awaited, so long desired, the girls who bring happiness, the girls who have golden wheat growing straight from their heads. In Russia. Here we have nightclubs, discothèques, bars, alcohol and drugs. And there's always a new girl. We can hold her hand in a café or on the street and we won't be obliged to marry her; we'll take her home, but only for one night, and in the morning she'll catch a taxi and leave without a word. We always dreamed of them, of the wheaten-haired girls. Now we have them. But where is the happiness?

There is no happiness: the fair-haired Russian women brought us none. We have ourselves become women like them.

23

There are the Chechens married to their tribeswomen, who speak their native tongue, take their children twice a year to Chechnya and, setting off, refer to it as 'going home'. They don't call the place where they live now home, even if it's their own property, purchased or granted during privatisation. Yet they are dwindling in number. The new generation befriends Russian girls, visits nightclubs, and does not mean to return to the village.

And then there are those of us who lost our roots long ago, even before the wars began. We drift 'like a cloud rent by the wind, finding shelter in neither this world nor the other'.[8]

There we have become outsiders, yet we will never be insiders here.

We wouldn't even remember – we would have forgotten long ago – that we're Chechen, but they keep reminding us. Russia does its utmost to forge the Chechens into a genuine nation, united and monolithic, and each fledgling who falls out of the nest is shoved straight back in.

If we forget, then they'll show us our very own passports. In my old Soviet passport, under 'Ethnic Origin' it said: 'Chechen'. Lest I forget. In my new Russian passport there's no section headed 'Ethnic Origin'. Yet nothing has changed. The very first page shows my place of birth: the Chechen Republic. That's not correct. There was no such Chechen Republic when I was born. I was born in the Chechen-Ingush Autonomous Soviet Socialist Republic, in an area of the USSR, run, like all the other areas, by the regional committee of the Communist Party of the USSR. At the time we were taught that we belonged to one great nation called the Soviet People. And we believed it. We set off for the institutes of Moscow and Leningrad – the great cities of our great motherland – then stayed there. But now we're taught that we are Chechens. And this vast country has suddenly become foreign.

24

During the first Chechen war, nearer its end, an end which shamed Russia, I lived in St Petersburg. I had no residential registration whatsoever, nor did I worry unduly about this. Thanks to my northern looks the police didn't stop me on the street. The poor policemen. Nobody had provided them with even the most rudimentary guidance on the anthropological type of the Chechen nation. In their search for terrorists they were detaining 'persons of Caucasian ethnic origin'. If you are really at war with an enemy, you ought at least to learn a little about him. The majority of Chechens are persons of non-Caucasian ethnic origin.

Please excuse me, compatriots and fellow tribesmen, learned and not so learned, who assert, out of perfectly understandable and worthy intentions, that the Chechen people are one of the most ancient ethnic groups on earth, an indigenous Caucasian ethnos. No, I won't argue about the origins of the Chechens. For such arguments are meaningless.

The very idea of the origin of the Chechen ethnos is wrong because no such Chechen ethnos exists – at least there was none until recently. There were the ancient Sumerians who lived in the days of the Babylonian kingdom, and the Hurrian tribes who later founded the state of Urarta. The remaining Hurrians settled in the foothills of the Caucasus, possibly mixing with the tribes who had resided here since earlier times. They gave the future Chechens the foundations of a culture and a common tongue, which is undoubtedly closest to ancient Hurrian. But a language does not make a nation.

Later, over successive millennia, the incoming tribes amassed. The Aryans were one of the first, it appears, during the period of the great migration of peoples travelling from the Black Sea's northern shores to the east, as far as India. Some stayed behind in the north Caucasus on the outward journey. Some also appear to have remained there on the way back.

I found the most unusual account of Chechen origins in the ancient Indian Puranas, the epic narratives. There the story goes that the caste of Kshatriya warriors became too numerous, with their incessant wars ravaging the earth. Then Bhumi, the goddess of the Earth, approached the Supreme God Vishnu in the form of a cow to plead for his protection. Vishnu manifested himself in the form of a Brahmin priest who deviated from dharma, the doctrine appropriate to a priest, by starting a battle and wiping out the generations of Kshatriyas nine times. The remnants of this warrior caste, driven out by the god's will, abandoned India and took refuge from the Lord's rage in Egypt – where they founded the Ancient Kingdom – and in the Caucasian mountains.

25

The Chechens paid dearly for the hypothesis of their Aryan origin, with expulsion to Kazakhstan, in 1944. I have found no official confirmation of this, but the Chechens themselves are convinced that Stalin decided to punish the entire Chechen nation not because of some yarn about a 'white horse' supposedly prepared by the Chechens for Hitler, nor because of mountain bandits who resisted Soviet power (Bandera's Ukrainian Insurgent Army was far more numerous, yet no one ever thought to exile the entire population of the Ukraine); rather, because scholars in Nazi Germany were working on the theory that the Chechens were an Aryan people, and in conquered Russia preparations were afoot for their role as equals with the Germans.

I don't know whether it was so, though it's quite possible that such a theory was used as a Nazi propaganda trick to create allies within the Soviet Union, but the theory of Aryan origin – just like the theories of the Caucasian, Hurrian, Turkic and Semitic origin of the Chechens – is at once true and false.

For there was no origin. Though all the tribes listed were present. After the Aryans, plenty of others stayed behind in the mountains. What happened to the Pechenegs? Or the Polovtsy? Exiting history's stage, many peoples were preserved through melding into the conglomeration of tribes known to their neighbours as the Sosani, the Dzurdzuki, or some other such name. What the Chechens call themselves is of no help to us: the ethnonym 'Nokhchi' simply means 'people'.

After the fall of the Khazar khaganate, several Khazar clans also settled in the mountains, even spreading Judaism across the Chechen lands. And the process never ceased. Fleeing Russian serfdom, runaway Slavs inhaled the free mountain air and became Chechens.

In the Caucasian mountains, another Babylon arose. Only, if in the Sumerian Babylon many tongues tried to build one tower, reaching to the sky itself, then in the Caucasus tribes who'd adopted a common tongue each built towers of their own. And the sky – the sky was close already; standing on the summits of the mountains, you could touch the white clouds with your hands.

Many nations are born of a hybrid ethnic substratum, which does not stop them from being nations. But for this, fusion is required. And in Chechnya no complete fusion – whatever academic historians may say – has ever taken place. Each tribe has been preserved. This is the whole point of the existence of *teips* – the Chechen ancestral clans, about which so much is written yet so little understood in Russia.

Of course, within the *teips*, too, blood has been mixed. Since each *teip* traces its origin from a single ancestor, intra-*teip* marriage is frowned upon. This rule holds fast to this day. The blood in the *teip* is mixed, intentionally moreover, to prevent the clan from degenerating. Yet this is only along the female line. Any Chechen can name you at least seven forefathers on his father's side; some can name you twenty. But scarcely anyone can remember their ancestors along the female line beyond their great-grandmother. For thousands of years Chechens have taken wives from among the Avars, Ossetians, Ingush, Georgians, Russians and, needless to say, the female members of the other *teips*. But their descent is traced along the male line. Over thousands of years a unique process for the reinforcement of the male genotype has occurred.

Like the reinforcement of the Jewish nation's female genotype, only in reverse.

26

Each *teip* has kept alive the memory of its historical origins; the *teips* have not melded together. Everyone remembers that the Gunoy *teip* originates from the Russians; the Benoy, probably the largest *teip*, comes from the Hurrians; the *teips* who originate from the Khazars are still known as the mountain Jews, or Taty; my *teip*, the Ersenoy (Arsenoy in other transcriptions) descends from the Indo-European migrants.

That is why the Ersenoy are tawny, tall and light-eyed, more closely resembling Baltic peoples or Germans than 'persons of Caucasian ethnic origin'.

Oh, poor policemen. If you wish to arrest a Chechen, don't look for someone swarthy. You can spot a Chechen by other qualities, qualities which I'm not about to reveal in detail. I'll simply recount how one day, when my father was in St Petersburg, he met an old acquaintance, a Russian who had spent several years in Chechnya. This lady had never set eyes on me. My father sat with her waiting for me, and they chatted about the Chechens. The lady said that she could still spot a Chechen in the crowd by his gait and demeanour. Glancing at the mass of people walking along the street, she pointed and said, 'See that man there, I bet he's a Chechen.' Father smiled and replied, 'Oh yes. That is, in fact, my son.'

That lady said a Chechen always holds himself as though today the whole world belongs to him, and tomorrow he'll be killed regardless.

27

Such subtleties are unknown to the custodians of the law, and so I lived without any registration, walking freely past the police checkpoints. But when my company rented office space at a high-security plant, we required permits, and they wouldn't issue me a permit without registration. I approached the landlord of the flat I was renting; he was a good man and immediately wrote the necessary declaration.

My landlord and I were invited to attend the Department of the Passport and Visa Service, where they register foreigners. We arrived, and the moment I walked through the door I declared that this was illegal: I was a citizen of Russia, why did my registration call for special treatment? I remember the major sitting behind his desk. He stood up, and, with spite in his voice, announced: 'We are at war, and you are the enemy.'

So that's how it is. We are Chechens, and we are Russia's enemies. Should we forget this, they'll remind us.

He explained in detail to the landlord of the flat what his provision of accommodation for me would entail. He guaranteed endless searches and passport registration check-ups, and should any explosion rock the district, my landlord would be tried as an accomplice. For I would automatically be identified as the perpetrator.

Nevertheless on that day my landlord wouldn't renege on his vow to get me registered. But a month later, apologising and hanging his head, he asked me to vacate his flat.

Lev Gumilev[9] would have termed what's happening to the Chechen nation passionary[10] overheating. Whence the heroism of the Chechens, their energy, their procreation, but also their fatalism and self-immolation. Their downtrodden instinct for self-preservation. At worst, such passionary overheating culminates in a nation's extinction.

I don't know whether this is provoked by solar activity.[11] More likely by historical realities, in the first instance by Russian politics. Right up until recent times, the Chechens were merely a ragbag of tribes, who'd never been able once and for all to unite, to establish their own statehood and form a unified nation. If the 'war till the last Chechen' is not carried to completion, if the Chechens survive and become a nation, they'll only have Russia to thank. Who ignited passion in them more than any solar anomaly, forced them to stand shoulder to shoulder, impressed on each Aryan, Hurrian, Khazar: You are a Chechen. The Russians are our last hope. They won't let us remain women. They'll force us to be Chechens and men, because every Chechen is a combatant, every Chechen is the enemy.

And all that remains is to triumph or die.

28

Large houses like rocks over the narrow rivers of Petersburg streets. In the rocks are tiny caves, inside which live people who've brought in furniture and household appliances. Like the river swallows. The people are like swallows. Perhaps because everyone here died long since, but nobody remembered to inform them of this.

There are no real swallows here. Real swallows never fly here. Sometimes I think: How can we build a home here, light the hearth? Swallows will never fly to these places anyway.

I am mad, haven't you realised yet? Only a madman could spend so long thinking about swallows. Sometimes I think I'm a swallow myself. Perhaps because I died long ago.

Mountains. Nobody could think so much about mountains.

In sixteen years I've lived in twelve cities. Married twice. Yet to this day I'm merely a lone bird who has strayed from the flock; it's so easy to stray from the flock when the flock itself has lost its way in the sky. A daughter was born to me; I gave her the name my mother bore. That name was Vera – 'faith'. But I have no faith left. And I see her less and less, often only in photographs. Once again I cannot sleep at night; my heart is gripped with yearning and pain, because I barely see my daughter growing up. You will understand this, for even the mad are only human.

Time after time, why is nothing destined to come true?

Perhaps somewhere in the faraway mountains a stray shell has smashed my clan's tower. And my entire clan is condemned to separation and drifting until I can find the place, pick up the age-old stones and put them together again. Even if I have to build my tower from white slate!

29

Let me tell you about the madmen.

Just before the war, many madmen materialised in Chechnya. Perhaps the foreboding of war begot them, perhaps the earth herself entered them, like an amber drop of resin swathes the fresh cuts on a tree, only the tree was yet to be cut. Perhaps it was Mother Tusholi speaking to us through them; she sent us her favourite children – but who listened?

In our neighbourhood lived Ibrashka. His full name was Ibragim. My Mama called him Ibrashka, Ibrashka the fool; that's what everyone else started calling him too. Ibrashka was the most ordinary village idiot. He was very strong and muscular, beautiful even. He would work for days on end: carrying water, laying up wood, building things; he herded and milked the cows himself. He was, no doubt, the best of sons to his mother; he loved her tenderly and wouldn't let her do hard work around the house or in the yard. They even tried marrying him off, but after three days the bride returned to her parents. Rumour had it that Ibrashka had proved too robust in bed, and the girl simply couldn't take it. Following his bride's departure Ibrashka fell sad for a week, then he forgot and once more occupied himself with the house, the yard and the cows. In a word, he was a normal halfwit. He spoke poorly, mostly stayed silent, and wore clothes of the wrong size. There was one other peculiarity – well, all madmen have their peculiarities, that is why they are madmen. Ibrashka was frightened of aeroplanes.

A silver bird had only to appear in the sky, or the faraway drone of a jet engine to sound, for Ibrashka to fly into a panic, search for somewhere secluded and press himself to the ground, like a child presses himself to the soft breast of his mother. Even the nearby rumblings of agricultural biplanes frightened Ibrashka.

We, by contrast, weren't frightened of aeroplanes. We liked to look at them, holding our palms to our brows as visors, liked to follow these metal angels with delighted glances as they journeyed high above the clouds. We especially loved military aeroplanes, which left white vapour trails in the silky-blue sky. We weren't frightened of anything.

Ibrashka had remained at the developmental level of a child and we children often played with him. But sometimes, oh the mindless cruelty of children, we mocked the clod in every way imaginable. We called him unkind names, we pelted him with lumps of dung and stones. Ibrashka would put up with it for a long time but sometimes even his patience would snap. Then, his face flushed with blood, he would tear off after the herd of wrongdoers. Silly, witless children. If Ibrashka had managed to catch one of us, he could have easily – without even realising – twisted his captive's head and broken his neck. But we had one trusty method of escaping reprisal. When Ibrashka got too close, someone would shout loudly: 'Ibrashka, look! An aeroplane!' And the rest would start to hum: 'Vvvvvvvoooooooooooooomm.' Ibrashka would drop straight to the ground, sometimes on to the hard asphalt of the road, and there he'd lie a long time, covering his head with his hands. And we'd laugh at him.

Poor, crazy Ibrashka. Aeroplanes weren't what he should have feared. When the air strikes began he patiently sat out all the raids in the shelter. But when the sky was clear of aircraft he would venture fearlessly on to the streets. Other than aeroplanes, Ibrashka was frightened of nothing. On one occasion, he left the bomb shelter to bring the children some water just as a mop-up operation was being conducted in the village. He was shot by the Russian soldiers' assault rifles.

Since the war, many of the survivors, when they hear the drone of civilian planes – the take-offs and landings of passenger aircraft near the aerodrome – involuntarily press their heads into their shoulders. And some can't control themselves and fall flat on the ground and cover their heads with their hands.

30

In the centre of Shali, for as long as I can remember, there lived another mad person, Dunka. Well, I don't know exactly where she lived, but you could see her in the town centre almost every day, near the department store or the market square.

Dunka was a Russian teacher who had been sent to Chechnya for work experience. When she was still just a young girl a Shali man had raped her. The rapist fled from the police into the mountains, while Dunka found herself pregnant. They say that it was then she became a little crazy, stroking her swelling stomach and saying, 'There's no need to send anyone to jail. See, I've got him right here, in the darkest of dungeons.' The man from Shali was eventually caught and convicted. The Soviet court tried him, and the rapist was sent to serve his time in a penitentiary. Had he been tried by a clan court, he wouldn't have been sent anywhere. But Dunka was Russian, an outsider, she had no clan – she hadn't a single relative, not even a distant one – so there was no one to cut the criminal's throat.

When the time came to be delivered of her burden, Dunka gave birth to a stillborn boy. For a long time she wouldn't hand the tiny corpse over to the doctors; only when she fell asleep did they manage to take the body and bury it by the cemetery railing. Then Dunka went fully mad.

Somewhere she got hold of an old pram, laid in it a doll with torn-off arms, and wandered all day long through the village centre, her hair matted, wearing the most extraordinary rags. The whole of Shali felt guilty that she was raped here and ashamed that the rapist remained alive, which meant, according to the law of the mountains, unpunished. Dunka was not sent to a lunatic asylum, they didn't even take away her staff flat. Each day passers-by gave her food and money, parents forbade their children to laugh at the holy fool, women chatted with her on the street. Women with children especially loved chatting with Dunka.

'How are you, Dunka?' they would ask. 'Where are you off to?'

'I'm going for a walk with my little one,' Dunka would reply. And she would immediately turn her attention to the other mothers' children: 'Ah, see how your boy's grown! Oh, you can tell straight away how bright he is! He'll be a big boss! And your little girl, what a beauty! She'll get the best groom in all of Shali, she'll live in clover, she'll have butter on her bread!' Mothers loved talking with Dunka. Of course, any mother likes to hear her child praised. But the words of Dunka, one of God's fools, were held to be a blessing from the Almighty.

Then Dunka would complain: 'See, my little one just won't grow. I try feeding him, giving him milk.' Dunka would produce a baby bottle full of milk, lifting it from time to time to the mutilated doll's plastic head. 'But he won't grow! And you know why? Because he's dead.'

And the mothers would calm Dunka as best they could. They'd say, 'Don't worry, Dunka, your little one will grow too. See, he's just a wee baby! He was only born yesterday, what do you want, for him to walk and talk straightaway?'

That was how Dunka lived, for a good thirty years from the start of her madness until the war. Her hair had greyed, her face had wrinkled, and her child still refused to grow, but the mothers calmed Dunka, and she believed that she'd given birth yesterday, and smiled happily.

Only pregnant women feared meeting Dunka. If Dunka bumped into a woman bearing a baby in her belly, she'd come up, put her hand on the woman's tummy and ask: 'So, will your little one be born dead too?' Dread would grip the woman; she'd return home, more dead than alive, and pray incessantly, while relatives fetched a saint or mullah to the house for protection from the evil eye.

Dunka breathed her last after one of the first bombings, her old body, mutilated by shrapnel, was buried in the cemetery beside the graves of the Muslims.

In the aftermath of the two wars, medical workers in Chechnya have observed that, owing to stress, wounds and the effects of chemical weapons and vacuum bombs, women have started to deliver stillborn children with increasing frequency, even when there is no miscarriage and the child is carried to term.

31

Shali was not alone in having mad people. In another administrative centre, Urus-Martan, lived blissful Dangi. Dangi was tall, with hair as fiery as the sun. They called him Malkh Dangi, Sunny Dangi. Dangi lived on his own, didn't marry and had no children. He worked as a nightwatchman at the state farm, sleeping by day, unless there was a funeral. Funerals were Sunny Dangi's real work. When a Chechen dies, a funeral ceremony is held, a *tezet*. All the relatives of the deceased and the elderly folk from his village assemble. The body is buried immediately, that same day, then the ceremony is held after the funeral, in the yard of the deceased. The men and the women sit apart. Mutton is boiled up and offered to all the mourners. They perform a *zikr* – a Sufi prayer.

In Chechnya over recent years much has occurred that I find astonishing and inexplicable. A mufti called Akhmad Kadyrov appeared, who announced, 'The Russian–Chechen problem? I'll show you how to solve the Russian-Chechen problem: in Russia there are one million Chechens and 150 million Russians; each Chechen should kill 150 Russians, that's how the Russian–Chechen problem will be solved.' That very same Akhmad Kadyrov then became the pro-Russian leader of Chechnya. When he was blown up in a stadium – whether by the rebels or the FSB[12] – Akhmad's son, Ramzan Kadyrov, set off for the Kremlin and, under the gaze of the world's television cameras, met Putin. The whole world saw Chechnya's new hereditary leader. Dressed in a tracksuit and *papakha*.[13]

Muftis? What muftis? The Chechens have never been

fundamentalists, they have never favoured orthodox Islam. There were always mosques and mullahs, but not many went to the mosques, and the mullahs were the butt of jokes. Chechen religious life took place for the most part in the Sufi communities. The Sufis have no priests or mullahs, no muftis or church hierarchies; the founders and leaders of the Sufi communities are the sheikhs, the saints. A sheikh need not even know Arabic, the language of the Koran – his authority stems from his personal holiness and his morals, for the Sufis what counts is religious ecstasy, not following rituals. The Sufi form of Islam could not be better suited to the freedom-loving Chechens, who have always opposed power of any kind save the authority of wisdom, experience and personal moral example. The majority of Chechens belong through family allegiance to the branches of a Sufi order. At the zikrs, to the accompaniment of musical instruments, the names of God are chanted, and during the prayer the participants in the zikr fall into a trance.

Dangi went to all the *tezets* in Urus-Martan and he joined in all the zikrs. He lived modestly, most days eating *siskal*, maize cakes, washing them down with sweet or sour milk. But at a *tezet* there was always plenty of meat. Dangi loved going to *tezets*. During the wakes Sunny Dangi behaved quietly and calmly; like all the men, he stood to greet people entering, conducted conversations befitting the occasion. But during the zikrs Dangi was always the first to fall into ecstasy and would sit for hours mumbling something unintelligible, rocking his head, crying out from time to time: 'Allah Akbar' – 'God is Great!'

When the war started, Dangi gave up going to work, and would wander all day long through the village wearing a drifting smile. He would tell everyone he passed that soon there would be lots of funerals and he needed to get a good night's sleep so he could sit through the wakes. He no longer needed to work, because now he would eat his fill of meat every day.

Then one day Dangi put on his best clothes and left the village. He had never gone anywhere before, and people asked him: 'Where are you off to, Malkh Dangi?'

'To Samashki,' Dangi told them. 'I have lots of work to do in Samashki, they are digging hundreds of graves there, and they'll hold a *tezet* like I never saw in all my life!'

Poor Dangi, thought the people of Urus-Martan, what a goose this war has turned him into. The Russian checkpoint near Urus-Martan allowed Dangi through: 'Let him pass, the fruitcake. Mind you, he'll deactivate the mines along the road.' From Urus-Martan to Samashki is fifteen miles; Dangi went by foot and told everyone he passed on his way: 'I'm off to Samashki, there they will hold a great *tezet* because they're going to bury hundreds of people. How could Dangi pass up a *tezet* like that? Afterwards, they'll bury Dangi too, and all of you must come.' So Sunny Dangi invited people to his own funeral.

The Russians entered Samashki. They killed everyone: men, women, the elderly and children. They showered grenades upon the houses. In the schoolyard, from the poplars overlooking the blind windows of empty classrooms, they hanged the younger schoolchildren, then they charred the little corpses with their flamethrowers. And they wrote on the brick wall: 'Museum Exhibit: Chechnya's Future'. In the course of a single day, over two hundred graves appeared in Samashki's cemetery.

But Dangi didn't make it to the *tezet*. On the outskirts of Samashki he was stopped at another Russian checkpoint. The soldiers accused him of being a combatant, said he was feigning insanity. They beat

Dangi, they shoved needles under his nails, but Dangi cried out: 'Allah Akbar' – 'God is Great!' Dangi fell into a trance, like at the zikr, and the soldiers became more and more enraged. They tortured him to death and flung his corpse out on to the road. The people of Urus-Martan collected Sunny Dangi's body and they buried it. Many attended his funeral – hundreds, even thousands! After all, everyone already knew that Dangi's funeral would be soon: he had told them so himself.

32

The village lives by sunrises and sunsets. The city lives by watches, the time on the electronic boards in metro stations, the miscellaneous melodies of mobile phones ringing their alarms, news broadcasts on the car radio. But the village lives by sunrises and sunsets.

When the scarlet cow of the sun wanders into the boundless blue pasture of sky, chewing leisurely on the white shrubs of clouds in order to feed the green calf of the fields with her fresh milk of rain, the housekeepers rattle their enamel buckets and go out to the cowsheds for the morning milking. The milk strikes the bottom of the vessels resonantly in white jets. After the milking the housekeepers open the gates and march the cows outside, driving them on with smacks. The cows assemble in ragged columns and walk unaccompanied along the familiar route to pasture. Somewhere ahead strides the herdsman, who from each yard receives a little money and a lot of milk, sour cream and curd cheese.

There is no special pasture near the village. The land is built upon, filled with forest plantations or tilled for cereal crops. The cows pluck the grass at the roadside, along the lands of the state farm, and on the large field marked on the map of the village as a football pitch. There is another football pitch – a real one – in the centre. The district competitions are held on it, the pupils of the Child Youth Sports School practise there. Here, on this outlying field, at the edge of the mulberry grove and the bank of the river Bass, we kids are the only ones to play football, but the cows don't bother us.

In the evening, as the sun heads down towards its stall, the herdsman gathers the herd and steers it back to the village. A dappled parade of cows fills the road and pavements. The only traffic jam possible in the village forms, and car drivers wait obligingly for the cows to drift past. The parade spills out from the main street into the side streets, lanes and alleys. In the air hang the discordant moos and the dust raised by the herd, penetrated by the rays of the setting sun. Dust raised by the cows' hooves will cleanse a person of all sins, like waters from holy rivers and sacred rain, after which a horseshoe rainbow arches across the sky. Is that why people stand outside their houses when the cows return?

Each cow knows its path home. If its housekeeper doesn't meet it in the street, the cow will moo fretfully. Then the small gate will open, and a barefoot boy will swing open the heavy gates. Just at that moment the clouds reflect the last claret rays of the sunset.

Each village yard has a cow, sometimes two, perhaps several. Plenty of people can afford to buy their dairy products at market, but without a cow in the home – well, how would daughters occupy their time, how could you tell whether a bride-to-be is lazy or flighty?

At market they sell the sour cream made from straining cream through a separator – thicker than shop-bought butter, delicious as the first December snow – and heads of homemade curd cheese, wrapped in muslin. But they don't sell milk at the market. Whatever next – selling milk! Every yard has a cow, and if your cow has yet to calve, then the neighbours will bring you milk, in a three-litre jar or an enamel bucket if need be. No one takes it into his head to sell air or water.

In our yard we have two cows, one red, called Zorka,[14] the other dappled, Lastochka.[15] We got them as little calves and reared them into beautiful brides. My sisters greet Zorka and Lastochka at the gate and escort them to the stalls in the brick cowshed built specially for them.

When my sisters went off to study in the big city, we sold the cows; Mama was ailing and she couldn't look after all the animals on her own. Besides cows we had dozens of hens, as imperious as aristocrats, geese, Chinese ducks, turkeys, rabbits and coypu in wire cages. Zorka had managed to calve – we sold her at the other end of the village along with her little calf – while someone on a neighbouring street bought maiden Lastochka. For a month, Lastochka would come to our yard and moo beguilingly. But once she had calved in her new home she accepted her new owners. For a long time Zorka continued to run away every so often, making her way across the entire village back to us. We would let her into the yard, feed and water her, and in the morning her owner would come and take her. A cow will remember for life the place where she first calved as home.

33

In our district's agro-industrial complex, there descended from on high plans for the harvest collection and the use of agrochemicals. The use of agrochemicals creates a vicious circle. Hiding among the seeds, many illegal immigrants infiltrated our lands: dapper beetles from the state of Colorado, runaway locusts and other insect riff-raff. Pesticides were sprayed over the crops to protect them. After eating the poisoned beetles, the birds – the natural enemies and population controllers to a host of pests – began to die. So our dependence on agrochemicals grew ever greater.

Then one year, just before the collapse of the Soviet Union and its agro-industrial complexes, there came a directive for super-intensive crop dusting. The local agronomists shook their heads, attempted to prove their point at the meetings, but they couldn't get the decision revoked. The chemicals were dropped using crop-spraying aircraft but even the low altitude at which the biplanes rattled in the sky could not guarantee, given the slightest breeze, 'pinpoint accuracy' in guiding the chemicals on to the fields. And so the poisons coated the grass bordering the crops, and the roads, and even the football-pitch pasture-field. The unsuspecting cows continued munching on the grass, and one by one began to fall to the ground and die in torment, gazing reproachfully at the low sky where swallows and biplanes flew, and from which, for the first time, rained death.

At first people stopped letting their cows out to pasture. But they couldn't keep them in the yard the whole day long, and besides there was nothing to feed them on. That's when it all began.

Blood – thick, nearly black blood – suffused the earth. I

remember it well. We children played near the state farm abattoir, and I remember well the lake of blood, overhung by a dense, humming cloud of gnats.

At the market, sour cream and curd cheese became scarce – milk disappeared altogether – but then plenty of beef turned up instead. Prices fell to absurdly low levels, but by now nobody would buy the meat. For the first two weeks they had continued to buy it. They marvelled at its cheapness. In every yard they boiled up meat in large kettles, enormous pieces like the nomads eat. And they gorged themselves stupid, till their guts split. But then they stopped buying it, and it was just left to rot on the wooden counters, teeming with flies. Then they began throwing the beef out in the rubbish; the sanitary inspectorate was run off its feet, treating and burying the dismembered cattle corpses to prevent an epidemic. But an epidemic was to begin, and the sanitary inspectorate would be helpless to stop it. Within a few years, an epidemic of blood and corpses was to begin.

34

On the football pasture they later built a car market, the biggest in Chechnya. There they sold cars, spare parts, and all sorts of other bits and bobs. On market day thousands would flock to the bazaar, crowding it from one end to the other.

On 5 January 1995, the day of the first Russian air strike on Shali, the market was chock-full. When aeroplanes appeared in the sky, no one thought to flee. These were our planes – Russian planes – probably searching for combatants. Well, what was that to us? We were innocent civilians. Why should we run and hide in bomb shelters, as crazy General Dudaev had urged us on television? It wasn't as if the Americans had arrived.

An aeroplane swooped low and dropped a cluster bomb right into the thick of the crowd. Hundreds were torn limb from limb, there were pieces of bodies, human meat, tangled with the mangled steel of the cars, so that it could only be buried as one mass. And blood – once more, blood poured across the ground. Rivers and lakes of it – so much blood that it seemed as though the very earth was sodden with blood, like an ailing mother from whose breast flows not milk but blood.

35

It was wrong to kill the cows. The cow is the mother of man, for she feeds him with her milk. A man has seven mothers: she who bears him in her belly, the earth, his country, his wet-nurse, the cow, the swallow, and any woman whose breasts are brushed by his lips. According to Chechen custom, if a man's lips touch a woman's breasts, she becomes his mother.

We are apostates. We have violated the law. We rape the earth, kill the cows, we sleep with fair-haired women, caressing their breasts with our lips. That is why the sky has fallen in on us. In Russia the sky is empty, distant – it couldn't care less what people do. The sky over Chechnya is more dense than steel. It is close, brushed by the peaks of the mountains. And it has caved in on us because we have violated the law.

No, I didn't take part. I alone didn't take part. One year before the mass slaughter of the cows, I stopped eating meat altogether. I had a vision of death, sensed how close and heavy the sky was. Well, as you already know, I was mad. I ate no meat, I was afraid of the sky and left for the big city – not meaning to return to the place where it was going to fall down. But I was wrong to run away. I was wrong. A man dies but once: only a coward dies every minute. When the sky did fall down, its shards were scattered over the whole world, they pierced my heart, and now I no longer know if I'm alive or if I died there, on the field where cows once grazed and kids chased after a shabby football.

36

Sky, you never loved us! You love the meek, but we were proud, and you punish us for it, sky! In the high mountains we stole too close to you. And earth – our kindly mother – couldn't save us from father sky's rage. For we made off with your fire.

When Dela, the Almighty Lord, created this world and breathed life into its people, the earth was cold and dark. Even when wrapped up in the skins of beasts, we froze, and our clay walls could not keep our homes warm, while our bellies had only raw food to digest. But in the sky there was plenty of fire; Sela, the god of the heavens, splashed it about, hurling lightning bolts with bravado during the storms. And there was a youth by the name of Parmkhat who scaled the tallest mountain and reached the sky. While Sela slept Parmkhat stole the fire and carried it down to the people. The people kindled hearths in their homes, began cooking their food, and beheld light and warmth.

Yet Sela seethed with rage, for Parmkhat had made people almost the peers of the gods. So he chained the youth to the rocks of the Caucasus and commanded the eagle to peck all day long at Parmkhat's liver, while by night the liver would grow back. Thus Sela punished him with eternal torment for his insubordination and for his pride. People still praise Parmkhat in all their tongues. The Greeks know him as Prometheus.

37

Before the start of the first war, unidentified aircraft bombed an aerodrome near Grozny and the trainer aeroplanes it was home to. Dudaev sent a telegram to Moscow: 'My congratulations to the leadership of the Russian Air Force on gaining supremacy in Ichkeria's skies. Now let's meet on the ground.' As an air force general, he should have realised that in modern warfare air supremacy guarantees victory below. But he led his doomed people into war – into a war with the sky.

There was no air defence. Dudaev sent two emissaries to London to negotiate the purchase of Stingers and who knows how the war might have gone had the resistance forces got their hands on those Stingers. But the procurement of the Stingers fell through: the FSB had organised for the emissaries to be assassinated in London.

This time Sela did not sleep; he did not let us steal his lightning again.

38

Memory of mine, I cannot gather up your threads, cannot weave them into cloth. I remember all this, and I remember nothing. I remember what happened thousands of years ago, I remember what happened to other people, remember what merely may have been, I remember what never was, and sometimes I remember what is merely to come. Such memory is called madness.

I remember sitting – I think it was me – on the floor of a flat. It is the city of Petrozavodsk; I lived there too. I must have lived there too. Petrozavodsk, a flat on the thirteenth floor of a new building, I sat on the floor in the kitchen and thought about the Shali tank regiment. In the combat report from the front I heard that during the battle of Urus-Martan the Shali tank regiment had been eliminated. An enemy formation. When Russians die, they talk of 'losses', or even say they've 'fallen'. When Chechens die, they describe them as 'eliminated'. Because Chechens are the enemy. I too am Chechen: the enemy. And when I die, they'll describe me as 'eliminated'.

At the battle of Urus-Martan the Shali tank regiment had been eliminated. I give it some thought, but simply cannot grasp the sense of this strange, daft phrase. The Shali tank regiment. The Shali . . . Lord, wherever from? Where could Shali have got tanks from?

I remember just one tank. It stood on a concrete plinth in the centre of the village, where the road forks. The muzzle of its gun pointed at the village. They say that this tank was pulled down when Dudaev took power. Well, even if they put a tractor motor into it, that would still only make one tank, not a whole regiment!

I call to mind Shali. Shali stretched across the river – there's the upper village, where the cemetery starts. The village begins with the cemetery. Inside the cemetery are graves, some over a hundred years old, but there are no tanks. Next come houses. Houses surrounded by fences, barns in the yards, cows in the barns, yes, cows, but tanks – tanks don't hide in barns. In the centre of the village there's the square, the department store, the cultural centre, the park, then School No. 8. This I remember. But I remember no tanks. Then, lower down, houses again, the district hospital, the bus station and the kebab house. And the mulberry grove – but we kids explored every inch of that grove. If there had been any tanks, we'd have noticed them. We also knew all the buildings of the state farm like the back of our hands. And outside the village? Outside the village we knew everything too: the forest belt along the fields, the manmade pond, the hill with the oil pumps. We used to scramble up the hill; from there we could see the whole village spread out before us. There was no tank regiment in view. Of course, there were places in the village where I didn't go, for instance, near School No. 3. I hardly ever went there; perhaps that was where the tank regiment hid? No, how could you hide an entire tank regiment near School No. 3? I may not have gone there myself, but all the same, they'd have told me – the kids would have told me if we'd had tanks in the village, an entire regiment. We loved tanks dearly, how could we have failed to spot that?

I shut my eyes and see them crawling out from under the earth: heavy, clanking monstrosities. They crawl out from under the earth, they have always been in Shali, but lived below the earth, which is why we couldn't see them. They were waiting for the war to start. When there is no war, the tanks slumber. They awaken to the thunder of guns – and here they are crawling out, bursting through the earth, blackened by time, shaking off clumps of clay and webs of roots, they form into a column and head for Urus-Martan. The battle will be there. They'll be eliminated there. And we'll be eliminated along with them. Because we are Chechens, and hence the enemy.

39

This era will become myth. War always becomes myth. They'll write thousands of books about it, make films of the books. That's all for kids. New generations of little boys will read about the war, watch films about it, stay awake at night imagining what they would have done if they'd been there; in the daytime they'll play at war, just as we played at fighting with the Nazis when we were kids. And once again, they'll be sorry that they weren't born earlier, that 'not a single bullet came their way'.[16] And they will get their war, a war of their own. Each generation gets a war, because writers write books about it, because war is celebrated in poems and songs.

They're already writing books, plenty of them. Former soldiers and officers, generals even, are publishing sketches and memoirs about how they fought for Russia in Chechnya. And some even write about how they killed civilians. Well, *à la guerre comme à la guerre*, what else can we expect from war? Such is the stark reality of the front. The heroism of mopping-up operations, the self-sacrifice of reprisals and the absurdity of being blown up by your own mines. *A la guerre comme à la guerre*.

The warriors of Islam too write of how they fought against the infidels, how sweet and joyous it is to become a *shahid* and join Allah, kicking open the gates of heaven.

And I alone write of swallows. Because I am a swallow. Neither a Federal knight, nor a holy *mujahid*: just a swallow who never returned to the eaves of his family home.

And we are not little boys any more, we were born at the right time, yes, we were born just in time to die. But we didn't die. Why?

Why did I wait for this war, why did I prepare for it since childhood, studying combat strategy and tactics, drawing up maps of the locality, arranging the troops, sketching arrows for the attacks and retreats, dotted lines for fortifications? Why, if I left, instead of standing on the plain and dying like everyone else?

If I had died, I would have died just once. What anguish to die time after time! But I left; that's why I was killed by a sniper's bullet on Grozny Street, I was blown up by a grenade in Samashki, I was fatally wounded by shrapnel in Shali and I burnt in a tank at the battle of Urus-Martan, where my entire tank regiment was eliminated.

40

And then, sitting on the floor in the flat on the thirteenth storey in the city of Petrozavodsk, I bit my pallid lips in impotence. The music was too loud. The mountains beckoned. I should have left – no, not to be a victor, I couldn't have been that. We have never won; how can you win against the sky? I should have died. Or rather – no, it's not that I should have, but that I had a right to. I had a right, a hereditary right to death in a desperate war.

Sometimes it seems to me like I alone used that right. I alone made my way back to the motherland, took up my weapon and was eliminated. I even know where: he fell in a trench at the bank of the river Bass, when the columns of Federal troops were moving down from the north, from the direction of Argun.

But that I – he'll never get to write about it. That's why I – another I, the one who remains – write this book. The one who died yet does not die, like the noon-time shade, who migrates from place to place and will now feel only one thing for eternity: that he is inhabiting foreign places. Alien places.

41

When did it happen and where? How did the threads of my memory entangle, knot, entwine? Perhaps it happened when I was twelve? Or six? No, most likely it happened before my birth. Just before my birth itself, some thirty-two years ago.

When my mother's belly began to expand – like a waxing moon, rounding out day by day – at the due moment, as entitled by employment law, she took maternity leave. Mama worked at the school, teaching maths. Sometimes she taught double shifts, worked overtime, even when Papa was director of the state farm and there was no want of money. Mama loved her work, loved her independence.

On maternity leave, Mama visited her favourite city, Leningrad. That's how I first found myself amongst these bogs – still in my mother's womb – first soaked in their sweet, noxious fog: prenatal memory. I recall particularly well Mendeleevskaya Liniya, the pavement along the railings at the building of the

Twelve Collegia. I still feel drawn to this place where I first enjoyed strolls, squeezed into an awkward pose, squashed by the walls of my mother's womb. I walk beside the railings, I shut my eyes and feel myself returning to this primordial condition, to pre-time, with this balmy, drunken phrase: Mama, deliver me back.

Not long before the day when the full moon was to give up its burden (was I a burden to you, Mama?), Mama returned to Shali. And even in the last days of her term, she often went on strolls, walking to the market and shops. Her pregnancy passed with ease, the fourth pregnancy of an adult woman.

On that day too, Mama strolled around the town centre, lost in thought, holding in her hand a light package of shopping. In one hand a light package of shopping, her other on her stomach, her eyes wistful, beholding the point on the horizon where sky meets earth. Have you observed the special wistfulness of a pregnant woman, ready any day now to empty her swollen belly? Have you observed the bulging of the spring earth, pushed from within by the pallid green shoots?

In her wistfulness, Mama didn't notice, didn't notice in time, there wasn't time to swerve, to cross to the other side of the street. Bang in front of her – as if the embodiment of some random negative thought – appeared Dunka, the village madwoman. Dunka stretched out her hand towards the belly and whispered, mutely moving her lips: 'A dead one . . .'

In dread, Mama recoiled and took off swiftly homewards. She had barely made it back when the contractions began. Father's driver took her to the maternity ward, the waters broke, and the expulsion of the foetus commenced. It was a difficult birth. On its way out of its mother's belly, the child dislocated her rib. But that doesn't matter. What matters is that he was born dead. Lifeless.

Silent. Not gasping in greedily his first helping of the caustic, weighty air of the earth's atmosphere.

The midwife beat me about the face for a long time, shouting: 'I'm not going to lose you, I will have you breathe.' Though I don't remember that. Like I don't remember the moment when I first convulsively swallowed in this life's air and cried, mournfully, inconsolably. I don't remember that. But I remember something else. The lives of ancestors, the flight of swallows, the mountains and steppe – and even the future, only someone else's. Because then – then everything became mixed up. Perhaps some of my brain neurons died, and those which remained meshed together in an unfathomable, unprecedented formation. And it became quite impossible to tell whose each memory was, who was doing the remembering.

42

It takes half an hour on the rattling bus from Shali to Grozny, always packed with people, the old men and the women sitting, the smaller children sitting with the women, while we stand. Riding along the tarmac road, we pass Germenchuk. That's what the little village just beyond Shali is called, almost like my name, an ancestral name, perhaps since the times when Ger Man, the fair man with the spear, stopped his cart here, at the bank of the river Bass. There's a stop in Argun, at the bus station littered with the spat-out shells of sunflower seeds, where you can get out and stretch your legs, sipping the fresh air. Then comes the road again, and fields with oil pumps, until, just before Grozny itself, an enormous pit appears on the right. Here they quarried minerals from the bowels of the earth, perhaps gravel or sand, and left a huge, gaping wound.

The earth heals its wounds. After the war, people brought to the pit the heaps of rubble from wrecked houses, all mixed up with corpses. Now the pit is no more: the earth has regained itself and become level.

And so the bus enters the city. We never said 'Grozny'. Just 'the city'. We knew no other cities. There's the road under the railway bridge and Minutka Square. Then the bus station.

Minutka Square is the entrance to the city. Now this name is known throughout Russia, probably all over the world. During the wars, Minutka would change hands sometimes several times in a day. That patch of paved land just before the bus station became the key to the warring city, a strategic foothold, a junction.

Back then it was simply Minutka Square, the terminal where we got off the bus and went on into the city by foot. When we rode to the city for shopping or simply to visit the cinema, to amble its beautiful streets, to sit in the 'Juices and Sodas' café.

But that day we didn't arrive by bus. We drove by car. Mama at the wheel, me on the back seat amid a pile of notebooks and sketchpads filled with drawings. Mama was the first woman in Shali to learn to drive. We were in the red Moskvich. Papa had gone to work in his staff car, Mama was on holiday – it was summer, school was closed. Mama was driving me to the city.

I like the road; my eyes glued to the window, I watch the scenery floating by.

Why are we travelling to the city? Because of Uncle Zhenya. Uncle Zhenya recently arrived from Moscow. Though he's no uncle to me, simply Father's friend. Older than Papa, he's an intellectual Moscow

Jew. Last summer he came and stayed with us for a couple of weeks, bringing his family. For the sun, forests and rivers, kebabs and booze in the glades. They sunbathed too, playing cards, and telling jokes. This time they brought their little girl, a plump Jewish girl, roughly my age. Our parents said that she was my fiancée and I had to marry her. They were just joking. Some jest: I nearly died of fright.

I didn't want to get married, much less to a plump Jewish girl. If I was going to marry, it would only be to Yulia, whom I saw in Grozny – though only once, it's true. But that would be later. When I grew up. For now, I didn't want to get married at all.

Left alone, I would sit for hours on the floor in my room, the furthest one in the house, surrounded by notebooks, sketchpads, maps and books. Among heaps of pens and pencils, I would carefully sketch. Once Uncle Zhenya came into my room and started questioning me about what I was drawing. So I told him.

After this, Uncle Zhenya advised my anxious parents: 'You need to take the boy to a psychiatrist. Don't be frightened – it doesn't necessarily mean he's ill. Take me, for example: I'm not, I hope, crazy, but I see a psychiatrist regularly. I know a good doctor in Moscow, I'll give him a call, he can recommend who to see in Grozny.'

There is soft furniture in the doctor's study, a big window draped with heavy curtains which match the furniture. We sit in a semicircle, a crescent; Mama and this man of about forty with a small beard talk in front of me. Mama narrates. 'It was a difficult birth, he's had all the normal childhood illnesses, he doesn't really play with other children of his age, just sits for hours in his room, reading or drawing. He started reading at four – his older sisters taught him how to, they played school with him. I bought him children's books but he doesn't like them. He reads about war the whole time. Especially books about military history, full of detailed descriptions and battle plans. Then he draws out what he's read. But the odd thing is he always switches everything round.' Mama shows a picture. At the battle of Cannae, the Roman soldiers are lined up differently, and Hannibal suffers defeat. At Austerlitz, the hussar regiment attacks the French from the rear. In the battle of Stalingrad, Paulus escapes the encirclement. And here's the strangest one . . . Mama shows the maps.

It's an atlas of the North Caucasus. The Chechen-Ingush Autonomous Soviet Republic, Northern Ossetia, Dagestan, Kabardino-Balkaria. The maps are marked in blue and red pencil. Long, blue arrows point north to south, short, red arrows point south to north, Grozny is ringed in a double circle of both colours, and at Urus-Martan is a little cross.

'And then there are stories. All the children like talking about when they "were grown-ups". When the adults frighten our neighbour's boy and tell him that if he's naughty they'll give him away to the wolf, he says, "When I was a grown-up, I killed the wolf." But ours – ours just talks non-stop about war.'

The man with the little beard turns to me. He asks what the pictures are of. With a friendly smile, he suggests I tell him the most interesting thing I can remember. I want to tell him about how thrilling it feels to wait in ambush with a musket pressed to your shoulder, about how the Maxim machine gun clatters almost like the conveyer belts in the state farm's barnyard, about how . . . But I stay silent, I say nothing. Somehow I understand that it is better to remain silent. Though I'm desperate to tell someone how painful it is to die from a nomad's arrow piercing your throat.

Then the psychiatrist talks with Mama. He reassures her that everything is within normal range, there is no pathological condition.

'My understanding is that there is no dementia. It's possible that asphyxiation at birth caused some degree of cerebral damage and there is a tendency to schizophrenia, but let's hope that once puberty has passed everything will normalise.' The psychiatrist explains the terms when Mama asks. 'Confabulation? Confabulation means false recollection – when the patient mistakes his fantasies for memories.

'And if the boy has leanings towards all things military, perhaps you should send him to the Suvorov Academy?'

Towards the end, he confides: 'There have been many strange goings on lately. They brought me a man – an intelligent, calm, rational man. He refused to move from his village to Grozny, where they were offering him a flat. He told his relatives that Grozny was a dead city – that it was going to be razed to the ground.'

Mama agreed to bring me back in a month's time. But a month later the doctor was no longer to be found in Grozny. They told us he had swapped his flat in a hurry and travelled north.

43

'Chug-chug!' clatter the wheels of the goods wagon. The rimless, spokeless iron wheels, the grooved, cast discs. 'The red wheel, without rims or spokes, ran away to freedom, rolling down the blue field' (the sun). Here's another riddle: 'An iron wheel with twelve spokes whose rotation kills all life' (time).

There are people in the goods wagon: glum men, dejected

women, bawling children. In the corners stand mounds of frozen faeces and iced urine. It is cold. There is no water. No food. By now there are several dead bodies: they'll be taken out at the next stop. If they are taken out at all. If not, then the dead will travel on, with the living, to the new lands, the Great Steppe.

It is 1944. A special-op eviction. The NKVD unit has sealed the village. They have dug trenches, positioned their machine guns. Only after that do they enter. They round up all the men over fourteen, holding them in the school to thwart resistance. During this time they oust the women, old men and children. Then they load up the men. Drive them to the railway station and cram them into goods wagons. They fasten padlocks and seal them with wax. A package for you, Great Steppe!

That time they came to our yard. They saw a Russian woman with her suckling children. Decided to leave them. But took the Chechen father. That Russian woman was my grandmother, and one of the suckling children was my father.

Thus were we left on our land, with our mother. Thus were we torn from the breast of our motherland, which was exiled in goods wagons to the Great Steppe. Russian newcomers occupied the empty houses, dividing up the belongings and livestock. My father grew up in their midst, ignorant of his Chechen tongue, answering to the Russian name of 'Boris' rather than the one he was given at birth. Were we to blame for this?

In 1957 the Chechens returned. Boris saw his father return with another wife and with new half-brothers for him. He rushed to him, wanting to embrace him, to kiss him. His father pushed him away gruffly. It is not done for Chechens to show tenderness towards women and children in front of strangers. How was Boris to know this? He had grown up among Russians. Were we to blame for this?

Thus we started living, divided within, outsiders to the Chechens, outsiders to the Russians. Mixing inside us the blood of two tribes, when the sky had decreed these tribes should not mix blood but spill blood. And on this count we were to blame.

44

Salaudi is building a big brick house. Salaudi's sons mix up the mortar themselves with their spades. An elderly bricklayer hired for a high price smokes Prima and oversees the construction. The neighbours come over and watch. Secretly envious that they'll never build such a house, they laugh aloud: 'Eh, Salaudi, what's this basement you've dug? Decided to kit yourself out with your own personal bomb shelter, have you, in case of World War Three? If the Americans come and drop their atom bomb on us your basement won't help, Salaudi!'

Salaudi is silent. Let them scoff. Their own houses have no basements, their mud huts. They'll collapse with the first blast wave. Salaudi knew what a blast wave was. He'd managed to see action in the Second World War. And his sons knew. One of them had served in Afghanistan. Perhaps it will be no help against an atomic bomb, but if an ordinary bomb drops, it'll save us, they thought. From the blast wave and the shrapnel fragments. So long as it's not a direct hit, of course.

At that time Salaudi knew nothing of vacuum bombs.

. . . FAE (fuel-air explosive, or thermobaric weapon). Liquid fuel (ethylene oxide) functions as the main explosive. Upon impact a small explosive charge bursts open the casing of the bomb. The liquefied

gas starts to disperse, forming a cloud. As soon as the aerosol fuel cloud reaches a certain size, it detonates by means of the second charge. The overpressure within the detonation can reach 3 MPa with temperatures of 2,500–3,000°C, while the rapidly expanding wave front can damage structures invulnerable to the effects of a conventional blast wave. During the dispersion process the cloud flows into trenches, hideouts and bomb shelters, thus intensifying its kill capacity. The special feature of a vacuum bomb is the powerful shock wave created by the fuel-air explosion. Because of the instantaneous ignition of a large volume of space, the air heats and subsequently expands, forming a pressure wave of supersonic velocity; then terrible laws of physics come into effect.

However, a vacuum bomb is named not after the blast wave but after its consequences, when the reverse process of compressing air occurs. Buildings of all kinds will collapse like a house of cards. It is difficult to say what can happen to humans: it can reach the point of internal organs exiting through all bodily orifices. Vacuum bombs are very cheap to produce as they amount to a gas bottle and rudimentary detonator . . .

45

How could the bombs have failed to start falling, when in the soft soil so many bomb shelters had been dug, like irresistible magnets beckoning the malign iron birds?

So it was on our state farm. Near the farmstead was a field, sometimes sown with maize, sometimes ploughed fallow, and sometimes just abandoned to the onslaught of the coarse thistle with its prickly, magenta clusters. Then, smack in the middle of the field, they dug out a long bomb shelter, covered it with cement tiles and shovelled a mound of earth over it. Though we already had a bomb shelter on the state farm, a short distance from the new one. I remember how the old bomb shelter had once saved us.

The favourite game of all little boys is of course war. But we couldn't always gather a large enough gang to divide into two camps and begin our noisy combat. Often there were three of us: Anzor, Sultan and I. Then the opponent in war would be the state farm, with all its manpower and machinery. It was also terribly exciting to play at being partisans. We carried out sabotage attacks on the railway; once with great success we derailed a wagon filled with mineral fertiliser. We stuck nails into a cam belt and punctured the tyres of passing trucks. We carried out raids on civil defence warehouses: we made off with a whole sack of gas masks. And one day we burned down the German headquarters.

The German headquarters in our game was the state farm bathhouse. Right up against the bathhouse stood a barrel of diesel oil; we set it alight using a fuming tyre, and the fire quickly leapt on to the building's roof. Then we took fright and, bewildered, began bringing water from the nearest pump almost in our cupped hands, trying to put out the roaring flames.

When we saw the state farm watchman running for us and swearing in two languages simultaneously, we turned and fled. But where to go? We could have just split up, but who could guarantee that none of the captured partisans would crack under torture and give away his comrades? Oh, there was no need for torture. If they'd brought one of us to his parents and said there were three of us, it would immediately have been clear who the others were. If I was caught, then it meant Anzor and Sultan. If Anzor was caught, Sultan and me. If Sultan was caught, me and Anzor.

So we sat shaking with fear on the damp concrete floor in the half-light, listening to the frogs jumping in the booming echo of the basement.

46

The residents of the farmstead did not hide in the state farm's bomb shelters. Better still was PP-2, the secure, underground communications centre, with a triple thickness of concrete and a whole mountain of earth above it. PP-2 was never bombed – the centre was designated a Federal asset. But that's quite another story.

Rather, the state farm's long bomb shelter in the middle of a disused field was used as a site for the disposal of unexploded bombs. In our district this task was voluntarily performed by Bislan Sabirov. I remember Sabirov well.

My family may have been mixed, but I was descended from a renowned and honourable clan: the Ersenoy *teip*. The elders of Shali knew twelve generations of my forefathers. The Sabirovs were newcomers – just some Kabardins[17] who had settled in Shali relatively recently. They were all short and stocky with skulls shaped like Neanderthals. Their Chechen status was yet to be affirmed. Bislan would try to affirm his status by picking fights with me, an aristocratic outsider. He was three years older, no mean difference at our tender age. But if you must fight, then you must fight. In the streets of Shali no one will laugh at you for losing. But they will spurn you for refusing to brawl.

Mostly I lost to the older and beefier Bislan. But at each meeting, of course, I would once again take up the challenge. By tradition, if you cannot overcome your opponent, then your elder brother steps in for you. I had no elder brother. Later Bislan was beaten by Dinka, my dear summertime friend, but that too is quite another story.

I also remember coming home after the first war. Wandering about the yard, mulling over my childhood, I kicked at random objects underfoot. Then I went inside and asked my mother, Why is the yard dotted about with upside down tubs for feeding the birds? And Mama replied. Under the tubs are unexploded cluster bombs.

Modern munitions (fragmentation, pellet, high-explosive, incendiary) which in terms of their capacity and effect may be classed as weapons of mass destruction. The special feature of such munitions is the enormous quantity (hundreds or thousands) of fragments (pellets, flechettes, etc.) ranging in weight from a fraction of a gramme to several grammes. Anti-personnel pellet bombs, for example, range from the size of a tennis ball to that of a football, and contain around 300 metal or plastic pellets, 5–6 mm in diameter. The strike radius of such a bomb depends on its capacity, ranging from 1.5 to 15 metres. Pellet bombs are dropped from aeroplanes in special casings (dispenser pods) holding from 96 to 640 bombs. The dispenser is detonated in the air and the showering bomblets shoot out, dispersing over an area of up to 250,000 m².

After the air strikes, some bombs fail to explode. To stop them from detonating by accident, my sister covers them with tubs. Then Sabirov walks through the yards collecting them and blows them up in the long bomb shelter out in the field. Mama talks calmly, matter-of-factly. I turn cold. Mama, couldn't you have told me any earlier? I've been wandering around kicking them.

Sabirov would gather bombs in the second war too. Here's how it worked: he would bring the lethal ball to the door of the bomb shelter, raise his arm, fling it deep inside and immediately slam the heavy metal door. Inside, the bomb would explode, causing no harm.

Sometimes the bombs wouldn't explode at the first go. On one occasion he'll have three goes at throwing an iron sphere into the dark womb. Then he'll go in, whirl it in his hands and drop it nonchalantly on to the floor.

And the bomb will explode.

47

Once more I write. Once more it is winter, it is cold, and I write. Now I write plenty. I know: it is disjointed, sketchy, fitful, jumbled, fragmented, broken. There is no central plot. It is hard to read prose like this, right? Easier to read linear prose. Prose that makes you want to turn the pages to find out what happened next.

And what happened next?

Nothing happened next. Once more it was winter and then spring in the city where no swallows lived. Once more I write. The wheel of my time has no spokes. Just a heavy, cast disc.

We shall write, to be sure. Perhaps I'll even write genuine narrative novels and stories. They will have heroes and heroines, plots and intrigues, unexpected twists, supporting characters, outcomes, the works. I'll write yet. There is nothing left for me to do but write.

That's for later. But now, now come spurts of blood. Not the crimson blood that fills our veins, smooth flowing and even; this is scarlet, arterial blood, shooting in a fountain from a throat pierced by a spear, spattering you with droplets – it won't wash out easily, okay?

Do not read further.

Oh, and another thing: it's like a cluster bomb. A big container; it opens in the sky and out fall smaller bombs, a mass of hedgehogs from the heavens, the size of a child's ball; inside each little ball is a deadly filling: pellets, shrapnel, flechettes.

Did something hit your heart?

48

Iron gates painted sky blue, across the street from ours – here is the house where Vakha and his family live. They had two girls and two boys. First the two girls, then two boys. In that order. The eldest was Satsita, almost the same age as me. Between our houses was a dead-end strewn with gravel. And scattered with little balls. On that day an aeroplane appeared out of the blue, in the early hours. They wouldn't have made it in time to PP-2. Everything happened fast. A random cluster bomb. Satsita fell. No wounds, no blood. She opened her eyes and murmured: 'It hurts, it hurts . . . here.'

Her hand fell on her heart. They took off her top, her T-shirt. Near her heart was a barely noticeable spot.

Vakha started up his car and raced for several hours to Makhachkaly, through mines, checkpoints, firing. The surgeon examined Satsita for a minute, then ordered his assistants, 'Get the operating theatre ready, prepare the anaesthetic.' A flechette had hit her right in the heart. But her heart hadn't stopped. It had continued, convulsively, painfully, to drive the blood in spurts. And Satsita hadn't died. She passed out from the pain on the journey, she was sinking into an abyss, but opened her eyes again.

The Dagestani surgeon pulled the flechette out of her working heart. Where, at which international medical conference will he present a paper on this unique operation? Which trainees took notes of every move he made? Who will write about this event in a specialist medical journal or dissertation? What prize will he receive, what honour?

Nowhere. No one. None. Because this operation could not have taken place. As there could not have been any flechette bombs. They were banned by the Geneva Convention and destroyed in all countries signatory to the agreement. Russia did not drop cluster bombs on Chechnya; Russia has no cluster bombs.

The surgeon said the steel pellet under the right shoulder blade of my father could be left there if it doesn't disturb him. Satsita keeps the long flechette, darkened with blood, in a cardboard box for New Year tinsel.

49

Do you know which occupation in Soviet times was the most prestigious in the North Caucasus, among the Chechens, Ingush, Ossetians, the many-tribed Dagestanis? Mountain-dwellers are greedy, evil and wild. Probably, the job of director, or general or public prosecutor perhaps?

The doctor's profession.

And the most prestigious specialisation among medical workers?

The surgeon, of course.

And this too I remember well. The cleverest children, the straight-A students, the medal winners, didn't even pick a profession: it was already chosen. Parents would say with pride: My girl gets straight As. When she leaves school, she'll study medicine!

How did they know that so many doctors, the very best doctors, would be needed within just a few years, to save at least a few lives? Perhaps the earth whispered this to them.

The war started and in this carnage, in this nightmare, in this hell, there was only one way to stay human: by being a doctor. Someone who doesn't distinguish between military and civilian clothing – torn to rags anyway – doesn't distinguish between nationalities and tongues – all people moan in the same language – saving anyone who could be saved. Fighting against the sky which pours forth death.

While cruel father sky, preparing to kill his children, hoarded up shells and bombs, missiles and mines, dressed his mercenaries in khaki, mother earth prepared her resistance army. In medical institutes throughout the entire country, instead of the military pledge an oath of humanism is sworn. The earth didn't want to hand over her children without a fight.

And here's the sky's army, in bog-coloured clothing, and the army of the earth, in white gowns like summer clouds. Where is the earth and where the sky? All had swapped places.

The Chechen doctors stood little chance. The sky knew whom it was fighting. The very first missile and bomb attacks by the Federal forces struck hospitals and clinics.

In the adjacent republics, in Dagestan, North Ossetia and Ingushetia, the earth's warriors stood rooted to the spot, going without sleep for days on end, hand to hand against the sky.

Now you too know whose war it was.

50

I always find it hard to write narrative prose, especially now that I am exploding from within, ready to shower out in a fan of pain. I find it hard also because I don't like to fill in the gaps. For example, here are events in one city, events in another, but in proper narrative prose you need to tell how the main character packed his suitcase, took a taxi to the station, and then shook in the carriage on his journey from one city to the other.

But I don't remember how I bought a ticket, waited in the airport, boarded the plane and flew to Nazran. I remember only the call from Lena, our eldest sister, to say that Zarema was wounded – wounded several days ago in Shali, but nobody had known – and she was now in hospital, in Nazran.

And then, instantly, without pauses and scene jumps – as if

someone had cut out a section of the celluloid – I'm walking into an overcrowded hospital ward. Inside the ward . . . No, that's not right, not true. First I see only her. Thin, wasted, lying flat on the iron bed, all taped up in white strips of bandage, with pinched facial features, deathly pale. Did I say the word 'deathly'? I shouldn't have said it – after all, she was alive, that was the main thing, she was alive; that I must have grasped before anything else. But I remembered another Zarema: youthful, radiating health, athletic, ever confident and determined, and I felt so, so terrible! I covered my face with my hands, couldn't hold back the tears, my shoulders and chest shook with weeping, I whispered, 'Zarema, what's happened to you, little sister?'

An adult woman spoke loudly to me in Chechen: 'Don't cry, you're a man aren't you!' And quietly, in Russian: 'See, she's alive, now don't you cry, it'll only make her feel worse.' Only then did I realise there were other people in the ward. I looked around . . . No, I looked around properly only later. First I ran out of the ward to the corridor, calmed myself, pulled myself together, then went back in.

And, quieter now, I walked towards her, sat down on a nearby chair, and asked, 'How are you?' Tears were in her eyes, but she calmed down too and said, 'I'm well, I'm much better already.'

She really was much better. Here in Nazran, while we were none the wiser, an Ingush surgeon in an ordinary regional hospital with no neurosurgery department, tired, sleepless for days on end, had carried out a highly complex operation on Zarema. After the missile exploded into fragments, she was left with pieces gouged out of her forearm. But that wasn't the most terrible thing; the head had sustained shrapnel wounds, there was blunt traumatic injury to the brain. The intracranial pressure was rising, with pain, loss of consciousness; the situation was critical. The surgeon performed trepanation of the skull. The pressure eased, the crisis passed, now Zarema was getting better.

Zarema spoke little, I was told all this by others. Yes, there were others, I noticed when I looked around properly. In the ward lay women. Bandaged, burned, some with amputated limbs.

Then I went back into the corridor. The regional hospital had become a crowded military field hospital. For the civilian population. There were old men, women, children. Wounded, maimed. A boy with his leg torn off sat on a little bench, crutches propped against the wall, and spoke with an Ingush kid of his age.

'How do you say "sun" in Ingush? And "water"? And "bread"?' The little Ingush replied; the little Chechen laughed. To him the Ingush words sounded like mangled Chechen.

You know, I remember how I was once taken by ambulance to the emergency ward of a St Petersburg hospital. My neighbours there whined and complained, one incessantly wailing, 'Why did it have to happen to me?'

In Nazran nobody complained, neither the women nor the small children. Sometimes they said, 'It was Allah's will.' How can you defeat such a nation, how can you subjugate them, conquer them? You can never defeat a Chechen. You can only kill him, eliminate him.

Then I felt ashamed – for my lack of restraint, for these tears. People had suffered deaths in their family, their bodies torn to shreds, but we were alive, we were still in one piece. And a Chechen should never cry. It is hard to be a Chechen.

What am I to say now, when they open my passport and ask, 'Are you Chechen?' I can only answer: No, probably not, though I would dearly love to be.

51

Zarema faced a long course of treatment, the healing of her forearm, neurosurgical intervention. All that could be done in Nazran's overcrowded hospital, with its shortage of medicines and inadequate conditions for complex operations, the doctors had already done. Father and I organised Zarema's discharge, and I came to take her to St Petersburg.

At last, they handed us her discharge report, a Ministry of Emergencies vehicle drove her to the airport. In the airport a prematurely aged Ingush woman official issues stamps for the never-ending shipment of 'Cargo 200'. And we see the covered trucks standing in line for loading. But we're alive, we're alive! They may have to carry my sister into the plane on a stretcher, then I'll hold her in my arms, but we're alive. The air stewardesses vacate three front seats for us. None of the passengers utters a word of protest: this is Nazran, everyone understands.

This is Nazran. Everyone understands. But in Moscow, in Moscow it is as if they don't even know that there's a war on, as if they haven't heard. Our flight is to St Petersburg, but we set down in Moscow. A car drives to the stairs, men in civilian clothes come on board: 'Anyone here with firearms wounds, step this way!'

What? Step this way?

Only if you are wizards, if you can suddenly magic Zarema on to her legs. But you are not wizards, just pitiful Moscow office drudges, pitiful office drudges from the institute of pen-pushing. Once more I lift my sister into my arms, I go with them. This is the FSB, they have received information, and they must make checks. I produce the medical documents, I can't restrain my feelings, once again I can't restrain my feelings.

'You scum, monsters, cretins, she's barely alive, maybe you want to lock her up in jail? Found a terrorist, have you? A lady sniper? She's a teacher. You bastards, you sons of bitches, you blew up my village, she was on her way from work, you launched a missile attack on the village when there were no combatants there, you murderers. You want to take her away, do you? Me too, perhaps? You'd better take me too, or better still, kill us right here, on the spot. If you didn't finish us off there, well kill us here. Because if you take my sister away and leave me alive, then I will become a terrorist, make no mistake, I will blow up the whole of fucking Moscow, together with your fucking pen-pushing office and your fucking president, you motherfuckers!'

At first they growl back: 'If she hasn't taken part in combat, then how come she's wounded? We're not at war with the civilian population.'

'Ah my little ones, my soft-headed Muscovites. You're not, right? You've no doubt been reading the government press and watching the television. And you know nothing, right? Your pen-pushing office knows nothing, right? Let's get back on the plane, everyone there is from Nazran, they'll tell you: the whole town is full of mutilated children, there are wounded lying in the hospital corridors, all of them elderly, small children, women. Perhaps they are all combatants, seeing as you're only at war with them? Perhaps babies take part in combat action too?'

Sullen, they shut up. They hand back the documents, apologise dryly. We return to the plane, I carry my sister in my arms through the tense atmosphere of the cabin – a sigh of relief, and we fly to St Petersburg.

52

Probably I should be ashamed of my lack of restraint. What do they know, how are they to blame? Boys from the FSB, in peaceful Moscow. At that time Moscow was still peaceful. Probably – but I'm not ashamed.

We are all responsible for this, all of us, and corpulent, smug Moscow most of all. In the New Year they abolished pensioners' concessions, and Russia began to seethe with protests, till they shook the very throne of the president. Free travel cards and free electricity – that, it turns out, is the foundation of Russian existence that cannot be touched. Tens of thousands of people on the streets shouting political slogans: 'Putin – out! Putin – out!'

Why did we not take to the streets when this madness started, when this madness continued, when this madness recurred? When they bombed and shelled peaceful villages, killed people by the thousands – citizens of our own country. When unending trainloads of coffins were travelling, Cargo 200, the coffins of Russian kids – yes, Russian – senselessly killed in a senseless war. The tears of a mutilated child? What do we care for the tears of thousands of mutilated children and mothers, bereaved and grieving? We're more worried about our concessions, are we?

We forgave our generals, up to their elbows in innocent blood, but we cannot forgive them our travel cards, can we?

Why did we keep quiet, why did the nation's conscience keep quiet? Or has the nation no conscience any more?

Why didn't we listen to those who couldn't keep quiet?

Lazy, cowardly, mean, good-for-nothing nation, we deserve our worst tyrants.

Or did we think this was not about us, had nothing to do with us? Answer, for whom does the bell toll? Well? For whom does the bell toll? But the bell is not tolling. Even the sleigh bells are merely tinkling, the jingle bells on the reins of the troika. Where are you tearing to, troika? The three, the seven, the ace.[18] You are tearing off nowhere, you are taking your new hotshot aces for a ride, with their diamond ladies in expensive furs, with their flunkies, along Nevsky Prospekt, along Palace Square. Give alms for the horses' feed! Give alms for the troika horses' feed, and for the coachman's drink, and that's all there is to Russia, that's all.

The madman General Dudaev told us, back then, 'Russians, the war will come to your home.' Well now it's come.

And I say 'us' and 'we', because I'm one of you.

53

No matter how hard I tried to leave – to fly away, drive away, slope away – I just couldn't hide from the war. The war came after me, came not only through the official news broadcasts packed with lies and the tales of people from my village visiting St Petersburg, of how 'Idris – you know, who lived near the water tower – he went out to mow hay near where an army unit were, had a deal with them that he'd bring them a case of vodka, but they gunned him down all the same.' The war came to me through the searches at airports and stations, through the detentions 'while we verify your identity', through blunt refusals to register me, and the awkward and sheepish refusals to offer me jobs after reading my application form. Whether there's anything mystical to this or not, I had occasion at around the same time to take a heavy Makarov pistol into my hands and risk a bullet in the head. To hell with it all, I decided, if everyone thinks I'm a Chechen, then I'll live up to the hype. You want a Chechen, well you'll get one.

At a brief meeting with a bitter Russian gangster, after he'd voiced his claims and described vividly how he planned to kill me if my firm refused to pay up, I shrugged my shoulders nonchalantly and said:

'My name is Sadulaev, German Umaralievich. I am a Chechen. I don't know how to feel fear. The part of our brains responsible for fear has atrophied completely. You can kill me – sooner or later, you or someone else. See, we're all dead already, and the dead don't fear death. But for each one of ours, there'll be ten of yours. That's how we do things.'

The gangsters stopped phoning. However, I did get a call from the FSB inviting me to a meeting. 'What's all this, German Umaralievich, why are you threatening honest businessmen?' Again I shrugged my shoulders: 'So you guys are protecting the protection rackets?' The captain smiled: 'Ah, the language you use. We aren't protecting them. Simply keeping things in order, upholding law and justice.' I smiled back: 'Then here's the low-down and you can see for yourselves who owes whom.' The captain pored attentively over the documents and let me go. He told me simply: 'You come to us if anything happens. Well, why did you have to be so uncivilised, eh? See, you're a cultured man . . .'

That is true: we are cultured.

I have carried my war with me; we installed it in the clinic; I sat with my sister for days on end, then travelled to visit her each day. And there is operation after operation. Papa writes to all the authorities, Papa attempts to get the treatment covered from a budget, we are running out of money to pay for the hospital ward and the endless expensive operations. The responses are evasive. Perhaps yes, perhaps no . . .

I cheer up my sister: 'We Sadulaevs are like cats – no matter how you drop us, we'll land on all fours.' And we really are.

54

I was about to graduate in law at St Petersburg State University by distance learning. Over the summer I decided to do voluntary work experience at the Vasileostrov district prosecutor's office. I was assigned as a volunteer to the assistant public prosecutor for supervision over the police. A very pleasant, calm and intelligent girl. She gave me the job of going over the paperwork for closed criminal investigations, which had piled up on her desk by the dozen.

I remember those meagre office folders, containing just a few sheets, written in the dry, often clumsy and always dour language of the field workers and investigating officers.

Every second folder held a suicide case. Whenever we discovered a suicide the procedure was to conduct an assessment with a view to initiating criminal proceedings: was it actually homicide disguised as a suicide, or had the victim been driven to suicide, which would constitute a crime in its own right, in accordance with current criminal law?

They were as alike as stillborn twins, these investigations into the circumstances of suicide. From one folder to the next, the same story repeated itself: forename, patronymic, surname. Date of birth 19__. Cause of death: asphyxiation. Body discovered by family members, hanged by rope noose attached to ___, no signs of struggle or violence. There would follow a brief biography of the victim. Attended School No. __; grades – average; no previous police record; not registered at psychiatric clinic; not registered at drug abuse clinic; was sociable, had friends, engaged in ___ at sports centre; described by relatives and acquaintances of that period as honest, open, good-natured teenager. In 19__ called up for military service. Sent to Chechen Republic. Demobilised in 19__; no injuries. Following demobilisation attempted to enter higher education/find employment as a ___; changed place of work frequently; became irritable and withdrawn; began using alcohol/drugs; no settled private life; relations with family became strained. On the day prior to suicide acted as normal; no incidents took place; received no letters or other communications. Decision: to deny prosecution in the absence of a criminal act.

Each week there were several such cases. And this was only in one district of one city. Who kept the statistics, how many of these superfluous victims were there, dead soldiers of a faraway war, across the whole of Russia? In America, someone did keep statistics, they calculated that the number of suicides among former military servicemen who had been through Vietnam was double the number of American combat losses during the Vietnamese adventure.

And these were the best of soldiers. Those whose hearts hadn't hardened, who saw bloodied children in their dreams. If this nation has a conscience, then they are it, and that conscience has already died, hanged in flats and rooms of communal apartments, unable to live with what it knows, what it remembers.

Then there are others. Those who went to fight for the combat pay, went voluntarily, to murder and rob with impunity, knowing the sweet taste of other people's blood. And they too have returned. Make no mistake, they too have returned.

The women in Samashki said to the journalists: How could the Russians not realise that these monsters who have brutally murdered our children will go back home – they aren't human any more, they are subhuman, they know no other life, they will carry on killing there too, it's what now gives their lives meaning and excitement.

I don't want to write any more about this. We all have children. I don't trust these words, shaping themselves into sentences with suspicious ease, line after line. Or this blood spurting forth, these innards tumbling out of me, like after the explosion of a vacuum bomb; you can predict the future with them, if you know how. I write about the past – it becomes the future, I write about the future – it becomes the past. My little daughter is growing up, going to school, every day she goes out on to the street, the street where . . . Better not to write about that at all.

55

I'd like to write about something else. About what I remember. About my childhood in the green valley near the Black Mountains and the blue ones, about games, playmates, favourite pets. About dogs, for instance. Yes, dogs.

Here in the big city, people keep dogs in flats. Sometimes little toy dogs, no bigger than a cat. Sometimes strapping, aggressive canines. They keep them in the narrow confines of a city flat. How are these people not afraid? You can't always tell what's on the mind of another human, so how can we tell what's on the mind of a large predatory animal, and sleep under the same roof as him? 'The Dogs of War' – it's the name of a Pink Floyd song. The dogs of war, they always live with us.

No, in the village we don't let dogs into the house. They have the spacious yard, they can take time off from their leashed duties and run around the street. In our yard there was always a dog or two. Of course, I loved them. It's hard for me to imagine now, but I almost kissed those smelly, doggy, toothy creatures. And they were patient with children, even when I harnessed a sleigh to the sheepdog – not a sledge-pulling animal by nature – and rode along the street.

We had Rem, an aristocrat, and a sheepdog, Mukhtar. Those I remember. Later Rem died under the wheels of a truck, and we gave Mukhtar away to someone. One day Papa brought home two reddish-brown puppies. So that the dogs would grow up fierce, they were given the names Pushtun and Koba.[19] A few months later the puppies fell ill with canine distemper. They ate nothing, vomited murky green slop, wandered and staggered about the yard looking hopelessly gaunt or lay by the garage wall.

Before long one of them died. It was Koba. I felt personally to blame for his death. For not having had enough resolve, enough focus in my meditation to save his life. No matter what, I had to save the other one.

Early in the morning, as day broke, I stood waiting on the garage roof, facing the sun rising over the gardens. And I prayed: 'Sun! You bestow life upon all the living, you sustain our breath and the beating of our hearts. Do not forsake my puppy, show him your mercy.' Pushtun lived.

Koba I buried myself. In the far south-eastern corner of our garden, under a crab-apple tree. I dug a grave, tipped soil over the corpse: a little hill took shape. I even made a bench, and placed it near the grave. Later I often sat on that bench reading, writing, sometimes just contemplating. My family did not approve of this, but said nothing. After all, I was still a child. Moreover, a crazy one.

56

During the war, when Russian aircraft began regular raids on the village, the villagers would try to hide in the bomb shelters. I have already mentioned this. But there's more. My father wouldn't go to the air raid shelter. He would simply stay at home, trusting to fate.

And one day it happened. Papa was standing in the yard, Pushtun was scampering nearby, an enormous dog with a pale-russet coat. A bomb fell directly into our yard.

From the moment the aeroplanes appeared in the sky, Pushtun had become restless, pressed himself to my father and whimpered. An explosion boomed, and in a flash the dog jumped on to his owner, knocking him off his feet. Pushtun covered him with his body. After, when Papa lifted him up in his arms, he was bleeding all over, wounded by the shrapnel blasted from the bomb. In him were dozens of metal pellets. Intended for my father. Only one hit Papa's body, in the shoulder.

That's how it will always be from now on. Must it always be? No matter what I recall, the threads of my memory lead me back to the war . . .

Many years earlier, on the garage roof, while praying to the rising sun, I solicited from him not just my puppy's life: without knowing it, I had petitioned the sun for the life of my father, whom the dog would save from death.

57

And I could write more. But somewhere must come an end. Everything comes to an end. This tale too must end, and the sooner, the better.

Somewhere inside, no doubt, though hiding this from everyone, even myself, I believe – still believe – that I should write a story about this and put an end to it. And then it will all stop. The dreams, the memory, the war. All my fears. See, they are my fears, but I'll close my eyes, I'll put an end to it, and the terrifying spider will disappear, it will all be over.

Yet so far the magic of my words has been powerless. I have already written, but as you see I write again. Perhaps this time it will work? I cannot forbid myself the hope.

58

And then I saw Father off at the station. He had visited me in St Petersburg, we spent two weeks together, we loved each other as though for the very first time. It was winter, but our feelings were as fresh as spring – people don't talk like that about filial love, but why not? It is stronger and purer than love for a woman. And it wells up again, as if for the first time. We talked for hours, cooked meals together, went for walks. We couldn't get enough of each other. We were happy just the two of us, he and I – one whole. And the dozens, hundreds of our ancestors too, going back to fair-haired Her and beyond, were all in us, conversing with one another. And this didn't seem like madness to us.

Then I saw Father off at the station. I embraced him, pressing my warm face to his unshaven cheek. At home I could not have done this. But we were in Russia. Nobody would see us. A few minutes remained before the train left, and Papa spoke.

'Yes, we cut down the cherry trees, but it's even better like that. The neighbours' kids were forever climbing them, in any case, breaking off branches – we kept having to shout at them. Now the garden's more spacious. The other trees have grown. There's a good harvest every year. And nobody touches it: there are no pests. There are birds, lots of them. When they started bombing and shelling the forests, the woodland birds flew to the village, they huddled up close to the people, settled in the gardens. Now there are loads of them, they sing, flutter about the branches. Thrushes, woodpeckers, bullfinches, blue tits – they're all here! And they've eaten the pests clean up so you don't need to use any chemicals now. And the swallows, you know, the swallows have started flying back! They've built a nest above our doorway . . . And . . . maybe it will all be the way it was?'

I could hear, unspoken: 'Maybe you'll come home, son?' I smiled sadly, and replied: 'One swallow doesn't make a summer, Papa.'

The train left. I went home. I switch off my telephone, close the doors; I'm going to sleep. I'll dream of mountains, the Black Mountains and the blue ones on the horizon. I'll dream of gardens filled with flowers and fruit, suffused in birdsong. And Mama will come out on to the doorstep, squinting in the spring sun. And before everything comes to an end and is furled up in the helix of ancestral memory, I'll see myself as a swallow, an angel on a brilliant path. And I'll fall into the sky.

Why the Sky Doesn't Fall Down

A Crown of Sonnets

1

Every evening after eight I'm left here alone. The long rows of rooms are filled with old furniture and archives, there are computers in the office, in the apartment a sofa, a cupboard and television. I work here, and this is where I live. I live here because it's very convenient – the journey home from work takes less than a minute. Because someone has to live here, anyway, to answer any after-hours phone calls. To turn the lights in the windows on and off, to keep evildoers away. That's how I explain it to the few people who ask. That's how I explain it to myself. It isn't true.

In reality I live here because I have nowhere else to live. Because I have no home. Everyone has a home. Where he used to live, where his parents lived. A little log cabin in the country, a room in a communal apartment. Birds have their nests, wild animals their dens. I have nowhere to lay my head. Although I'm an ordinary ghost, one of billions of ghosts.

And I do have a house which now stands dark and empty.

The autumn is heavy, cold. The windows haven't been reglazed since the commandant's headquarters were blown up. There it is, the commandant's headquarters: you can see it if you stand on the veranda. Only now there is no veranda. And no glass in the windows. Nobody glazes windows any more. There is no point glazing windows. The panes shatter during the explosions. The house is empty. Whatever could be sold or swapped for a bag of marijuana was taken by the Russian soldiers who entered my yard in armoured personnel carriers. What the soldiers left behind went on booze for my alcoholic uncle, whom my father had entrusted to live in and look after the house. Yesterday I had a dream. The garden: right in its centre is the large, spreading cherry tree. Flanked by little sibling cherry trees. I remember planting them with Father. Remember them growing, donning their bridal blossoms each spring. This was only a dream. The cherry trees have been chopped down, and their gnarled stumps jut above the grey earth.

I walk down the long corridor. From room to room. We often had guests, and almost without fail they'd say that you could lose your way in our house. I didn't understand them at the time. But I did later. When I was living in cramped flats, rooms, corners of rooms. Where no one could lose his way. In our house you really could though. Each child had a room of his own; our parents had their own room; in the main room we would gather to watch television and to read the newspaper aloud; in a separate room was the library, where we received guests; in addition to the kitchen there was also a dining room, although in the summer we loved to take lunch on the spacious glass-covered veranda. And to read books, lying on the saggy couch in a heap of old quilts.

Books. The books went as kindling the winter my sister and her husband were trying to warm a single room. Here, on the wood stove, is where they cooked, where they heated up water for washing. And here are the scraps of glossy paper, singed at the edges. The *Great Soviet Encyclopedia* – that lasted well. Its thick pages and cardboard cover ignited poorly but burned long, almost as long as willow logs.

The lane had three long cottages, each divided into two: six families in all. We lived without street name or house number. One day we decided to write a collective request to the executive committee. Opinion over a name was divided. Father suggested 'Willow Lane'. Huge weeping willows grew in our yard, visible from afar, from wherever you looked flooding the view of the lane with emerald green. How my sisters loathed them! Whatever the season, they shed leaves and twigs, and Mama would issue orders to sweep the spacious yard. I too swept, though more often than not I carried the rubbish out on my good old homemade cart, which my uncle the alcoholic had built. And then I'd run to the library, to the books.

Perhaps something had survived that winter? Impressive folios of academic translations of the Rig Veda and Mah bh rata. Collected works bound in green with gilt lettering: Tolstoy, Bunin, Turgenev, Chekhov. Bound in blue: John Steinbeck. Various editions of Sergei Yesenin. Most beloved of all were a small volume of the selected poems of Nikolai Gumilev and a slim red hardback bearing a trefoil: Jorge Luis Borges.

The lane never did get a name. The penultimate stamp in my Soviet passport reads 'State Farm Jalka Estate'. That's what they called our state farm, so named in Soviet times. Named after the river. The river Bass runs through our village. Whereas the Jalka flows near Gudermes. But the powers that be got into a muddle. They named the state farm in the village near Gudermes 'Bass', and ours 'Jalka'. Our relatives lived in the village Bass, on the bank of the Jalka. My first cousin.

They were betrayed. The youths from the sabotage squad, mere kids, were sent to mine the roads in front of the advancing Federal troops. He was very gifted. At home he made all sorts of cunning contraptions and he also grew flowers in the greenhouse. He always had flowers in his greenhouse – even in winter. They made a good demolition man of him. They were sent on ahead. But at that very moment the commander was selling their corpses to the Russian generals though they were still alive when he betrayed them. Gudermes was surrendered without a fight. The sabotage squad was encircled and they were killed from a safe distance, slowly and merrily. Victory had been paid for. The corpses were brought to town on a truck and dumped in the square. Mothers, howling, dug their children out from the heap of bodies and carried them home. How could they carry them, weighed down with death, in their thin, wrinkled arms? Well, that's nothing. That's another question. Empty, frantic eyes, hearts frozen with grief – how could they carry their own hearts now, so large, so heavy, so useless?

Beyond my window is a late white St Petersburg autumn. The calm of an old lane. The calm of an imperial building. And memories. Like explosions. Once my memory was a strawberry field. Now it is a minefield.

When I was fifteen or sixteen, I wrote two novellas. They were terrible. The first, a long one in gothic style, recounted a tale about werewolves: a wolf and a vixen who came to a carnival in the town of Alraune. Their masks were the best in the carnival. Genuine beasts' heads on human shoulders! And in every inn they visited, when they left, the wooden floors became sodden with blood, red as young wine. They found themselves in a castle and sat down at the long table of a knight – the castle's owner. The son of a great Crusader, who in one of his heroic campaigns for the glory of Christ had killed, among hundreds of innocent village dwellers, the father and mother of two infants. Heathens. Who had remained true to the customs of their forefathers and would not accept the Saviour. He had christened them with the sword. He ordered that the children be tossed into a wagon. During the night, wild beasts attacked the camp where they had stopped in the forest. The next morning many knights lay with their throats sliced from ear to ear. And the children – a boy and a girl – had disappeared. The young owner of the castle seated at the long table recalled this family legend and asked all the guests to remove masks. Only two revellers – wearing the wolf and fox heads – would not remove their masks. The knight fought and defeated the werewolves. With his sharp sword he chopped the bestial heads from their shoulders and, impaling them with a long spear, cast them into the hearth. A flame shot out of the fireplace in a furious whirlwind. That night the town of Alraune burnt to the ground and people from neighbouring villages claimed to see in the flames and smoke over the town the silhouettes of monstrous beasts – a wolf and a vixen – running across the sky.

The second novella was short. It recounted how early one morning a Pioneer detachment walked out of a secret cave and marched through a provincial Soviet town to the beat of a drum. The detachment sang: 'Raise our bonfires higher, navy nights!'[20] When they left, fire came flaming down from the skies. The novella was called 'Alraunsk, Burnt Again'.

We all saw it, each in his own way, we felt it in our skin, in our memory of the future we foresaw the fire from the skies. It already streamed over us, invisibly but palpably, when the fields were still filled with strawberries. Delicious, large strawberries grew in the forest glades near Serzhen-Yurt. Serzhen-Yurt was destroyed twice. In the first war it was wiped from the face of the earth by carpet-bombing, multiple-rocket launchers, heavy artillery. Yet people are amazing. In the brief interim between the wars they rebuilt houses – beautiful stone-and-brick houses, the kind that last for centuries. On this wonderful patch of land where large strawberries grow, where the water in the rivers is clear as crystal, where the freshness of the submountain air dizzies you; on this accursed patch of land, crossed by the road to Vedeno, the road to the mountain stronghold of the Resistance, a road that one group wants to seize, and another wants to hold on to at any cost. On this road stood Serzhen-Yurt. When that village still existed. In the second war it was again wiped from the face of the earth by carpet-bombing, multiple-rocket launchers, heavy artillery.

Alraune is the Arabic name for the mandrake plant. In medieval times magical powers were attributed to mandrake; a powder made from its root was an ingredient in many magic potions. The mandrake root resembles a human figure and according to legend it grows on the site of a murder. When you pick mandrake from the earth, it emits a human moan and anyone who picks mandrake will, without fail, die. Therefore, the plant is drawn out of the earth by tying it to the tail of a dog. Who is then doomed.

Now strawberries grow in these fields, even more, it seems, than before. Sweet, intoxicating strawberries. Nobody picks them. Everyone laid mines – the Federals and the rebels. Nobody knows the patterns, the maps. Legs blown off young soldiers, children torn to pieces. Strawberries grow well in fields watered with thick, rich human blood. But perhaps they are no longer strawberries. Perhaps it is mandrake growing in the forest fields near Serzhen-Yurt. Mandrake brings death, mandrake moans and explodes in the form of mines under the feet of anyone who treads this paradisical earth, this hellish earth.

When I finish writing this story, I too can die calmly. Everyone has already died. What am I doing here, alone in this void, in this quiet? I knew that I must compose one book. I waited for wisdom, which comes with the passing of years, waited for grey temples and composure of mind. Now I have begun. It feels like I don't have long left. And what about the grey head? My temples have already turned grey and I'm not yet thirty. But our generation fell into the line of fire. Everyone has already died. When I finish this tale, I too can die calmly.

2

Our families were friends. We had a lot in common. Their mama had the same name as mine. Our fathers bought identical cars. Weekends and holidays, picnics in the countryside, New Year's Eves and birthdays we spent together. In the cold, empty house we still have the photo album, there are many photographs of us in the forest, on the river bank – our parents playing cards, us running through the fields, chasing a ball, knocking a shuttlecock about. Their only son was roughly my age and we both had two sisters. I have never met another driver like Valid. It was quite terrifying to sit in the car as he chased down the road at night. Though he never had a single accident. Valid was very tall and beautiful, women loved him. He was desperately brave. After serving in the army, he stayed in Moscow. He used to send money to his parents. He shipped cars for resale. The day came, and he returned himself, for good, his lofty, bare forehead shot clean through. The war was beginning there. The only good Chechen is a dead Chechen. Well, Valid became a good Chechen and returned home. His lofty, bare forehead shot clean through. Since then, I often see him in dreams and talk with him. We talk about everything. And he always smiles. I no longer notice the hole caked with red blood in the middle of his forehead. All the same, these are difficult dreams.

3

I have never been in the mountains. None of us has ever been in the mountains. We lived in Shali, which translates as 'place of the plain'. Shali is an ancient settlement in the heart of Ichkeria. In Soviet times it was considered a village, though one of the largest in the world, with more than thirty thousand inhabitants. The only one larger was somewhere in Africa. We took pride in this. Then Shali was designated a town. An ordinary small provincial town, like many along Russia's fringes.

But I've never been in the mountains. It's true, we sometimes saw the mountains. In fine, cloudless weather, the Greater Caucasian range soared up like a wondrous vision over the southern brink of the horizon. And it was strange to see the snowy caps of the summits on hot southern days. The gorges, glaciers – all clear to see, in detail. In the morning we would go out to school, and the road led straight to the horizon, to the fairytale blue mountains with shimmering white peaks.

There were hills too. Wooded hills at the foot of the mountains, at Serzhen-Yurt. And strange unwooded elevations in the fields. In

India they say that mountains once knew how to fly but the tsar of the skies, the god of war Indra, severed their wings with lightning and they fell to the ground. I saw those mountains when travelling by train through the country around Kurukshetra. The landscape looks truly bizarre – no ridges, no foothills. Just a field with a hill in it, as though it had fallen from the sky. I believe it, now I believe it. I know that plenty can fall when nobody holds the sky up. Even mountains, mountains too can fall from the sky.

Such a hill stands west of Shali. In the flat, bare field is a high, treeless hill. The Bald Mountain. It is believed that such mountains are an assembly point for evil spirits. In reality, these are the memories of the heathen shrines set upon the summits of such hills; our ancestors carried out sacrifices here, kindled the sacred fire. For here they were closer to the sky, the abode of the gods. I think in days gone by that that mountain too had a shrine. Near the ancient settlement, it is the site closest to the sky.

We were drawn to the hill. As kids, we saw it while playing. Then one day we gathered for an expedition. We trudged for a time on the trails through the forest belt, through the overgrown thicket, along the edge of the golden wheat fields, across the bare plain with the abandoned oil pumps. We scrambled up the steep slope. And we made it. On the level summit of the hill stood two huge containers for oil, empty and rusty. We scrambled to the very top. The entire village spread out before our eyes. The silver ribbon of the Bass snaked. Beyond the village the groves shone green, the state farm fields glowed yellow. And the sky. The sky was so close.

On the rusty sides of the tank we – my best friend, Dinka, and I – scratched out the names of our sweethearts in huge letters. I wrote the name Larisa. Larisa had studied with me in Class 7C, School No. 8. She was the daughter of the chairman of the district

KGB. Ginger-haired, with a sweet, freckly face and a light, joyous character. I think she's still alive. Because they left, long ago. At the end of Class 8, Larisa said goodbye to us. Her father had been transferred to another location, and they were leaving. She looked at me sadly on our last day, a warm, sunny day in May. Later I received a letter, one letter. I think she's still alive. Because they left long ago, long before the sky fell. And because I've never seen her in my dreams. Not once seen her in the city of the dead.

You could check your watch by him. Every day without fail after lunch he would appear in the sky. Every day the dragon came for new victims. He would drop a full bomb load onto the village, on to the quiet, peaceful homes. And the homes would blaze; cluster bombs banned by international conventions exploded there and flechette bombs unknown to international conventions. And each time he'd finished his bombing, the dragon would mock us. He knew there was no air defence. Oh, he knew there were no serious armed formations at all. Just a defence squad – guerrillas with a hotchpotch of small arms bought at the market and some double-barrelled hunting guns. He would come in at low altitude, skimming the treetops and at full throttle, he'd shoot his machine gun just for fun at the people fleeing through the streets – the women, children and the elderly escaping from the burning buildings. Until his ammunition ran out. Then the dragon flew off. But the next day the dragon would be back.

The dragon flew in from the west, where in the evening the setting sun flared like a funeral pyre. Passing over the village, he would turn around and come back. He would turn around above the bald hill.

He was brought down by a single shot, an incendiary charge from an ordinary Kalashnikov, while he manoeuvred for another run. Flying low, fearing nobody, skimming the treetops. He knew there was no air defence. And no Stingers. If only there had been Stingers! But there were none. So they brought him down with an ordinary Kalashnikov. Two guerrillas squatted on the Bald Mountain, under the empty tanks, on the flat summit of the Bald Mountain, where the ancient shrines of our ancestors had once stood. For it is closer to the sky, where the gods live. Where the dragons live.

The bullet hit the fuel tank, the aeroplane caught fire. The pilot tried to pull the burning machine out of its dive. But an explosion boomed. The plane fell into the vast flat field, where earlier, when there were no dragons, wheat had grown. The ejection seat worked, expelling the pilot into the sky; the parachute's white canopy opened. Two guerrillas were waiting for him where he landed. I don't know if he was dead already or merely unconscious when he reached the ground. One of the guerrillas pulled a long knife from his boot and – in a wide slice from ear to ear – cut the pilot's throat.

They carried him through the streets on a homemade cart, a sturdy homemade cart, used before for carrying refuse. He had an Asiatic face, no longer expressing anything. His head – hanging from his neck bone – was dragged along the dusty road. Out of each house came women who spat in his face, delivering the most ancient, the most terrible curses upon the dragon's soul and upon his entire clan, in all its offshoots and generations. There wasn't a street – wasn't a family – to which he had not brought death. Now he rode through the village on the refuse cart, and women spat in his face. The blood no longer poured from his sliced throat. But did he have blood, like the blood a human has? Perhaps he had blood, but of another kind: the dark green blood of a dragon, and a cold snake's heart.

4

Why am I writing this book? For whom? Why have I left my bed, thrown off two blankets? It is cold. This winter in St Petersburg is very cold. The old building has large windows and no amount of radiators could heat the room. But under two blankets I feel warm. I lie and look at the white tiles on the lowered ceiling. A few tiles are missing. I look up for hours and mechanically rearrange the tiles in my mind, imagining what geometric shapes could be made from the combinations of the gaps. And I think. Well, no, I don't think. Thinking involves something dynamic. My consciousness is static. I simply remember. I remember it all.

For whom am I writing this book? Nobody will read it, nobody could understand it. Nobody will accept it, on either side of the line of fire. Nobody needs a book like this, it does not fit into either side's propaganda system. Not one of its heroes' names is sensationally famous – oh nobody knew of them while they were alive, they were ordinary people. This book can't even offer sophisticated youngsters any postmodern touches.

Why have I left my bed, thrown off two blankets? For whom am I writing this book?

For them. Nobody knew them while they were alive; they were ordinary people. Now nothing is left, and it's as though they never existed. But they did exist. This is my town – the town of the dead – and I should engrave a memorial plaque for each home. This is the book of the dead and it should have a line about each of them. This is my duty. For this reason I was left among the living. Left for a while.

The living don't need my book. The dead do. I know this. I

remember this while I imagine the geometric shapes emerging from the compositions of gaps.

A crown of sonnets is a complex poetic form. Together, the first lines from each sonnet create a final key sonnet. In Russian poetry only one such work exists, composed by an obscure poet at the turn of the century. His crown of sonnets is named 'To the Dead of the First World War'.

5

On that visit, I didn't immediately recognise Mariam in the tall, slender girl with large eyes. Which was hardly surprising. When I'd last seen her, she had still been a child of seven or eight. She had looked funny, big-eared. Glancing at her now, the last thing you'd do was laugh. Taller than me, and I'm certainly not short when standing up straight. A beautiful, fine-featured face. Lustrous, piercingly blue eyes. A bride. Mariam herself laughed, said there wasn't a guy here whom she couldn't look down upon, referring to her height. But that was maidenly modesty speaking. In reality she was engaged.

Mariam was Valid's younger sister. Some years earlier Valid had returned to the homeland, and the eyes of the parents who'd lost their only son were consumed with grief. Mariam was the youngest child. Bereaved, her parents now devoted all their desperate love to her.

Evil spirits, demons from dark caves, descendants of dragons and snakes, bloodless monsters tormenting the earth and its inhabitants in ancient times. Now they have returned. They are dressed in green clothes like the skin of giant bog toads, with epaulettes like spines on their shoulders. The one with the biggest spines, the one who has more of these spines is revered by these monsters as the boss, the other monsters obeying his commands.

They calculated everything with precision. After the strike of the surface-to-surface missile on the very heart of Shali, on the crowd of people who'd arrived – some on their own business, some because they'd believed the rumours that the authorities were finally issuing pensions and child benefits – they waited two hours. That would be enough time for the relatives to carry the hundreds of dead bodies, the hundreds of wounded, into the houses, to try to save those who had survived. They calculated with precision that the wounded would be carried to the nearest houses, not far from the centre: you cannot carry people losing blood all the way to the edge of the village. Two hours after the terribly powerful strike of a surface-to-surface missile on a peaceful village and unarmed people, the town centre and adjoining streets were showered with mortar fire.

In the house of Mariam's relatives, not far from the centre, they were bandaging my sister, found among the wounded.

Shells rained down on the house and yard. From under the rubble they dug out my sister, unconscious but alive. Mariam and her cousin were in the car. A shell fell straight on to the vehicle. Tattered clothes, spattered in blood. Just like before when we climbed in the garden as children – spattered with ripe cherry juice.

Two people exist on this earth as living ghosts. First their only son, then their daughter. Early in the morning they came here again, to the cemetery. Where else do they have left to go? Ah, how sweet for them the thought that they too will soon be able to rest in this earth. Right here, nearby... We'll all be close, our little son, our little daughter... We'll be together... As we used to be, remember, when we lived in Serzhen-Yurt, the village which is no more, in the house of which only ashes remain. Remember how we used to gather berries in the forest glades? Where are you now? In which glades do you gather berries? Who will smooth your ruffled hair, who'll kiss your little white hands, who will cuddle you in the land of the dead, in the place where the sun never rises? Are you cold in the earth, do you long for the sun, for the sky? Don't long for them, because the sun has burnt out and the sky is no more; it fell down and smashed and killed us all. And it only seems that you are there and we are here. We too are there, we're already there, in the place where there is no sun or sky.

They came in the morning – early in the morning, very early. But they were not the first. Beside the fresh grave, by the mound of earth, lay a boy. His thin shoulders were shaking, and one name burst out endlessly along with his sobs. Happiness had escaped – happiness which had been so close; the first and only love of his entire life now lay in this earth. The lilac will never flower, there will be no light-filled spring joy. Life has ended, no hope remains. She was sixteen. What did they kill her for? For the blue, piercing blue of her eyes? For her smile which filled my heart with warmth? What did they kill her for? Earth, take me, I am young and strong, take my blood, my flesh: let her go, let her walk upon the grasses, let her plait flowers into her glorious hair... don't stay silent, earth! He gets up. He should feel ashamed; he's a man, he should not cry, he knows how to endure pain. He should feel ashamed but he doesn't. He no longer feels anything. He is seventeen. No, he is seventeen thousand, he is already old, knows how to feel nothing but pain.

He walks away, through the fragments of sky, to the place where he'll now live, to a world in which spring never comes, where the sun never rises.

6

Narts, narts, ancient *bogatyrs*,[21] tear the rock asunder, come out from the mountains, look – the sky has fallen, no one is holding the sky up! See what has happened to your earth, your people!

Evil dragons are flying over the houses, gardens and cornfields, burning everything with their foul breath, raining incandescent steel from the skies. Horrific monsters are crawling the earth, spewing out death. Hordes of cannibals are scouring the villages, killing and devouring your children.

Narts, arise from your centuries-long slumber, save the world as you saved it at the dawn of time! Slay the dragons, the monsters, chase the cannibals away to the faraway, cold, snowy lands, to the place where they ought to live, devouring each other.

They were a tribe of earthly gods, peerless warriors. But the era of heroes passed and ominous signs of decline were everywhere. And the earth could no longer support them. They took a step and sank up to their knees from the weight of their bodies, from their own might. They took another – and sank up to their hips. They left for the mountains, but there, too, the age-old stone slabs cracked under their tread. They realised that their time had passed. Yet no one could kill them, there was no warrior or weapon that could strike them dead. So the narts boiled up seething copper in a huge cauldron and drank it. Yet even then, the narts didn't die straightaway. They lay for a long time in the cave, tormented by thirst and a rock pigeon brought them water in its beak. As they died, the narts stroked the pigeon. Ever since, on the head and neck of the pigeon there has remained a stripe of molten copper.

7

It became a ritual. Every day after class Ruslanbek and I would fight, after goading each other with hurtful words. The whole class would gather to watch. The boys would stand in a circle, cheering each successful blow or throw loudly. The fighting went on, with varying results. That day, I kicked Ruslanbek in the stomach, but my opponent stepped back just in time and grabbed my leg. Another instant and he'd have jerked the leg towards himself; not having expected such a turn of events, I bent my leg at the knee and with all my weight laid into him. He fell on his back straight on to some large lumps of burnt coal scattered around the schoolyard. Finding myself on top, I began to strangle him. Ruslanbek resisted. Suddenly I saw tears welling up in his eyes from wild, unvoiced pain. Something flipped in me. Somehow all these spectators seemed vile, yelling enthusiastically at the sight of our tussle. *Found yourself some gladiators*, I thought angrily, relaxed my grip, and got up. Ruslanbek leapt up, overcoming his pain, and got ready to throw himself at me. I stretched out my hand to him. 'No hard feelings,' I said in Chechen.

We became friends. Sat at the same desk, skipped lessons together. Rode after school on passing military trucks to the soldiers' lake to bathe. The lake was dug specially for tanks and infantry combat vehicles, as a water obstacle for crossing during training exercises. Our mountain brooks are brisk and shallow, but in these artificial lakes you could swim for ages in the calm water.

I remember how we swam in the autumn, how we climbed out on to the bank and – shivering from the cold – smoked a packet of Kosmos cigarettes. For us it seemed terribly forbidden, but grown-up and manly. I remember how we returned, once again catching a lift in a truck from the nearby military base. Ruslanbek had an open, easygoing character; he asked the soldiers cheerfully and simply, and they laughed and gave us a lift.

Ruslanbek had a nickname, a word which translates from Chechen as 'holes'. He was awarded this name by our classmate – and his neighbour – Rasul. Rasul's parents were rich and bought their son expensive tape decks and Western clothes. Rasul's papa worked as the manager of the warehouse. Ruslanbek's mama was a teacher, his father a bus driver. And there were two sisters as well, who also had to be clothed. So Ruslanbek had few clothes – a navy school uniform and not much else by the looks of it. Arriving home from school, he'd go off to play outdoors in the same clothes. Ruslanbek was a lively boy, so it was hardly surprising that his clothes would become worn to holes depressingly quickly.

One day, however, Ruslanbek's mother heard the neighbourhood children teasing him. She hurried her son home, and made him take off his navy jacket, trousers and shirt. She sewed up all the holes, crying quietly, spilling tears on to the dusty garments. From that day on, even when playing on the streets, Ruslanbek would wear a suit that, though it was the same old threadbare one, had always been washed and darned by his mother's hand.

The name stuck regardless. But not as far as his mother was concerned. She called him Rusik. He had light-blond hair and blue eyes. Among Chechens you will often see people with 'Slavic' looks; some explain this as the influence of mixed marriages, but the elders say that a real Chechen is fair-haired or red-headed, with blue or green eyes and gentle facial features. Whereas dark hair, large noses – these in fact are the consequences of many centuries of interbreeding with our neighbouring peoples.

Everyone still remembers Ruslanbek's extraordinary eagerness for community work. Without ever being asked, he'd be the first to run up and push a stuck car; for days on end he would accompany his neighbours if he noticed them planning some building job or maintenance; no old lady could pass him carrying bags. Ruslanbek would take the bags and walk the woman home, diverting her with polite conversation along the way. Rasul always laughed at him for this unsolicited kindness, which at times could seem meddling.

He was one of the first to join the defence squad, probably because of this personality trait. The guerrillas were setting up watches at the edge of the village though the purpose of such patrolling was mundane enough. There was no combat action, but the Russian soldiers, reduced to a half-animal state, would run off with weapons from units stationed at peacefully surrendered villages, plunder everything in sight and kill everyone they met on their way.

Lord, what was there to take from Ruslanbek's house? Rasul's house, though, offered easy pickings now. But Rasul had not volunteered for the watches. Most likely he had left, long ago, and was living in Russia.

Besides the hungry and drunken soldiers, there were snipers too. The snipers sat in hiding and got bored and to relieve the tedium would shoot at people. Rather, at Chechens. Ruslanbek died swiftly, easily. He probably didn't even feel anything. The sniper's bullet went straight through his heart, and he fell on his back as though he'd choked. His wide-open, surprised eyes reflected the sky for the last time – so clear and blue.

Ruslanbek's body was taken home; they began preparing his ablutions and burial. His mother, aged and crazy from grief, stood over her son. To her it seemed he'd merely fallen asleep. Only, here on his shirt, on his chest, was a tiny little hole. But that was no big deal. She'd sew up the hole. She always sewed up the holes in his clothes so the mean neighbourhood kids wouldn't tease her sweet, fair-haired treasure. Let me sew up the hole! Why are you holding my arms, why are you crying on my shoulders, where are you taking me? Let me go, I have to sew up the hole while my son is asleep; he'll wake up and go out on to the streets to play, you see, and I can't let him out in rags, the boys will laugh at him – let me sew up this small hole, let me go, let me go to him . . .

8

It began long ago, during the first days of the war. 'Mama, I had a strange dream. I was in our neighbourhood and I'm walking, as usual, along the path through the field, to the state farm canteen where we used to buy fresh warm bread. But the field is covered in bomb craters, all that's left of the canteen and the warehouse opposite it are smoke and ruins, smoke drifts over the land, over the heaps of charred bricks . . .'

'Yes, my son. That's how it is. The field is full of craters, the canteen and the warehouse were destroyed. Lots of buildings have been destroyed, my son. Lots of people have died . . .'

Since then I often dream about our town, only now I don't dream of it like that – no, I see it calm and untroubled, the way I knew it and saw it in childhood. All the buildings are intact, there are no craters in the fields, no craters in the streets, no traces of shrapnel on the fences and the walls of the houses.

And in this town live people. Plenty of people! I meet them everywhere I go, on every street, on the pavement by the road. I know all of them. We greet each other, we chat. And I walk on. I meet plenty of people on the way.

Only all these people are dead.

In the town of my dreams, in the town of the dead, I have never seen anyone who is still alive. And if I see someone there for the first time, I'll soon hear of his death.

I feel bad when these dreams start. I feel like I'm ill. I walk about all day in a dream-like state, but as soon as I fall asleep I find myself in the place where yesterday's dream ended. I feel good there, with them. And I feel bad here, with you. I tell them this; they nod their heads in sympathy, and say, 'Yes, we know. No one will understand you there. Stay here with us. We're all already here, you see, and only you are still there. Come over to us and stay.'

9

For some reason, my neighbours would reminisce about Ibragim most often of all. Ibrashka – that's how he was known after my mama successfully nicknamed him. Ibrashka was our village idiot.

He suffered from oligophrenia, and even at his advanced age remained at the developmental level of a child. We grew up, became adults, but Ibrashka was for ever a child. He was very funny and kind; we would often exploit this and poke fun at him. He played football with us, went out to tend the cows. And he was big and brawny, just as nature compensates in strength for any lack of brains. And he was stubborn. When he made up his mind to do something no one could stop him.

The Fascists were carrying out a reprisal. People hid in the cellars from the blind rounds, from the grenades which were hurtling down everywhere, from the mortar fire. The tormentors would not leave for a long time. The children in the cellars were crying. They were pleading for water. Ibrashka stood up, got a bucket, and moved towards the door. They tried to stop him going. But how could they?

'Ibrashka is a good boy . . . the children want to drink . . . Ibrashka's going to go and get them water . . . everyone will say, "Thanks, Ibrashka!" The children will drink . . . Ibrashka knows where there's water . . . Ibrashka goes and gets water every day, it's not far! . . . Everyone will be glad, everyone will say, "Good Ibrashka!"'

But the Fascists saw him, in his daft clothing, with the grimace of feeblemindedness all over his face. One could not help but realise he was ill. They drove after him in their armoured personnel carriers and, laughing heartily, hurried him along with bursts from their assault rifles. Ibrashka quickened his pace.

It's nothing . . . Ibrashka will get some water . . . Ibrashka is a good boy . . .

One of the first rounds, it seems, hit his leg. Ibrashka fell. The empty bucket rolled over the cobblestones with a clatter.

Why does it hurt so much?... Why are they laughing?... Ibrashka is a good boy... Ibrashka's gone to get water... The children want to drink...

The tormentors drove closer to the man writhing on the road. A few breezy rounds from the assault rifle finished him off.

That was how they found him. That was how they buried him. Pain and childish bewilderment are eternally stamped on Ibragim's face.

10

I remember what a cheerful girl Lakshmi was. She was younger than me and lived in a nearby house, with her father, mother and brother. I remember clearly how terribly cheerful she was. I recall this because she has become quite different now.

She is just as friendly, just as hardworking. Probably even more hardworking than before. As if trying to busy herself in her chores. But it is as though she has forgotten how to laugh. The spark in her large dark-brown eyes has gone out for ever. In its place are uncried tears.

They were travelling to their relatives, trying to get out of the bombing zone. A Russian driver was taking them. The car was stopped at a checkpoint and the soldiers dragged the driver out and started to beat him. 'What's this,' they said, 'sold out to the wogs? Transporting combatants, are you?' And they laid into him.

The combatants were sitting in the car. Fat, rather funny and kind – as chubby people often are – Mansur, Lakshmi's father;

combatant Lakshmi – a girl of fifteen; twelve-year-old combatant Issa; and the chief combatant – their mama, Tamara.

Mansur got out of the car. He started pleading: 'Guys, don't beat up our driver. He hasn't done anything. We've got our documents on us. We're going to our relatives. You can search the car. And look, here, take this.' Mansur reached into his inner pocket and brought out a worn banknote, the last of his cash, saved for an emergency.

'Ah, a wog's got out.' The soldiers began laughing malevolently. One cocked his assault rifle . . .

There's a burst of fire and Lakshmi sees her father, his hands flapping ridiculously, sink to the ground. She doesn't hear her own scream, doesn't hear her brother and mother's screams. She sees her father. No, don't . . . In the stomach . . . a burst of fire . . . From right up close. But the blood comes out of his mouth for some reason. He hasn't died yet. In the stomach . . . He still hasn't died . . . For some reason he's even trying to get up – with his stomach torn apart . . . And he's fallen. He was alive when the soldier walked up, calmly took the worn banknote from his spasmodically trembling hand, and, kicking the dying man, said:

'I hate those wogs.'

11

To the north of our lane was a large field belonging to the state farm, usually planted with maize or left to lie fallow. When the field was left fallow, it ran wild with thistles as tall as a man.

During autumn in Ichkeria the sky turns grey, the earth dark brown. Low clouds bring cold, interminable showers. Returning from school, I headed for the yard to tend to the animals. I had to feed our farm's inhabitants. Change the water, muck out the barn – hard work for a boy at an age when many kids know nothing but play. Our family had it hard, and we all worked tirelessly.

But I had my games, too. When I finished my chores in the yard, I went out into the field. I played at war. In my hand I held a wooden sword. I approached the edge of the field. The wind swayed the heads of the dead thistles. I challenged the field to battle.

Wedged among the tight rows of dry sticks jutting from the earth, I began to hack, left and right, with my wooden sword. In my mind, the field of dead thistle was a horde of enemy forces, and I an ancient *bogatyr*. I hacked, hacked again and moved ever further, ever deeper into the enemy formation. Until, exhausted, I fell on the dark-brown earth. On my clothes clusters of prickles glowed red like bleeding wounds. I lay and watched the grey sky. The wind swayed the dead branches.

And I seemed to hear. The patter of horses, the din of an enormous army. Alien, unintelligible speech. They've come again, the hordes. And I seemed to remember. Once more I took my sword and went out into the field, one against a thousand.

And once more I was killed.

12

Spring has come to St Petersburg.

There are puddles and mud outside. But in the sky the sun is warm. Yes, the world still has a sun, and not just a white stain above us, as it was in the winter. It gives off heat like a country stove.

I probably need to wander the lanes and courtyards, inhale the smells of thawing refuse, listen to the noisy springtime cawing of the crows. I did all this in my previous lives and perhaps I'll do it in the next.

In this one, I sit in the old building. I look into the flickering glow of the computer monitor. Sometimes I read books, books on history, books about times long since past. It is absurd. Things are different now. Everything is entirely different. Now things are utterly different.

... And to the north of the Great Mountains was the land of Sim Sim, settled by people who cultivated the earth and worked metal. The large city in the heart of Sim Sim had ornate walls and tall towers. The people of Sim Sim never attacked anyone, never started wars.

But others attacked them. Sim Sim occupied the gateway between north and south, and conquerors from each side strove to break through – Alexander the Two-Horned, Timur the Lame, Khan Baty. The proud people of Sim Sim would not swear allegiance to the empires but went into battle against the enormous armies. And they fell in battle.

Sim Sim became deserted. Its survivors hid in the mountains. Centuries passed, and they returned to their native land, but a new conqueror once more eliminated the rebellious.

The great conqueror Timur the Lame was so embittered by the little nation's resistance that he sent a reprisal expedition to the mountains. Timur's warriors threw everyone they found in the mountains from the tall cliffs. Thus had Timur commanded, for the only good Chechen is a peaceful Chechen, and the only peaceful Chechen is a dead Chechen.

Three times the warriors of Sim Sim went out to battle with the army of the Golden Horde. They were betrayed by all their allies, who had been bought by the Tatar khans, yet only when not a single warrior was left living could the Horde break through the gateway to the north and attack Rus.[22] The years passed. Mothers nursed their children, and before their beards were grown, these very children had raised a revolt against the khan's rule.

To quell the uprising of the rebellious Chechens the khan appointed his faithful vassals – the Russian princes. The princes and their retinues hurried to help the Tatars deal with the people who had fought on the frontline till their last breath, shielding Rus and Europe from the Horde. And so Russians first came to Sim Sim. They burned the villages and killed the people – men, women, children and the elderly. The only good Chechen is a dead Chechen. They helped the Tatars; the khan was pleased with them. He expressed his gratitude in his own peculiar manner. Soon afterwards, one of the Russian princes arriving to pay tribute in Sim Sim, site of the summer headquarters of the Horde, was dishonoured and killed.

After the fall of the Golden Horde, several new khanates formed from its ashes, continuing the traditions of this cruellest, wildest and most barbarous empire in the whole of mankind's history. One of them, under its slant-eyed leaders, has endured to this day. The Moscow Khanate – the Oil Horde.

13

When will this book end? I am tired – why, to what end, who writes all these new pages, more and more of them? They said the war is over. So why does this book write itself, on and on?

Early one morning above the fields of Ichkeria stood a dense, milky fog. The lowing of the cows echoed softly, as though wrapped in felt. And the shot of a sniper thudded, like cotton against a carpet from which a bride diligently beats out dust.

Toyita had been a diligent bride. She'd had no shortage of chores. Four children, two still suckling. Her mother-in-law was already old, not the woman she had been. When her husband – in whose arms his beloved wife had died – buried her, he also buried his appetite for life itself. So the neighbours said, 'Poor children, what'll happen to them now? People die – we've all grown used to that. People are killed by the Russians. We're used to that here. But the children – they haven't been killed. If they were, it wouldn't surprise us. The Russians kill everyone. But so far no one has killed them – so how are they to live, without a mama?'

She simply went out to herd the cows to pasture. She did this every morning. But that morning the sniper's ganja had run out. Or perhaps he'd grazed his leg. Either way, he was in a bad mood. And he decided to kill someone.

And all Chechens are werewolves. By day of course they pretend to be innocent people. But at night every Chechen turns into a wolf and goes out to kill Russians. He cuts the Russian's head off and drinks his blood. That's why all Chechens have to be killed, the peaceful ones too. The only peaceful Chechen is a dead Chechen.

It was they, the werewolves, who blew up a truck full of soldiers driving away from the unit based just outside the village, next to the pasture field. Well, the soldiers had already finished their war and were driving to pick up their combat pay – 666 roubles for each day of war. Such a round figure. They were driving, these good, sweet Russian guys. Snipers, assault riflemen. To collect their money and go home. To their sweet brides, to their mothers.

But their truck was blown up by evil Chechen wolves. Who gunned them down, right here on the road. And on the side of the blown-up truck scratched out with a knife: 'Welcome to hell. Admission: 666 roubles.'

14

If I were a writer, I'd write a book about this. Or a short story. But I am merely a fragment of somebody's life. And in my heart's mirror are reflected eyes – but I don't remember who that person was.

At school I was the best in my class at writing compositions. The teachers would pass them around and one was published in the local newspaper. It was called 'We Need Peace'. The epigraph was a quote from Jonathan Swift: 'War, that mad game the world so loves to play.'

I probably wanted to become a writer. These days I don't know, cannot remember, I'm not sure whether that was me. If I were a writer, I'd write a book, a short story at least.

But I'm merely a schoolboy, back at my desk, these thirteen years have not passed, and I'm writing a composition. Free choice. My composition is called 'Why the Sky Doesn't Fall Down'. It's about a pilot. Perhaps I am that pilot.

I have fair hair and blue eyes; I have flown from a faraway snowy land. This mighty bird of prey obeys my hands. I am a warrior, carrying out my mission. To destroy the objective marked on the map. Beneath the wings of the plane lies unknown land. I make for the target. In the crosshairs I see a peaceful village, residents absorbed in their daily chores, children playing on the lawn outside their houses.

This is the objective.

And I hear an inner voice. No, not quite inner, rather, it comes from behind, a little to the left. A whisper works its way through the crackle of the headset:

It's what you have to do. And it's what you've always wanted to do. Kill. You're tired of living at peace, bound by thousands of restrictions and rules. By morality and law. But you've always wanted to kill. Back home you'd be tried and sent to prison for it. Here, for doing the same, you'll be recommended for an award. Just do it. Kill. Now you've been given might and power. Take control of the lives and deaths of these unknown people, who mean nothing to you. Feel yourself a god . . .

And I swoop lower, take aim at the house. My hand rests on the target-bombing button . . . But . . . perhaps, could it be . . . there's a sharp fall in altitude, my head is humming . . . I see the skin of my hand turn green, blister, my fingers lengthen, growing sharp claws, dragon's claws. I lift my head and look at the sky. The sky fills with cracks, more and more; I hear a ringing; the sky is ready to shatter like a glass dome.

And I understand. Understand why the sky doesn't fall down. The sky doesn't fall down while we remain human. And it shatters when we choose to take the place of God and mutate into dragons.

I lift my aeroplane, pilot it away from the village. Landing on the wide wheat field, at the woodless hill, I climb out from the cockpit, tinker with the fuel tanks, and move off to a safe distance.

The iron bird with the full load of bombs explodes, deafening the world. I take off the helmet with the incessant radio calls and toss it far aside.

The weather is clear and cloudless: on the horizon, like a miraculous vision, an unknown mountain range appears. I've never been in the mountains. So strange to see the snowy caps of the peaks on this hot summer day. And I walk, walk through the field of wheat, heading straight for the horizon, to the fairytale blue mountains with shimmering white peaks.

When the Tanks Awoke

In the name of Allah, the Beneficent, the Merciful.
Praise be to Allah, Lord of the Worlds,
The Beneficent, the Merciful.
Master of the Day of Judgement,
Thee alone we worship; Thee alone we ask for help.
Show us the straight path,
The path of those whom Thou hast favoured; Not the path
of those who earn Thine anger nor of those who go astray.

Koran, Surah 3, Ayat 13:

There was a token for you in two hosts which met: one army fighting in the way of Allah, and another disbelieving, whom they saw as twice their number, clearly, with their very eyes. Thus Allah strengtheneth with His succour whom He will. Lo! herein verily is a lesson for those who have eyes.[3]

1 - Grammar Lessons

Times. The tenses of verbs. Words invoked to sear people's hearts. Such times are gone. Or are they? So many words, so many people, no longer searing, merely verbalising. Talk shows. No matter what

I say today, no matter how I convince you, would you change? Would you stand up tall and go out into the streets, to the barricades? No. 'What an interesting point of view.' In today's talk show, the winner is . . . (*applause*).

Past, present, future. There is no past, no future; the present slides past on a razor blade of momentariness, carrying us from one instant of non-being to the next. What time do I live in?

I live in the past continuous tense. The past continues, strangles my every day like fungal filaments; it is the slimy jelly of life, it is the white vapour trail in the silky-blue sky: I cannot escape it, cannot fly away, even at the speed of sound.

All that has gone before is near me, with me, in me. Everyone who has lived before me lives in me, lives through me. And I shall live in those who will come in my wake. I myself come in the wake of those who paved the path, the straight path here, to the field of happy hunting; my life doesn't belong to me, but for those who come after me I'll be a pioneer, a leader, a trailblazer.

2 - The Myth of the Twins

Since he is no more, I live for the two of us. Sometimes it seems as if his soul entered my soul the day he died, became my soul. There were always two of us, and even now there are two of us, my friend and I. My brother and I.

After everything that happened, I am no longer well. That's why I don't trust myself. Could he have never existed? Could this be another confabulation, the effect of my shell shock, my mental confusion?

I remember always knowing that there were two of us. As a child I had a hazy vision, something told me I had a twin brother whom the grown-ups were hiding from me. Perhaps he lived in the next village or on the other side of the looking glass; perhaps now he lives merely in my dreams.

The fact is I never had a brother, just two sisters; I love my sisters but I always wanted a brother. And I dreamed that I had one, that one day we would meet and be together for ever.

The years went by but my obsession didn't let up, it held a secret power over me. I had to find out its meaning, what coded message lurked in this nebulous feeling. I began reading all the books I could on twins. I discovered that the natives of Malaysia consider the second-born to be the elder twin: they say that the elder sends the younger one ahead to check what it's like out there. From ancient Indian legends I learnt of the divine Ashwini twins: one embodies the dawn, the other the dusk. The Egyptian Book of the Dead claims that each person has a double – Ka; when the time comes, he will take his brother by the hand and guide him in the afterlife. The Upanishads tell of two birds sitting on the same branch of an enchanted tree: one bird eats fruits, rejoicing when it gets a sweet fruit and bewailing the bitter fruit, whilst the other bird simply observes it. But the first has only to tear itself away from the tasting of delight and sorrow and turn its gaze on the second for all illusions to vanish and the first bird to behold the truth. And among ancient Slavonic paintings I came upon this: two birds on the same branch, one holds something in its beak, the other watches. There was the myth of the creation of the world, which told of a flood covering the earth's surface and a bird which dived to the bottom of the ocean and brought up a lump of clay.

There were moments when it seemed that the key was close –

another instant, just one more, the tiniest effort and all would become clear, the divine light of knowledge would illumine my life. But the solution slipped away, and the secret remained a secret, twilight, madness. The dream of the twin.

That's why now, after the shell shock, the thought occurred: Perhaps he never really existed? I always wanted him to exist so I invented him, invented this person. Gave him everything that I lacked, composed a single, perfect whole from two parts.

But here is the photo: we're standing at the lopsided fence, in summer clothes, he leans on a crooked stick, I lean on him. The yellowed photograph from the old family album. On the back, traced in my childish clumsy hand: 'Zelik and Dinka'. As though I was afraid of forgetting who we were and what we were called.

3 - The Cruel God of Pleasure

I – we – Zelik and Dinka – were born in the village of Shali, in the Chechen-Ingush Autonomous Soviet Socialist Republic. Chechen-Ingushetia is located on the map at between forty-two and forty-four degrees latitude. To the east at roughly the same latitude lies the city of Alma-Ata, further along is Vladivostok, still further is the southern tip of the island of Hokkaido, Japan, with the cities Hakodate and Aomori. To the west at the same latitude is the famous Soviet resort of Sochi; on the other side of the Black Sea, the Bulgarian resort Varna; still further west and a little to the north is France's Toulouse; beyond the ocean lies the city of Chicago. The climate differs in all these places, due to the mountains, the steppe, the deserts and the ocean currents. Chechen-Ingushetia is colder than Sochi or Varni: the Greater Caucasus range shuts out the balmy southern winds – here the northern steppe winds blow freely. Yet it is probably warmer than in Vladivostok or northern Japan. Perhaps it's like Chicago or Toulouse – other inland parts of the earth.

Compared with central Russia spring arrives early here. And in May comes real summer, because in May the swallows arrive. For the whole village, summer starts the day after the swallows arrive. I too love the swallows but as a child summer came for me the day when – from far away, from the warm fairytale land where it's always hot and sweet melons grow to the size of a horse's head – flying over the Caspian lake on a silver angel, Dinka appeared in Shali.

Because Dinka always flew here for the summer and left when the air began to cool and smell of autumn, he embodied for me, somewhere deep inside, at the level of archetypes, of the unconscious, the seasonal god of dying and resurrection. And he had an appropriate name: Denis. Denis – Dionysus. Dionysus, the cruel god of pleasure; he journeyed the surface of the earth, circled by a retinue of bacchante and satyrs; he pitched camp on the hill near the town and enjoined all the citizens to hold festivals, the Dionysia, in his honour where the people would drink wine and copulate freely; whoever refused Dionysus would be punished with madness. So the myth goes.

In outward, plain reality, everything was simpler: Dinka lived in Turkestan, in the town of Bezmein, with his parents: his mother and stepfather. He went to school there. But during the summer holidays they sent him to Shali, to his grandpa and grandma.

I know all this, yet even now, when I remember Dinka, he appears in my mind's eye as an eternally youthful ancient god; perhaps because he died young, before my very eyes; perhaps too because now I shall wait eternally for the winter to end and for him to arise, as he always arose for me, appearing out of non-being, the unknown, the inaccessible, every summer.

4 - Abrek

I remember Zelik for as far back as my memory goes. I was born in Shali, where my mama lived at that time; I never knew my real father, Mama had me on her own, and I was raised more by Grandpa and Grandma. Grandpa and Grandma, and later Mama, lived in a special place in Shali enclosed by a tall concrete wall, the secure compound of PP-2. What 'PP' was, and why '2', nobody knew. On the compound's iron gates was the inscription LMS. LMS stood for 'Line Maintenance Station'. But that was a cover, a front. The site, enclosed by a wall of reinforced concrete, contained no line maintenance station. There was a hill seeded with grass, a four-storey apartment block, a tarmac square in front of it, a gazebo, garage, playground, a lawn and fruit trees along the perimeter of the rectangular zone, around four hectares in size. The most important part was located beneath the hill. The hill itself was a front, as well as a shelter. Well 'hill' isn't really the word – we always called it 'the mound'. The mound was artificial, created from the earth extracted when they dug the deep, well-equipped subterranean chamber which it concealed. The chamber was where PP-2, the top-secret government strategic communications facility, was actually located. They said you could dial anywhere on its phones, you could call, for instance, the President of the USA on his direct line and he would pick up the receiver in the Oval Room, on the other side of the world. PP-2 had been built for just such extreme emergency scenarios. To declare the outbreak of war or the end of hostilities, to administer the disaster response management of territories, for secret military communications when the usual channels had been destroyed. The chamber was approached by two entrances, from the western and eastern slopes of the mound; both were covered with concrete canopies and camouflaged with vines. The mound itself, again for camouflage, was sown with tidy grass. From the air it was meant to look like peaceful countryside. For authenticity's sake, I ought to add that we never referred to the subterranean chamber by that grim expression: we referred to everything located beyond those armoured doors wired with their sophisticated alarm system simply as 'under the mound'.

PP-2 was a top-secret installation under the immediate command of Moscow. The local authorities had no access to it. What's more, only Russians were employed to work in PP-2. Not just as communications engineers and other technical specialists, but even the cleaners, the gardener who planted and mowed the lawn, the guards – all of them were Russians, specially transferred to Shali for this work and housed in the four-storey building. The locals, with rare exceptions, weren't even allowed to pass through the iron gates guarding the installation's grounds.

Zelik was one such rare exception, or rather, his sisters were at first, probably because Zelik's family were half-Russified, he had a Russian mama, they spoke Russian well and Chechen poorly, and generally fitted in better with the limited contingent of Russians living in PP-2 than with the natives. I don't know whether the duty guards did their homework and consulted the KGB, or whether they made the decision to allow the Magomadovs (Zelik's surname) into PP-2 simply on a hunch, but in the summertime Zelik's sisters came almost daily to play with their Russian peers, the children of the special settlers who worked in PP-2.

As Zelik was wholly entrusted to their care, they would take him along in some pram or other, unloading him into the sandpit at the playground while they ran off with their friends on girls' business. My grandma released me into that same sandpit, and together we crawled, building sandcastles and driving our plastic toy cars. That is why I remember Zelik as far back as my memory goes.

His full name was Zelimkhan, the name of the Chechen *abrek*[24] famed in the nineteenth century for single-handedly waging war against the tsarist forces after Chechnya had already been subjugated, holding up stage-coaches and handing out the booty among his needy countrymen. A Chechen Robin Hood. Abrek Zelimkhan died when he was betrayed by one of his close friends.

It probably sounds trite to say that a person's name shapes his fate. Yet Zelik in some way repeated the tragedy of his namesake celebrated in folk songs.

Zelik died. I cannot stop myself saying it straight out. No matter what I remember, our childish games or boyish adventures, I see Zelik as though in a stained glass panel, in shades of red and green, a picture of his death, and everything acquires new meaning, new overtones.

5 - The Myth of the Androgyne

Dinka didn't quite live in Shali. Dinka lived in PP-2, on a very special site, sealed off and guarded, inaccessible to mere mortals. As befitted a divinity.

I was, it seems, no mere mortal. I spoke the language of the gods – the Russian language – and the guard allowed me in. But only to visit him. From the very beginning of summer I'd run to the iron gates and ask the guard: 'Can I go in?' At first the guard would shake his head: 'Your Dinka hasn't arrived yet.'

He was mine, my Dinka, yes, that's how it always was.

Then the day would come when the guard would nod me towards the door in the iron gates: 'Come on in.' Dinka was here!

The bond between us was a veritable disaster for our parents. 'Dinka has arrived!' – to mine this mantra meant I'd be running out of the house every morning having barely breakfasted and returning after dark, hungry and mucky up to my ears, my elbows and knees all scraped, but happy, because I had only to sleep, to wait a night before I could play with Dinka again tomorrow. And it was no use scolding me. 'Zelik has come!' – for Dinka's household this meant that their child would disappear for the entire day, without eating as he ought, hurriedly pulling on a T-shirt and shorts, forever scheming up dangerous and dubious games, crawling about the compound in places where he and Zelik were allowed and some where they weren't, turning up only at nightfall to collapse immediately into bed without so much as a glance at the telly.

Our elders barely mixed with each other, perhaps jealous of their children. All they'd do was shout at us, both his parents and mine, each within the confines of their own household, yet almost in unison: 'Oh leave each other alone for a minute, won't you! What is this, love?'

But love it was. And friendship. And rivalry. We had everything. We needed nothing, no one in the whole world. The two of us were that same androgyne, that mythical being, whole and perfect, whom the gods had divided in two out of envy and jealousy.

But each summer we were reunited, and we couldn't give a damn for the gods.

In that myth, man and woman emerged from the divided androgyne, but why? In the course of my entire life, having known hundreds of women, I have never yet found one whose curves would fit my cavities, and whose cavities would accommodate my curves, whose cables would connect to my ports – with whom I could merge as simply and freely into an indivisible whole as we, Dinka and I, merged.

6 - City of the Gods

It's now vital that I retrace everything in detail. Revive my memory, extend my past into the present, into the future, pick up the pieces and stick them together again. For I want to live, I want to live so badly! But life is all in the details.

So, the PP-2 compound was a very special place. No matter how hard they tried to disguise it, I imagine it was easy to identify even from the air. A rectangular island of order and harmony amid the living chaos of a Chechen village. Contoured footpaths, well-tended bushes, the planned geometry of the buildings. The entire grounds resembled a re-creation in miniature of a Western European landscape. The special settlers here were meant to feel that this was special, that they were special.

But for us children, PP-2 was the perfect site for fun and games. Here we had everything. A children's playground with sturdy swings on steel frames: you could swing all the way around the bar – and how else were you to practise being a cosmonaut, to acclimatise to g-force? A lawn for badminton. The tarmac paths converged at even crossroads, so you wouldn't just chase about on scooters and bikes but depict the movement of traffic. A slide, a garage, trees – varied terrain for games of hide-and-seek, Cossacks and robbers, war, with the most wonderful backdrops. An illuminated evening gazebo where we could play cards for money or tell each other ghost stories before bedtime.

Our parents fretted in vain that they couldn't herd us home for lunch. What lunch? PP-2 gave us all we needed. Immersed in our games, we would satisfy our hunger with plums, cherry plums, apples, pears, quince, cherries, raspberries, blackcurrants, strawberries. Or we could bake potatoes in a bonfire. Shoot, pluck and roast a pigeon. Well that was far more interesting than eating from a plate under the gaze of the grown-ups.

And they could do little to disturb us. During the day almost the entire adult population of PP-2, apart from the duty guard at the gates and the gardener, was 'under the mound', coming out only for a brief lunch break. We were sole masters of the installation's entire above-ground world. They, the titans, toiled away under the ground; we, the gods, played in the sunlight. Well, that's how it should be, isn't it?

PP-2 was our city, the city of the gods, the city of the children.

7 - Games

So what did we really do the whole day long? We played.

No, not just the two of us. In PP-2 there were many children, and when the game demanded it we would split into two teams, with Dinka in one and me in the other. Otherwise the game would be pointless. Then we'd simply be playing together, as we always were, he and I.

There were games for daytime and games for the night, or rather, for the evening, because late at night we were not allowed to play, we had to go home. But the southern evenings are stunningly dark, as thick as the blackest of nights, that's why there were games for daytime and games for the night.

For daytime: war, badminton, football, government (we printed our own money, published newspapers and appointed each other to all sorts of impressive-sounding posts).

For the night: hide-and-seek, 'hunt the red banner', billiards, cards, ghost stories. For example, in 'hunt the red banner' we would take two red flowers, a carnation and a rose (which we broke off from the bushes and blooms proliferating along the paths). These flowers were the banners. The players divided accordingly into the army of the roses and the army of the carnations. The 'banners' were hidden in the secret headquarters and the usual territory for playing was divided evenly in two. To win the game you had to locate the enemy headquarters, find their standard and steal it. But once on enemy ground, the player risked being captured: the banner's location was discovered from prisoners-of-war, who could be tortured by twisting their arm or forcing them to eat a sharp, green cherry plum. Captured comrades could be freed: to do this the rescuer had merely to touch the prisoner. But if the rescuer himself were touched during the operation, he too would become a prisoner.

There was a whole set of rules for every game – oh my memory is weak, I can't recall them all now, but each game had an integral, inviolable logic of its own.

And only we, Dinka and I, could stop the game or change the rules. This world had been invented by us, for us and for everyone else.

Weary of games, we would gather to tell each other stories. Everyone retold the scary tales they had read in books, seen in films, heard from others – about cannibals, for example, who made pies from human flesh or about the 'blackest black coffin'. But the best stories were narrated by Dinka. He had to be asked. After resisting a little, he would begin the tale of his heroic deeds. He was a god after all and he was expected to accomplish superhuman feats. And he told us of them, of how he flew into space with aliens, how he swam underwater across the Volga and the Caspian Sea in a submarine built from a barrel and a washing machine, how he battled in Bezmein against a cavalry of Turkmen – only it wasn't a cavalry but a donkey squadron, for as everyone knows the Turkmen ride donkeys. But Dinka had a nail-firing machine gun with which he could shoot the donkeys and their savage riders. Dinka described everything thoroughly, in detail, protesting, 'It really happened, and if you don't believe me, then you can ask—(here naming one of the characters featured in the account of his latest feat). If you like I'll give you his address in Bezmein.'

But we believed him. I still believe him now.

8 - The Prophet

Well, there were the titans, our parents, who spent their days below ground, and there were us, the gods. Then there were the people who lived beyond the walls and spoke some strange, unfathomable language. They lived quite differently, according to their own customs, though it was assumed that they were the subjects of the gods and titans.

And there was Zelik, like an intermediary between the worlds. He lived in their world and came to play with us, in our world. He spoke with us in our language and with them in their guttural idiom.

I always think of Zelik as a prophet. Perhaps a prophet in reverse. Well, people call a prophet someone who brings them news from the gods. But what do they call someone who brings the gods news of the people?

Yet leaving aside the fact that he came from another world, Zelik was still a prophet because he said strange things. Things he had never read, things no one had told him. He said that everyone – the gods, the people, the titans and even the swallows – had the same kind of souls. And that there is the Big Soul, shared by us all. And all souls are exactly like the Big Soul, only smaller. And that this knowledge equals happiness. That in school they teach us all sorts of nonsense like mathematics and spelling. Why do we have to study? We already know everything. All we need to do is to remember. Somewhere deep inside, we know everything, Pythagoras's theory, and the distance to the nearest star, and, most importantly, what happiness is. But to remember it we have to look at the One, the Other, Who is inside us. And when we look, we will remember, no, we'll realise that we never forgot a thing and we were neither titans, nor gods, nor grown-ups, nor children, nor ministers, nor guards, nor cats, nor swallows, nor boys, nor girls, nor Russians, nor Chechens.

That was just the game.

9 - Bezmein

What did I know of Dinka's life for the nine months he was far from me? I knew nothing. On the one hand, that faraway land, Turkmenia, was a kingdom of warmth and light: yes, that must have been right, Dinka, the summer divinity, had to fly away to the warm fairytale land where the summer spends the winter months. On the other hand there was its strangeness, its otherworldliness: and that too must have been right, for each autumn the divinity of flowering and life sets out for the abode of death. Even in the name of the town – Bezmein – I always heard *'bezdna'* – abyss. Or *'bezdna zmey'* – abyss of the snakes. And *'bez imeni'* – nameless. For the place where the dead live has no name, we can only call it something negative, something neither-this-nor-that, something other. And the dead too are nameless.

Secrets lurked in Dinka's birth too. It's always the case with divinities, their origin remains a riddle, a myth. Dinka had a mama, but no father. His mother's husband, a quiet and placid engineer, was his stepfather.

I knew from my parents that Dinka's mama had got pregnant in Shali by a Chechen, they even mentioned the man's name. But that Chechen didn't marry her and didn't even want to know of his son.

10 - Father

I am resurrecting everything, picking up the pieces, sticking them together again. And at times I feel serene and calm. But at times it hurts, it hurts very much and I don't even want to think about it, don't want to remember it. Yet I must, otherwise I won't be able to find myself, to become complete, to make myself whole.

Father. Why did you abandon me, Father? You and I are one, that's how it ought to be, but you abandoned me. No, you didn't abandon me, you didn't even know that I existed, you didn't want to know, it didn't interest you. Why, why did you do it, Father?

Thanks to you, Father, I don't have and never had a crumb of warmth in my soul, just ice, just resentment. Thanks to you I began hating my mother. Because all this is her fault, she's a slut, a whore, she had a good fuck with some lousy bastard – with you, Father – she was on heat, and she had no brains – no brains and no honour. She didn't even have the brains to get an abortion in time.

Then she got married, to a gutless jellyfish, a mute slave, she bore him a son, but I – I was always unwanted. And I love my half-brother, as God is my witness, I'm ready to tear anyone who dares touch a hair on his head limb from limb. He may be a mongol, he may have a harelip, he's dystrophic, but he's my brother and I love him. But I hate Mother. And she's no mother to me. Just as you're no father.

I was never wanted by you, never. I watch the dramas made in Hollywood and they all have the same plot, some kind of maniac or loser who, years later, is still moaning: 'Pop, why didn't you come to my baseball matches?' But I – how can I complain, what do I have to complain of? What matches, what baseball? You forgot about me straightaway, as soon as you'd discharged your foul sperm into my mother's stinking hole. You never wanted me, you just felt like unloading your pistol, you filthy bastard.

And Mother never wanted me, she handed me over to Grandpa and Grandma, left for Turkmenia and got married there. Then she started taking me back for nine months at a time, but why? She wanted us to be a family? What sort of family – I hate you all, you and Mother and her husband.

If I had any family at all it was only Grandpa and Grandma, they loved me, especially Grandpa. Oh if only he'd been my father! If I was fated to be born from my mother's accursed belly, then it would have been better for him, Grandpa, to have fucked my mother, his daughter. Then I would have had a real father. But he didn't fuck her, you did, you scum, and I had no father, only a grandfather. When Grandpa died, I had nobody left.

But that dog took me to Bezmein so that we would be a family. If only she had dropped dead, along with her spineless husband, instead of Grandpa.

What was my mother to you, Father? Just a Russian bitch, a slut? Oh, you're a Chechen, no doubt you were proud of yourself – were, because I hope that they killed you, killed the lot of you, you had it coming after all. Russian women are whores as far as you're concerned. She was a fool, a young teacher, sent on work experience to a Shali school. You sweet-talked her – oh you certainly know how to sweet-talk, you jackals. Then you gave her a good fuck, kicked her out on her arse, told your Chechen friends and you all had a good laugh over it, the story of how you, a *djigit*,[25] nailed a Russian bitch.

Where is your honour, Father? You Chechens pride yourselves on your honour, on your traditions, your respect for women. You won't even touch a girl's hand unless you mean to marry her. When you go on a date, you stand chastely several yards apart, barely even able to hear each other speak. You call all girls 'my pretty one', call all women 'mother', and when you get divorced, you keep the children, you don't leave them to the women. But all that's only for your own kind. Russians are outside the law, you can do what you want with them, cheat them, kill them, fuck them. That's your way. You are hypocrites and shits.

And I hate you, Father, I hate myself, because I have your blood and the blood of your nation flowing in my veins, damn the lot of you.

11 - The Bastard

We were one whole, we suited each other down to the ground, we were on the same wavelength. Does that mean we never quarrelled? No, we did quarrel. Once war even broke out.

It started with something trivial, I don't remember what. We couldn't agree about something, argued over it, began taunting each other. And when our rage reached boiling point, bubbled over, and we ran short of put-downs, we remembered what we'd heard the grown-ups say. Grown-ups have more venom, more hate and disgust – and we copied all this from them.

Dinka pulled a grimace of contempt and said: 'Shut your mouth, you filthy ape, you wog!'

From somewhere below my stomach fury erupted in me, but revenge is a dish best served cold. I had ammunition to strike back with. Putting my hands on my hips and spitting on the ground through my teeth, I sneered lopsidedly and asked: 'So I'm a wog, am I? Then what does that make you?'

'I'm Russian!' replied Dinka.

I paused, savouring the blow to come, realising how much pain it would cause Dinka. Then spoke: 'Don't you know who your real father is? Your father is a Chechen, which makes you a Chechen too. I also have a Russian mother and a Chechen father. But my papa loves me and Mama, while your father knocked your mother up and dumped her. He didn't want you! You're a bastard, that's what!'

12 - War

My mother never told me about Father. I learnt who he was from Zelik, during a quarrel. It hurt, but I immediately realised he was telling the truth, which made it even more hurtful and painful. I bit my lips till they bled and could barely hold back the tears. Then stamped my foot and said to Zelik: 'Don't come here to play! We're not friends any more! This is war!'

'War!' Zelik repeated and also stamped his foot. We turned our backs on one another and marched off, each in his own direction, I to the gazebo in front of the building, he to the exit at the iron gates.

I cried a bit in the gazebo. Then went home, ate my dinner in silence and sat and watched television. When Mama sent me to bed, I went to my room but I couldn't sleep for ages. At first I thought about Father, then I began driving these thoughts away; I decided to act.

In the morning, after breakfast, when all the children of PP-2 had come out to play, I called an emergency meeting. 'Where's Zelik?' they asked. I replied that Zelik had turned out to be a snake and a traitor, he was on the side of the wogs who lived on the other side of the wall, that's why we had quarrelled and I had declared war on Zelik and all his wog friends. The children greeted the news of war with delight. Evidently they thought this was another game, a new and interesting one. After all, Zelik and I were always dreaming up games.

We immediately drew up a plan of campaign: we would organise the first battle at the fire exit gates. The gates had no guards and what's more they opened on to the street where Zelik and his wog friends lived. The boys armed themselves with catapults and filled their pockets with stones; three girls were appointed to carry ammunition and bandage the wounded; someone brought a real first aid kit from their home, with bandages, surgical spirit and iodine.

When everything was ready the detachment moved towards the fire gates; the shooters took up position at the doors, gates and walls. I gave a whistle and shouted: 'Zelik!' The enemy appeared suddenly, from the direction of Zelik's yard, and charged into attack, hurling stones as they ran. One stone hit Seryozha's head, who was sitting in a tree. He tumbled from the branches, cried loudly and, clutching his bleeding forehead, ran home. Then we all climbed down from our positions and scattered before Seryozha's parents could come and tell us off.

The wog army was ecstatic. From the other side of the wall we heard: 'Whoohoooh! Russian chickens, Russian chickens, Russian chickens!'

We all lied cheerfully to the grown-ups that Seryozha had fallen and hit his head on the asphalt, but none of the PP-2 children wanted to go to war any more.

Long dull days stretched out. Without Zelik not a single game worked properly. Without him the summer stopped being summer, the holidays lost all meaning. And I missed him. I confess that I missed him.

Then I got a white rag and went back to the fire gates. I tied the rag to a stick, climbed to the top of the gates and began to whistle. Zelik was playing in the street with the neighbourhood kids. When they saw me with the white flag, the Chechen children hollered: 'Russian chicken, Russian chicken! You want to surrender, do you?'

'I propose peace, I have to talk with Zelik,' I yelled.

'We won't talk with you, Russian pig! We don't need your peace. You're a chicken, same as all the Russians!' the children shouted. And they added something in Chechen, no doubt something insulting or funny, as everyone laughed at this.

'I have to talk with Zelik!' I repeated. The crowd of boys stirred. It seemed they were trying to talk Zelik out of it. But he remained silent, unsure what to do. Then he broke away and approached the gates. 'Well, talk then.'

'Zelik, let's make up. Come and play with us.'

The Chechen children heard my words and began vying to speak with Zelik. Zelik stood there, silent, then turned and went home.

But the next morning Zelik came to PP-2, and once more we played together.

13 - The Return

When he found out from me about his real father, Dinka declared war. I went to the local gang of kids with this news. For nine months of the year I played with them but for three months, every summer, I left their company, vanishing into PP-2. Of course, I was teased for this. 'What, off to play with the Russians again? Dinka's arrived and you don't need your friends any more?'

The return of the prodigal son gratified the natives, and they supported the idea of war with the Russian children from PP-2 unhesitatingly.

The victory in the battle at the fire gates was won so easily that it wasn't even interesting. But the real tussle began later, when Dinka proposed peace and invited me to come back and play in PP-2. That tussle occurred, of course, inside me. On the one hand, I was cross with Dinka, and the Chechen kids would again think me a traitor for selling them out to the Russians. On the other, I needed Dinka. I moped without him, and I wanted terribly to play with him as we had before.

The next day I went to PP-2 though I no longer vanished from morning till evening each day, like I used to. I started playing more with the neighbourhood kids. So I learned to live between two countries, between two worlds.

Dinka and I said no more about it, never discussed it, never discussed the wogs and the Russians, or his father. That was probably a mistake. At the time I couldn't have explained everything to him, I simply wouldn't have found the words. If I could speak to him now, I would try. But he is already dead, that's why I can only address him in my mind, in my memory.

Dinka, you cannot think of people as barbarians, as wild, uncultured wogs just because their culture is different. From their perspective you also seem savage. You have to understand that people are different. Each nation has its own history, its own traditions, its own language. The Russians called foreigners *nemtsy*[25]– dumb ones – because they believed that a man who cannot speak their language must not be able to speak at all, must be as good as dumb. That is the psychology of savages – every primeval tribe considered themselves the only real humans. 'Hell is other people.' The self-designation of many nationalities means simply 'people'. Nokhchi, for instance, comes from *nakh*. Later there appeared 'Vay-nakh', our people. Already implying that others are people too, albeit alien ones. This was a small step forward.

The customs and acknowledged boundaries of savages apply only to their fellow tribesmen, while aliens are always outside the law – you can do what you like with them. This is the true meaning of savagery, barbarity. Those Chechens who believe that they should act ethically only within their own group, and they can be immoral and cruel to non-Chechens – they're hypocrites, shits, they don't understand the laws of the mountains, the customs of their own people. And those Russians who contemptuously call other tribes 'wogs' or some other name, who believe that Chechens are inherently beyond the law and can be killed or tortured at their own sweet will, are the worst of the primitive savages, they are the genuine wogs.

About your father . . . I shouldn't have told you like that, forgive me. But you too, you should also have understood, at least made an effort to understand. It's not your fault, it's no shame. Just fate, a trial. In the Koran it says that Allah never sends a man a trial that he cannot bear. You are strong, Dinka, you were always strong, that's why Allah has subjected you to harsh trials, see. You can overcome everything and preserve the purity and love in your heart.

We are all like you, you know. Nobody knows who their father is. We know only our mother – here she is, this earth, this nature. You can see her, hear her, touch her with your hands. But no one has seen the father. And when we suddenly find out, like you, who he is, we will realise that we are of one blood. We are all of one blood. We are brothers.

14 - Land of the Sun

How did I live in Bezmein for nine months of the year, from one summer holiday to the next? Unremarkably, as all children in the USSR lived. Went to school, to sports clubs. I was into freestyle wrestling, later Sambo and fencing.

Bezmein was an ordinary Russian town, though located in Turkmenia. The majority of the population were Russians sent here to work at the large electric power station and manufacturing plants. Some Turkmen lived in the town too, their children went to school with us, but the urban Turkmen were Russified. The genuine Turkmen lived in the farming areas. Sometimes they drove into town and in their vivid coats, with their heads bound in rags, sitting on their donkeys, they looked like escapees from a carnival or from the shoot of a film based on Eastern fairytales.

Sometimes, clapping our eyes on some such Ali Baba, we kids would throw stones at him. He'd get down from his donkey, swearing loudly in his own language, and chase after us, shielding his head from flying stones.

At school festivities, when they put on a play about 'Our Fifteen Sister Republics', they'd dress up dusky Rita in the Turkmen national costume, even though she was Jewish.

Bezmein was a beautiful new town with snow-white high-rise blocks, broad, straight avenues, fountains and parks, cafés and cinemas. Life there was modern.

We grew up fast. By the fifth form[27] I was already French kissing with girlfriends, and in the seventh form[28] a girl from the neighbouring street took me to a basement, undressed me and made a man of me.

In Shali everything was different.

15 - Madness

Something began changing, first imperceptibly, then little by little, then more and more tangibly, unmistakably. I was taken over by another force, rending me from within, stretching my body upwards, erupting in acne on my skin.

Arriving for his usual holidays, Dinka began telling stories not about flying in space or sailing in submarines. Now the theme of his exploits was girls, who, if he was to be believed, were declaring their love to him by the dozen, and wanted to 'do it' with him. About 'doing it' Dinka told precious little, though we all, me especially, craved the details so badly. But having lengthily described the prelude to the event, he'd limit himself at the most interesting point to some phrase like: 'And then I took off my trousers and fucked her.' We believed and didn't believe. For us this was even more fantastical than space flights.

But our doubts were dispelled a year later. Not only had time, our age and how we viewed the world changed but Dinka himself had changed. It had become all too obvious who he was. A couple of years earlier, he had been an angular kid with funny jug ears. Now he was a god amongst men, a genuine Apollo. A noble profile, perfectly proportioned body, enticing skin – always sun-kissed, ever so touchable – and ears hidden by wavy black hair.

The grown-ups no longer forbade him to leave the walls of PP-2, and we went on walks about the entire district. This became a genuine calamity for the local girls. Catching sight of Dinka for the first time, they would stop in their tracks for minutes at a stretch, feasting their eyes on him shamelessly. Ahead lay genuine mass madness. Through the grapevine the news spread of who this beautiful guy was, where he lived, what he was called. Girls flooded to him, almost in droves. Spying Dinka from afar they'd uninhibitedly yell: 'Denis!' They used any excuse to chat with him. The epidemic grew more serious and then the open declarations of love began. What's more, it seemed that jealousy was unknown to these girls. They would come in twos, in threes or fours, with girlfriends or sisters, all pronouncing, sincerely and theatrically, the Russian phrase, firmly memorised: 'Denis, I love you!' and they would laugh resonantly. And nobody felt embarrassed, it was as though this was entirely ordinary and natural. Dinka would smile in reply, so winningly, revealing two rows of even, snow-white teeth, drop some cheesy compliment, and ask her out.

All the neighbourhood boys and I were completely stunned. This was the last thing we had expected of our bashful Chechen girls. When they met us, they'd lower their eyes, you couldn't get a word out of them, while as for inviting them on dates in secluded places – the thought didn't enter our heads!

But Dinka was different to them, he was beyond the law. They could do everything with him that they couldn't do with us, and they were willing to. I am sure that if Dinka had suggested sleeping together straight off on the first date, almost none would have refused. But Dinka didn't give in that easily. He would charm them, torment them, seduce them and then . . . it was over. He dumped them just like that.

I think he was taking revenge. But on whom and for what?

16 - In the Barnyard

During one summer holiday Zelik told me he was going to work at the state farm, in the barnyard, on the night shift. To earn some money for next year's school clothes and footwear, to lay in grain for the livestock. From the ages of fourteen or fifteen all the local kids worked summers at the state farm. The pay was modest, but after the shift you were allowed to take home a bag of wheat, maize or even sunflower seeds. Rather, it wasn't exactly allowed, you couldn't get grain through the control post, and even at the pilferers' secret hole in the fence the old granddad guard would sometimes be waiting for you, and he'd make you take back the stolen goods and pour them out on to the conveyor belt. But on the whole they turned a blind eye. Otherwise no one would have worked there.

I had no need of money, much less of grain. Mother and Stepfather clothed me in the most fashionable outfits as it was, and, of course, we kept no cattle or poultry, living in a city-style apartment with all mod cons in a four-storey block. But staying on my own in PP-2 was boring. So I asked Grandma for permission to go and work with Zelik.

Zelik arranged everything through his friends. Officially you could only work from the age of sixteen, but they registered other people who were of age on the payroll in our place. Everyone in the district did it. Without child labour the state farm couldn't have dealt with the harvest.

The state farm barnyard consisted of a floor asphalted in waves, a grain elevator, warehouses and areas for the production of grass meal. We worked on the loaders, motorised units with a conveyor belt, loading grain packed in golden dunes beneath the open sky into the machine. When dark clouds gathered, we'd cover the dunes with tarpaulin, and after the rain we'd dry the grain, shifting the dunes with the loader.

The conveyor belt of the loader was overflowing with grain, so we had to wield a wooden spade for hours on end, tossing the grain raining down from the edges back on to the belt. Sometimes we were sent to the elevator or to load grass meal into sacks. The work was heavy but it was fun at the barnyard.

It felt more like a party than a hard day's work. The Chechens in Shali had no discos or clubs. While here the entire local youth assembled each evening, boys and girls. The night shift began at four in the afternoon and finished at one in the morning. And the whole shift long, the cassette player in the tractor croaked out loud music: Gentle May, Mirage or Modern Talking. We chatted, joked, got to know each other as we worked. The girls flirted. The guys showed off.

During breaks you could fall on to a golden dune somewhere away from the din of agricultural machinery and lie there, looking at the starry sky.

At the barnyard I made friends for the first time with Chechen guys besides Zelik. Though it didn't happen straightaway, and I had to brave some fights first.

17 - The Duel

And so, the girls of our district already knew the sweetness of a god's company. But the guys had yet to find out. It happened nine months later, when Dinka joined me working at the barnyard.

The Chechen guys gave the outsider a hostile reception. It was bad enough that he wasn't one of us, he was Russian, but on top of that almost none of the girls could tear their eyes from him. So they decided that Dinka should be taught a lesson. I knew it would be useless to oppose so I remained neutral. The lesson was to be delivered by Bislan Sabirov, a newcomer from a family of Karbadins eagerly aspiring to become Chechens. Sabirov was older than me and Dinka, and had fought with me earlier and most of the time had won. Now my friend's turn had come.

We had barely worked a few shifts before Sabirov found fault with Dinka, showered him with insults and created an excuse for a fight. They went out beside the old combine harvesters to brawl.

In a matter of minutes Dinka had taken down the bully and held him in a painful lock. Dinka was terribly athletic and fit. He knew Sambo moves, he was strong and supple and had quick reactions. The crowd of onlookers pronounced Dinka the winner and started laughing at Sabirov. Bislan promised to get revenge the next day.

And so it continued, shift after shift. The duel between the outsider and Sabirov became a regular show. Dinka displayed a range of moves, knocked his opponent down, demonstrated how to strangle and various other tricks of self-defence. But he never beat up the loser.

And yet the spectators, apart, of course, from me, sided with Bislan. Dinka's victory was met with disgruntled cries, and everyone waited for the moment when the Kabardin would get his revenge. And he did. It was bound to happen, by the law of probabilities. One day, while trying to pull off a complicated move, Dinka failed to notice a piece of metal from the combine harvester lying on the ground. He twisted his ankle and fell. Here Sabirov laid into him and began pummelling his face. Dinka almost lost consciousness from the pain in his leg, from the punches raining down on his face and he was unable to put up a worthy defence. I demanded that the fight be stopped. The lads waited until Sabirov had reduced Dinka's face to pulp then finally dragged him away. That's it, they declared, the fight's over, the Russian is beaten.

Everyone had already turned their backs on us – on Dinka and me, as I helped Dinka to get up – and they were walking off when suddenly, to everyone's surprise, Dinka, gathering the last of his strength, pushed me away and said, struggling to move his mashed, bloodied lips: 'I'm not beaten. I'll fight on.' The whole pack looked on in astonishment. Sabirov glanced braggingly at the guys and walked up to Dinka. He feinted, Dinka tried to block him and received a sweeping kick to the groin. Dinka buckled in pain, and Sabirov delivered another kick to the head. Dinka fell. The gang laughed maliciously.

But Dinka got up again, barely able to stand, tried to assume his stance and gave a sign that he would fight on. Sabirov quickly moved in, punched his stomach and headbutted him in the face. Dinka doubled up. Sabirov grabbed him by the hair and kneed him several times, then threw him on to the grass.

Dinka rose slowly, sideways, clenched his fists, raised them to his battered face and uttered something like: 'Come on, arsehole.' I couldn't take any more and threw myself forward between Sabirov and Dinka. 'That's it, enough! If you like, Bislan can carry on fighting with me.'

The eldest of the guys, Adam, came up to me and said, 'This is none of your business. If he wants to fight, let him fight. Everything's fair, it's one on one. You'll get to fight too in due course.' They dragged me away, and Sabirov punched Dinka several times, but already more in jest, half-heartedly. He ran up from behind and kicked his heels into Dinka's buttocks. But Dinka suddenly turned round and executed a beautiful right-legged roundhouse kick, hitting Bislan square in the jaw. Unable to keep his balance, Dinka tumbled down and couldn't get up. Bislan howled and he would have leaped on the prostrate Dinka, but here Adam shouted harshly at him: 'Stop!'

Dinka lay on the grass, Bislan stood holding his dislocated jaw with his hand, the entire gang stood around watching in sheer bewilderment. 'This is some strange Russian. I was in the army, saw plenty of Russians. But I never saw a Russian like him. Russians don't fight like that,' said Adam.

'Who said he's Russian?' I said, and everyone stared at me dumbly. 'He isn't Russian,' I continued. 'His father is Bachaev Aslan, from our *teip*, Ersenoy. It's just that Dinka lives in Turkmenia, with his mother, and doesn't know how to speak Chechen. Bachaev didn't marry his mum. Dinka is the son of a Chechen, and he's a Chechen, a genuine Chechen, not like some, who come here from Kabardino-Balkaria and learn the Chechen language, but don't know genuine Chechen customs, who kick someone when they're down. Dinka is our *teipan vosh*, our brother.'

'Why didn't you tell us before?' asked Adam.

'You wouldn't have believed me before,' I replied.

We were speaking in Chechen, and Dinka didn't understand a thing. Adam himself went up to him, helped him get up, firmly gripped his shoulder and embraced him, touching cheek to cheek.

'Denis, I apologise. You are our brother and from now on, if there's any trouble, just tell us. We'll kill anyone for you.' This Adam said in Russian. Then he turned and switched back to Chechen, addressing Sabirov: 'And as for you, get out of here, Kabardin dog. You have no nobility, you don't know how to win an honest fight, only how to kick a man when he's down. Who do you Sabirovs think you are, raising your hand against our *teip*? *Tebyakhkin nakh* – newcomers. Abandoned the land of your fathers, the graves of your ancestors, you roam like gypsies. Be gone.'

18 - Like Father, Like Son

The summer when Zelik and I worked together in the barnyard was our last holiday together. Both of us had started school at six and by sixteen we'd reached school-leaving age. Zelik was a straight-A pupil whose parents were preparing him for higher education in the city. I had never been interested in studying, I liked sport, so my progress was barely satisfactory and going to the institute wasn't on the cards.

In my last year at school, I visited Shali in the winter for the first time, during the holidays, because I knew I wouldn't be visiting that summer. Zelik wouldn't be there and I'd also be starting a new life.

The bell rang after the last lesson. I wasn't fussed about where I went for further education and I applied for an electrician's course at college while Zelik got into the law department of Rostov University. I found this out from a letter as we had agreed to write that winter. I carried on with my sport, taking part in competitions, got a Candidate for Master of Sports[29] in freestyle wrestling.

Then, at seventeen, this is what happened. One of the girls I was seeing got pregnant. She didn't even tell me, the idiot. Her condition became noticeable and it was too late for an abortion. Her parents came to see my mother. I realised what was going on when

I ran into them as they were leaving our flat. As soon as I came in, mother opened her trap and started yelling about me being a filthy skirt chaser and other shit.

But I stopped her. I said, 'Like father, like son, Mama, is that what you're thinking? That I'm just like my daddy? Well, you've got another think coming! I'll marry this girl and I don't give a damn what you think.'

Barely eighteen, I got married. We started living with her parents, who were soon well-disposed to me and took care of us, the young, unemployed, penniless couple. The day came and a daughter was born. Then I was called up. I didn't try to get deferred, I went to serve in the army, leaving my wife and child in the care of my parents-in-law. I had always dreamt of serving in the Pskov airborne paratrooper division and that dream came true: I was in outstanding form and they accepted me into the division.

All went well, on the whole, during my service. The first six months were tough, same as for everyone. But I never let anyone humiliate me. And when I fell in with the guys from the Caucasus, who took me for one of their own, my status was now beyond question despite the army pecking order. I enjoyed the constant physical exercise and strict discipline and the atmosphere of genuine male friendship.

Letters came from Zelik, he described his life as a student, I answered, wrote about my service. At first we wrote frequently, then less and less, but we were hoping to meet again when I finished my service. Once I went home on leave to Bezmein, to my wife and daughter.

The longed-for demob day came. A sergeant, paratrooper, top-scorer in physical combat proficiency, I left for Turkmenia. But I didn't find what I had left behind two years earlier.

During that time a dim-witted drunkard and his clever-arsed Jewish advisers had toppled the Soviet Union. Turkmenia had turned into the independent state of Turkmenistan. Real genuine Turkmen Ali Babas flooded into Bezmein. Even our own city-dwelling Turkmen began to behave differently – suddenly they couldn't understand Russian. Russians were hounded out of the town. Pogroms and violence broke out. Russians were fired from their jobs. It became impossible to find work, and I didn't bother continuing my pointless studies at the college which they had already renamed.

Several times the other Russians and I gave these donkey herders a kicking, but it always ended with the police – who were now all Turkmen – throwing us into the cells. We were powerless to change the situation. Russians left, families, whole trainloads. You couldn't even sell your flat. Turkmen buyers would come and offer a ridiculous sum and when we turned it down, they'd say: 'Well, it's up to you. You'll leave anyway in the end, and we'll get the flat for nothing.'

Russia couldn't have given a shit for us. Once she sent Russians here, took them from their native lands so that they could work for the good of the greater country. But now she forsook us, abandoned us. So we felt like a forgotten division, trapped way behind enemy lines. Here we were being driven out, while back in Russia no one wanted us either.

We left eventually, my wife, my child and I, packed our things in cases and left. How did I choose where to go? I didn't care. Nobody wanted us anywhere. My wife and I laid out a big map of the Soviet Union on the floor and asked our daughter to point somewhere on the map. Her little finger fell on the city of Perm. And that is where we went.

In Perm I was taken on by the OMON paramilitary police. I had served as a paratrooper, so finding employment with the police special forces wasn't a problem. Accommodation was another matter. We barely managed to get a single room in a hostel. All the same, it was better than rotting in Turkmenia.

The country continued falling apart at the seams. And then the war started in Chechnya. When they started sending OMON fighters on 'missions' to this war, I expressed a desire to go. They promised good combat pay, which we could certainly have done with. But that was not the only reason. I felt like going back, seeing the places of my childhood. Perhaps I wanted to meet my father.

And kill him.

Zelik and I had lost contact long ago. He didn't know my new address in Perm. I didn't write to him. In any case Chechnya's postal service was barely working.

19 - Winter

Something in this world broke, went awry, turned pear-shaped. Dinka came in winter. It was weird. He was so beautiful and tanned, the god of summer, Dionysus – yet surrounded by thawing snow, puddles coated with ice, and I was wrapped up in warm clothes. It felt strange inside but my heart rejoiced nevertheless to see him. I embraced him and shook his hand. We went for a walk down the street. I so badly wanted not to let go of his hand, but we weren't children any more and we couldn't allow ourselves such tenderness. So we simply walked together and talked. It was our last meeting. Unless you count the day he died.

Leaving school with a medal, I got a place at Rostov State

University and lived in Rostov, visiting Shali only for the holidays. I have nothing good to say of the towns where I've lived, so I'll say nothing about Rostov. My course lasted five years. During this time they first tried reforming, then they abolished Marxism-Leninism and the study programme was rewritten; the legislative framework changed, Socialist law became history; the USSR fell apart, then came the August putsch, privatisation vouchers, privatisation, re-denomination. The money put aside by my father in a savings account for me to buy an apartment after graduating metamorphosed into the price of a bottle of plonk.

It was also the era of romantic gangsterism. The most alluring image was that of the 'Chechen mafia'. Many of my contemporaries left for the big cities of Russia, where they became hardboiled gangsters and businessmen; an even greater number returned home in coffins. Much later I realised that there was no 'Chechen mafia'. Using the paws of flashy, hot-headed mountain dwellers anyone who cared to could pull chestnuts out of the fire. In Petersburg the Tambov gang and Kazan gang fought their turf wars using Chechens as their combat units. The Alkhazurs and Kazbeks[30] fell to the pavement with bullets in their heads, while the Vladimirs[31] and Talgats[32] rode the gravy train. In Moscow bank fraudsters with Jewish surnames fiddled the financial system with faked credit notes, while those ever-present 'Chechens' were the ones who took the blame. And it was the same story everywhere.

This, I admit, concerned me little. I was studying, and my natural inclination to romance and adventure was gratified by amorous escapades, which weren't in short supply here. Five years later I graduated in law and returned to Shali.

Chechnya was already being run by Dudaev. My father was

pensioned off from his post in the district administration because of his pro-Russian sentiments. I didn't know where to look for a job. In Ichkeria, Shariah law had been declared. We hadn't been taught Shariah at university except superficially, as part of the module on the history of the state and the law.

Together with my alcoholic and Jack-of-all-trades uncle and my cousin Akhmed, we started a business which I christened the 'Ford Factory'. We bought up old battered cars cheaply and out of these heaps of metal assembled automobiles which we then sold at the car market in Shali. There were no traffic police whatsoever and we had no need to worry about numberplate registration, ownership certificates or changing the engine and chassis numbers. The main thing was for the vehicle to move under its own steam, preferably on the low-quality homemade petrol which they sold on every street corner in buckets and three-litre jars.

And our cars moved no worse than the rest. Oh, the monstrosities that came out of our workshop! Zhigulis and Volgas were hybridised with foreign makes, we changed engines and chassis, anything that at least roughly matched. When things didn't match terribly well, our chief automotive engineer, Uncle, would rework the parts using simple bench tools. The bodies were straightened out, sanded smooth, repainted in beautiful colours – and there you had it, a new luxury automobile ready for sale. Warming to my work, I stuck an advert on the back windscreens of our cars: 'Ford Factory. Auto repair and restoration of all makes. 24 Naberezhnaya Street, Shali.'

20 - Tanks

We didn't get involved in politics, stuck strictly to our business. The beards in green gowns putting on wild dances with rifle salutes in the squares held no interest for us. But like everyone we were not averse to enjoying the fruits of the ensuing chaos.

Not far from Shali was a garrison. A military unit, barracks, officers' quarters, practice ground and hangars. We saw all this only under Dudaev: in Soviet days Chechens hadn't been allowed into the grounds. Through some kind of astonishing agreement with the Russian government, the unit based near Shali was withdrawn and repatriated to Russia, while the bulk of the military equipment was left behind. Shali headed off as one to plunder the garrison.

We couldn't just stand aside and watch. One evening, my cousin and I got in a Moskvich pickup and made our way to the garrison, hoping to net some useful spares among the remains of the military fleet, perhaps even an entire truck if we were lucky. Having driven past the unguarded garrison entrance with its wrenched up barrier, we headed for the large group of hangars. Standing next to them was an old granddad in khakis with a green band round his cap, apparently posted by the Ichkerian authorities to stand guard over the equipment.

'*Vasha*' – a term of respect for the elderly – 'please let us look at the spares!' I asked.

'A hundred dollars!' replied the guardian of the military supplies.

We bartered and settled on fifty.

'You can open the hangars and help yourselves.'

We broke the lock on the doors with a crowbar and entered. We looked about . . .

'Fuuu-uuuck me sideways!' I spluttered. In the hangar stood tanks – real tanks – rows of them, with canvas-shrouded guns, reeking of diesel oil and engine grease.

'What the fuck?' I added, and wondered what would happen now.

The tanks slumbered, but their sleep was shallow. It felt as though they wouldn't remain sleeping for much longer . . .

21 - Bombs

We didn't drive a tank out of the hangar. What did we need a tank for? Of course, given that it would have cost us fifty dollars and we could have sold it at market for two thousand, it would have been a good deal. But we didn't want to spoil the image of our firm. The Ford Factory (24 Naberezhnaya Street, Shali) was a civilian enterprise and didn't deal in military hardware.

The smell of war hung in the air. Russia was threatening the use of force. On the Ichkerian channel the mustachioed Führer Dudaev raved, calling on us to join the National Guard, to fight and defend our freedom and independence. He explained how to build a bomb shelter and take cover from artillery attacks and air strikes.

People said he had a screw loose. Were we to drop everything and go dancing with our assault rifles? Sure, we'll hold a *sinkeram* – a party. Only don't send us those beards, send pretty girls! Who are we to celebrate a *lovzar* – a wedding – with, these unshaven guys? Maybe we should sleep with them too? Sleep with them yourself. We need to work, earn money, marry pretty girls, build houses, have children – you can deal with the Russians on your own. Moscow put you in power, Moscow will remove you from power. We knew nothing about you, not you, not your *lamaroy* – your men who descended from the mountains. Who are you anyway, which *teip* are you from? A mountain Jew from the *tebyakhkin nakh* – newcomers. Get your head examined. In Afghanistan you flattened the ravines with carpet-bombing, and now you think the Russians are going to do the same here? This is not Afghanistan. If the Russians think Chechnya is part of Russia, then why would they bomb their own territory?

The storming of Grozny began on New Year's Eve. The rumble of explosions from the city went on endlessly, day and night. Some Shali men joined the guerrillas and fought on the streets of Grozny. But most stayed at home: they couldn't believe what was happening and were waiting for it to finish.

In January the Federal air force bombed the car market, striking at the civilian population. It was the best recruitment campaign the Armed Forces of Ichkeria could have wished for, all Dudaev and Udugovy's propaganda efforts paled in comparison. All day long the village buried its dead by the hundred; the next day guerrillas set off for Grozny.

The air strikes damaged our business irreparably. Two vehicles ready for sale were turned into mangled metal, the kids hired to sell our cars were killed. I was saved miraculously; during the bombardment I had been taking a prospective customer for a test drive along the road to Germenchuk, showing off the performance of the Opel mutant with its transplanted engine.

On the evening of the third day, Akhmed and I were sitting in the yard which doubled as the Ford Factory. 'Zelim, all our guys are joining the guerrillas. Are we going to sit snug at home like whores?' asked Akhmed.

'Decided you want to be a tough Ichkerian too, have you, Akhmed? And have you spared a thought for your poor mother? If they kill you, what will she do?' I talked sense into my business partner and relative. 'The Chechens won't win this war in any case. You know, when Imam Shamil was taken prisoner, they drove him through the whole of Russia to St Petersburg, to the tsar. They drove and drove, and Russia never ended. "If only I'd known how large Russia is, I wouldn't have fought her," Shamil said.'

Akhmed wouldn't let up: 'There was a preacher on the television reading verses from the Koran. I memorised one translation, Surah 3, Ayat 13: "There was a token for you in two hosts which met: one army fighting in the way of Allah, and another disbelieving, whom they saw as twice their number, clearly, with their very eyes. Thus Allah strengtheneth with His succour whom He will. Lo! herein verily is a lesson for those who have eyes."'[33]

I sneered. 'Become a mullah now, have you? A holy sheikh?'

Akhmed huffed. 'Don't laugh at the Holy Koran! That preacher said that even if there are more of the enemy, we'll win all the same, because Allah is with us! That's the meaning of the ayat.'

I thought my answer through and objected: 'I'm not laughing at the Holy Koran. But your preacher on the television is a fool, he didn't understand the meaning of the thirteenth ayat. Miracles don't happen on earth. Victory belongs to the strong. What is the ayat saying? The Muslims saw that their enemy was greater in number and they protested: Why did Allah make our enemy stronger than us? But the Koran says: Allah helps whoever He likes. He won't be asking you beards about it in any case. If He wants to, He'll give the Russians numerical superiority, and they'll win.'

Akhmed was still sulking. I tried to explain it to him more gently: 'Well, what exactly would we be fighting for, anyway? Fighting whom? It's all a dirty, bloodthirsty game, not our game. It'll all be over soon, *Dal mukkhla*' – 'God willing.'

'*Dal mukkhla* . . .' Akhmed echoed.

We didn't go to war. The war came to us.

22 - Grozny

The OMON paramilitary police dispatched from Perm were sent by train to Rostov-on-Don. From there we were taken to Khankala by bus. From Khankala we moved in the direction of Grozny, accompanied by a tank and an armoured personnel carrier.

It was spring and there was mud on the bumpy roads, but in the sky a warm sun squinted sweetly. We were travelling in full combat gear, in body armour, with assault rifles and ammunition. It was hot and stuffy in the bus. The fighters took off their helmets and fanned themselves with whatever was to hand. We moved forward slowly. From time to time the column would stop, whenever the sappers in the lead armoured personnel carrier noticed something suspicious. Along the approaches to Grozny, from one side of the road, as if from under the ground a bunch of kids emerged. About fifteen or sixteen years old. Village lads in civilian clothes. But adorned with weapons. One of them managed to fire a grenade launcher at the armoured personnel carrier but the grenade launcher must have been jogged and the round missed, flew past its target and exploded on the other side of the street. The kids opened fire on the column with assault rifles. Bullets peppered the side of the bus, we started jumping out and taking up position behind the tank and armoured personnel carrier. After a brief exchange of fire the assailants were eliminated.

I went out to the roadside and collected the weapons of the dead. In our bus Sergeant Pilipenko, whom I had got to know in Perm, was bleeding. These armoured vests did more harm than good. Without it he might have had a perforating wound which wouldn't have been all that dangerous, but in the tin can of the armoured vest the bullet thrashed about from side to side, shredding his innards.

Such was our baptism of fire.

We entered Grozny from Minutka Square. I had been here before, as a child, when Zelik and I had travelled to the city to go to the cinema or a concert. Now the place was unrecognisable.

Grozny. Russian for 'terrible'. Think carefully before naming your children, your cities or even your dogs. In giving a name you are shaping fate, that's what happens. Why didn't they call it Peaceful, Green or anything else? Now the city was truly terrible, fulfilling its name. It was horrific, a genuine nightmare. The first thing it called to mind was Stalingrad during the Second World War, as seen in war films. Ruined buildings, streets filled with craters, and the threat of death from any corner.

Our mission was to hold the checkpoint at the Drama Theatre building, which we did, shooting back at the rebels. We patrolled the streets, engaging in combat every so often. Once, while flushing rebels out of a building, we found ourselves encircled and huddled against the wall on the ground floor, afraid of attacking. We were rescued by a detachment of paratroopers. 'Call yourselves a special force? A pant-wetting force, that's what you are. Shat yourselves from fright,' our saviours sneered in scorn.

The enemy was everywhere. Snipers and men with grenade

launchers fired from the ruins. The front line, if there was one at all, however provisional, travelled not through space but through time – along the boundary between day and night. If during daylight hours we still maintained some kind of control over the city, then at night we could do nothing but hide behind the checkpoint's gargantuan concrete walls.

The mission was extended. It seemed there weren't enough Federal forces in Chechnya to let us go home on time. But I didn't mind. I liked fighting.

> *The reason I love the thought*
> *Of stormy military sport,*
> *Is that human blood is no holier*
> *Than the emerald sap of grass.*

So wrote Nikolai Gumilev, Zelik's favourite poet.

Where was Zelik all that time? I didn't know. It was hardly a holiday, after all, and I couldn't just go off and visit Shali.

At the Grozny checkpoint a new batch of paramilitary police from St Petersburg relieved us. And we were sent to the district centre of Urus-Martan.

23 - The Repair Unit

Akhmed and I were tinkering about with hardware in the yard as usual, assembling a self-propelling wagon in the body of an old GAZ-2410 under Uncle's supervision. Several jeeps drove up to our gates, and out poured armed men in camouflage. 'Who's in charge here?' asked a rebel with ashen bristle barely breaking through the skin of his chin. The field commander was holding a leaflet with our advert and guarantee of quality: 'Ford Factory. 24 Naberezhnaya Street, Shali.' Looks like I've overdone the publicity campaign, I thought, coming out to meet him. 'Assalamu aleykum!'

'Wa aleykum salam! So you are the one and only Ford, I take it?' he inquired. His company hooted in unison.

'And you, no doubt, have come from America to sue us for trademark infringement?' I said. 'Or do you want to buy a car?'

'I'm not here to buy anything. By order of the Southern Front command of the Armed Forces of the Republic of Ichkeria the entire staff of your company is being mobilised for defence against the Russian invaders. You will be attached to the Shali Tank Regiment as a repair unit. Well, where's your factory?'

'This is it, everything you see here,' I replied.

Once again the rebels roared with laughter.

'Can't you do without us?' I continued.

'Actually we specialise in carburettor engines. But tanks – they're diesel . . .' Uncle backed me up, trying hard to get his tongue around the words after yesterday's alcoholic meditation.

'Diesel-schmiesel. Sort it out yourselves if you're such experts. But our orders aren't open to debate. In the event of refusal we will be compelled to consider you deserters and to deal with you in accordance with martial law!'

'Which paragraph and article are you referring to?' I was tempted to quip, but I held my tongue. The rebels, for all their laughter, had not come in jest. The commander continued: 'Be at the executive committee tomorrow morning, with the necessary tank repair tools and firearms.'

Here Akhmed flared up, as if stung by a wasp: 'You mean we're not going to be issued with weapons?'

'No, bring your own. That's what everyone does. If you don't have any, then buy some,' came the answer. Akhmed was pained: 'You're saying Dudaev hasn't even stocked up on weapons? Is that how he prepares for war? What's he done with all the money from the oil?'

I checked him: 'Quiet, Akhmed!' And addressed the rebels: 'All right. My *shchich*' – cousin – 'and I will be at the executive committee tomorrow. Just leave Uncle alone. He's not young any more. Oh, and he's not the best of fighters – in the evenings he goes on drinking sprees and in the mornings he gets hangovers.'

'*Dik du*' – 'All right' – the commander answered, and the rebels left.

'See,' I said to Akhmed, 'we were arguing over whether to go to war or not but Allah decided for us. We're going to have to fight. I don't want to run away. Run away from the Russians, run away from the Chechens, that's hardly the thing to do. I didn't serve in the Soviet army – my student status exempted me from that – but it looks like there's no escaping the draft, so we'll serve in the Ichkerian army.'

The next morning we loaded a pickup truck with tools, drove to the bazaar, bought a Kalashnikov each and arrived at the executive committee. From there we were escorted to the garrison, where they were preparing for the appearance on the battlefield of the Shali tank regiment.

24 - Urus-Martan

The district centre of Urus-Martan was heavily defended by rebel forces. The combined-arms teams sent into attack were drowning in their own blood and they pulled out with serious losses.

This was a war of all against all. Fighting on the Chechen side were National Guard detachments one moment, independent bands of guerrillas the next, and not always in communication with each other or headquarters. It was the same with the Federal troops: combined-arms teams, Interior Ministry troops, the artillery, the OMON, airborne paratroop forces, special detachments of the Main Intelligence Directorate, the FSB. Each had its own chain of command, and I suspect no one was coordinating and controlling the actions of any of the forces. Every so often they would take each other out – by accident, or so they claimed.

Yet the operational procedure follows a certain logic. Usually they throw the conscripts into the line of fire first. These are lads of eighteen or nineteen, fresh out of training, they don't even know how to shoot properly. When the battle starts, they weep from fear, fall on the ground and lie covering their heads with their arms. If the Chechens capture them then as a rule they take their weapons and let them go free. Or they deliver them into the arms of their mothers, who come to Chechnya to pick up their little ones as if from kindergarten.

Having sent the conscripts to their deaths and satisfied themselves that the resistance is serious, the troops go to work on the defending village with carpet-bombing, artillery and multiple-launch rocket systems. Afterwards the tank and mechanised units advance, the special detachments. When the rebels are smashed and the hub of the resistance is crushed, the mercenary soldiers or OMON paramilitary police go into the village – to carry out a mop-up. The mop-up consists of shooting all the men over fourteen found on the streets and in the houses, shooting the ill and wounded in their beds, throwing grenades into cellars and dark barns. Along the way you can loot houses and if you come across pretty girls then they too are trophies for the victors. However, if you're starved and hankering for intimate joys, then an ugly girl will do. There's no point being squeamish about little girls and elderly women, either – who knows when you'll next get a chance to fuck someone?

In short, war is war.

The battle of Urus-Martan was terribly important. It's possible that the outcome of the entire operation was decided by it. The rebels brought up large quantities of personnel and hardware to the district centre. After the first unsuccessful attack the Federals pounded the rebel positions from the air and with rocket launchers. Then, as usual, the tanks and armoured personnel carriers moved into battle. It was relatively easy to drive back the Chechens from their first line of defence. But here something unexpected happened. Down the road, through the village, towards the advancing Federals, came tanks. Turning in the field, they opened fire with their turret guns. This was no Stalingrad. This was the Battle of Kursk.

The radio waves filled with curses abusing our intelligence-gathering units for failing to tell us that a tank force was approaching.

The troops began hurriedly retreating, leaving behind burnt-out combat vehicles, mountains of corpses and casualties. Artillery was called in, and fire began showering everyone, our troops and theirs. Once again aeroplanes soared into the sky. The massacre continued for several hours. The rebels tried to break out of the circle of fire but only a few managed. Practically all the tanks were eliminated by artillery and air fire. The remaining Ichkerians abandoned Urus-Martan, and then, backed up by fresh armoured units, we moved into the village – to carry out a reprisal operation.

25 - The Battle

We rushed to the aid of the Armed Forces of Ichkeria who were holding Urus-Martan. Tanks thundered down the road, driven by former tractor operators from Jalka State Farm and lads who had served in the Soviet Army's tank forces. On the tanks sat the Shali guerrillas. Behind the tanks, bouncing through the potholes came the pickup truck, formerly of the Ford Factory but now of the Shali Tank Regiment repair unit. Akhmed sat at the wheel, I was sitting next to the driver's seat, holding on my lap an assault rifle which I had not yet used.

'Do you think, Zelimkhan, with a force like this, with an entire tank regiment, maybe we could win this war?' Akhmed asked, returning to our old conversation.

'No one ever wins in war, Akhmed,' I responded. 'And we have zero chance of winning. The Russians have enough guns, mortars and bombs to wipe out ten Ichkerias and a couple of Turkmenistans to boot. This is all just Chechen bravado. The Shali Tank Regiment! They put diesel in the tanks left behind for some unknown reason by the Russians themselves, they unfurl the green banner – and forward march! Now we'll win against anyone. An entire tank regiment, for sure. Let's frighten the moon by barking at it!'

This time Akhmed was not in the mood for arguing. He drove

the pickup, carefully circumnavigating the most dangerous of the potholes.

'Yes, Zelim. Look at our side, they're like children. Children playing games. Everyone you meet is a brigadier general, a colonel at the very least. If every Chechen colonel had, say, not even a regiment, just a platoon of soldiers, then our army would be the biggest in the world.'

'*Bakkh du*, Akhmed. You speak the truth. But what can we do? We can try and get through it alive, but not by acting like cowards, not by fleeing death. Then we won't be ashamed to look in the eye the women who've buried their husbands and sons. That alone will be victory enough.'

The battle began in high spirits. Passing through the village, the tanks fanned out and opened fire. The guerrillas leapt from their tanks and went into attack with cries of 'Vurrroooo!' and 'Allah Akbar!' The Russians fled, leaving their knocked-out vehicles and casualties in the field. The guerrillas dragged the Federals out of the vehicles and shot them. The regiment tried to prolong the onslaught, pursuing the fleeing enemy.

But soon the entire field outside the village turned into the stage for a carnival of bombing. True hell was unleashed. The shells fell thickly, covering almost every yard of earth. Planes appeared in the sky, a deluge of bombs rained down, the tanks blazed one after the other, the bodies of guerrillas burst in gory tatters.

When the attack began, Akhmed and I stopped our pickup at the edge of the village and hid in the trench, gripping our assault rifles. Isolated pockets of Federals were breaking through on all sides, some ran to the village, and we shot at those who came near us. Then they started bombing the sector, and we couldn't shoot now; there was no point trying to get up and move to another place – shrapnel flew like dust in a hurricane. I thought this must be the dance of Shiva, the Indian god of destruction – the dance by which he annihilates the universe. After a nearby explosion, I was shell-shocked and lost consciousness.

Dark was falling when I came to. The bombing and shelling had ended, tanks burned in the field, the Russians were finishing off the wounded – our wounded and theirs too when they couldn't discern camouflaged and unidentified bodies in the dark: 'The Lord above will know his own.'[34] I looked around and saw my cousin. Akhmed's eyes were open, the back of his head had been shattered by shrapnel, and brain matter stained his collar. I hoisted my cousin's corpse on to my shoulder and crawled along the trench skirting the village.

I don't remember how long I crawled, but I managed to escape the scene of the fighting. Up ahead, where the trench veered away, I saw several silhouettes of men with assault rifles. 'I'm done for,' I thought.

'*Kho mil vu?*' – 'Who's that?' – reached me from their direction. I responded in Chechen:

'I'm Zelim. They've killed my *shchich*.'

'Crawl over to us, keep your head low.'

And just then I heard Russian speech behind me. I threw down Akhmed's body, grabbed my assault rifle and turned around. Above the lip of the ditch, not far from me, stood men with weapons.

26 - The Mop-Up

We carried out the first mop-up in Urus-Martan in a rush so as not to allow the rebels time to entrench themselves in the houses when night fell. In the morning we would do a new mop-up, the full works. We shot at the windows, then burst into the houses. We entered the rooms by the book: first throw a grenade, then go in yourself. In some houses there were women, children, old people. We killed them. We came across wounded or holed-up rebels. We shot them. There were girls, too, not too bad, fit for the job. But today we had no time for that. For now we were killing everyone, we'd deal with that the next day. We weren't in the mood for tasting the fruits of victory.

In the evening we walked along the trench at the perimeter of the village. We noticed something stir at the bottom, we cocked our assault rifles. Just then a nearby barn flared up, the blaze illuminated the area and, standing up to his knees in mud at the bottom of the trench, I saw a rebel with an assault rifle who looked somehow familiar . . .

27 - The Glow

We stood like that and stared into each other's eyes, our muddied faces lit by the fire. For a whole second, lasting longer than eternity. We had time to remember ourselves – from the first summer in the sandpit to the last winter, all our games and conversations. We had been as muddy as this plenty of times before, messing around in the clay at the edge of the state farm field. In the evenings when we'd baked campfire potatoes, the specks of fire had played on our faces too. We remembered everything, even the most important thing of all, that we had always been one whole. We were united with each other and in the blissful bounty of our union we absorbed the universe into ourselves, with all the beings dwelling in it. The entire world contained no one but us, nothing but our game. The stars, the sun and moon, the earth, her rivers, fields, forests and mountains – they were created for us. The other children, they were playing with us, and each one also embodied the entire world. And He was there – the One who allowed us to play. He was in the soul of each of us and in the heart of every mote of dust. And this knowledge was joyous.

It didn't matter that there were several OMON paramilitary police fighters with assault rifles behind one of us, and where the trench veered away, armed guerrillas were covering the other.

That was just the game.

That second – it broke the thick thread of time, it pulled the entire world into a black hole, the past, present, future fused into a single glow, but the fire no longer danced across our faces, it froze like an electric light, as if someone were taking our photograph, and we were to live in it for ever. The second lingered on and on . . .

The one who shot first is the author of this story.

Crazy Diamond

Too many stories begin in the cafés strewn around this wet and chilly city, tangled in a web of neon lights. Perhaps for that very reason. In the Leningrad air's toxic moisture they look like hunting lodges, staging posts, camps for primitive tribes on perpetual Ice Age journeys across the permafrost on the trail of the migrating mammoths.

One day the archaeologists of the distant future will unearth our own encampments and from the artefacts will form their opinion of us. Of the people who lived through the third Ice Age.

Postgraduate researchers will write: In those austere times, people would descend every morning from their multistoreyed caves, travel through subterranean tunnels and across wet asphalt to reach other caves crammed with iron and plastic boxes in order to earn food, clothing and the liquid which they poured into their coloured, self-propelling wagons. They needed the food, clothing and liquid in order to provide their bodies with the strength to survive the northern winds. They also had a strange hierarchical system: the ones who earned food and clothing for themselves in the caves filled with plastic boxes believed that they were successful in life, whereas the others, who laboured in the caves with the metal boxes, drank huge amounts of fiery drinks and tried not to think about life at all. In the evenings, however, both peoples assembled in small herds at places which they called 'cafés', with glass windows, bars and small tables on a stone floor. There they fell in love, rowed, met and split up, mingled and clashed. Now and then pairs of persons of opposite sexes would emerge so that somewhere in a multistoreyed cave these primitive people could bring a new screaming whelp into the cold world of this Ice Age. Why? Because on the streets it was cold, whereas in the cafés it was warm, and they served hot water tinted brown through the addition of a powdered tropical dried fruit. This was probably why their stories began in cafés.

The girl sitting at the table in front of me is seventeen years old. Tall, with wavy fair hair and blue eyes, teenage awkwardness in her figure and a boyish expression on her face. At the start of the conversation I invited her to come and visit me at the weekend, and she hastily accepted. If she'd refused, I'll perhaps have thought of her as underage. But she's no kid, she's already had sex, she's quite capable of calmly going straight back to a grey-haired man's place for a screw, yes, she's already grown up.

I find it hard to desist from imagining myself peeling off her jeans, placing her on her knees and taking her from behind. Repeating, as usual, multiplication tables in my mind, working out how fast the tilt of the Earth's axis is changing. She's said something: I watch her lips move – and see myself asking her to take my soft member in her mouth. And she'll do it. She'll obediently and earnestly carry out ridiculous, comic movements to show how experienced she is. Nobody would guess that this little girl is performing oral sex for the third or fourth time. She'll suck and I'll look at her blonde head and grow hard again.

I noticed long ago how, during a date, whoever does most of the talking feels the least confident, wants to please and impress the other one first. On this evening the girl talked plenty, while managing to down one Bloody Mary after another. Her restless eyes tried to catch my gaze, she was forever asking about something or other – as though frightened that the ensuing silence would be too much to bear. I drank my coffee in little sips, answered briefly and smiled politely.

'So what music do you listen to?' she asked, a question taken from the special volume entitled 'When There's Nothing Left to Talk About.'

'All sorts.'

'Yeah, but what? Give me an example.'

'Classical, rock. Everything except pop and rap.'

'Wow, really? I like rock! Most of my friends listen to such garbage! Their kind of music makes me sick. I like Metallica, and our Russian group Spleen, and there's a group called Pilot. Do you know Pilot? You've probably never heard of them!'

'Yeah, I've heard of Pilot. I used to know Ilya Chort. He's their vocalist.'

'What, no kidding? How cool! You know, it's great you're into rock. 'Cause no one really understands me.'

Time repeats itself. Once again, teenagers who listen to rock are in the minority and stand out from their peers. I remember how things were nearly two decades earlier.

In a little provincial town in an ethnic outpost of Russia, we rockers numbered just a few. In those days, rockers didn't mean motorcyclists without silencers, it meant fans of rock music. Motorcyclists became known as rockers later on. Later still, motorcyclists began to be known as bikers. While those who listened to rock were left with no name at all. Then cyclists started calling themselves bikers and everything slid into sheer confusion.

But in those days everything was as clear as war. There were us, the rockers, and there was everyone else, the uninitiated. We were reprimanded at school for our leather, our discreet metal chains and shaved temples. And we had to brawl in the streets with the most belligerent of the uninitiated for our right to be different.

Every now and then, skiving lessons, we'd meet up at someone's house and all together, silently nodding in time to the music, we'd listen to Pink Floyd, Accept, Led Zeppelin, Deep Purple, Iron Maiden, Judas Priest, Def Leppard, Santana, ELO, Frank Zappa . . . It was like some sort of sectarian prayer group. Yes, we were a sect.

I was walking home from school one day with Islam, who was one of us. Islam announced: 'Governments ban rock because rock is power and freedom. If the people listened to rock, they'd overthrow all the governments, there'd be no laws, no armies, no police, no money, only music and love.'

It is unlikely he thought this up himself. He was probably parroting Elder Brother. I can't remember the eldest rocker's name any more, so I'll simply call him Elder Brother.

The fact was that Islam's family swelled the ranks of our sect considerably. All the Ibragimovs listened to forbidden music and thought forbidden thoughts. After Elder Brother, Movsar came next, then my classmate Islam, and the youngest, Shahid. All four brothers. Needless to say, they had the best record collection and we met most often at their place.

Elder Brother said little. He wasn't married, had no job, lived in a separate wing and seldom left the house. When persuaded to talk he would say that authority is violence and deceit. And that people live in a state of illusion. They want to run away from themselves, they're forever travelling. That's why they need oil, lots of oil. They'll soon start killing each other for money, oil and power, until the last man is dead. He said that oil is the stinking sludge of putrefied fern, money is coloured paper, and people who chase after this crap are just crazy. People said that Elder Brother was crazy and he probably was.

Movsar had a beautiful predatory profile, long curly hair and a powerful voice with which he'd yell: 'Balls to the wall!' He sounded like the vocalists of all the rock groups rolled into one.

Once we had a pipe dream. I told Movsar that when I grew up and earned lots of coloured paper, I'd buy instruments and equipment and we'd start our own rock group. He'd be the vocalist and I'd play the electric guitar. We'd be famous and wouldn't need to work or study. Instead we'd spend all our time on tour, perhaps even to foreign countries. And after our concerts people would overthrow the government. Well, no, they wouldn't even need to! Once they'd heard our songs, the police and soldiers would take off their uniforms of their own accord, throw down their weapons and join the crowd singing in unison.

But Movsar didn't believe me. He sneered grimly and said that when I had lots of coloured paper, I'd be the first to forget about rock and that we'd have to wait and see who would be wearing which uniforms.

Then perestroika happened. Listening to rock became fashionable among the sophisticated youth. Girls in my class, fans of Modern Talking, started asking me to make them tapes of Led Zeppelin. But the government didn't collapse, everything just got entangled and mixed up. Whereas before it had been as clear as war, so to speak. Real war was to begin a few years later.

And there came the first aerial bombing of our little town by the

Federals. Aeroplanes swooped low over our homes with a terrible howling and dropped cluster bombs on to the peaceful residents. King Crimson was playing in the Ibragimovs' yard. Elder Brother came out from his annexe and squatted in the yard. Over the roar of the aeroplanes and the thunder of bombs, a guitar solo was sounding. Elder Brother mumbled something, perhaps 'I told them so, but they wouldn't believe me', or perhaps he was simply singing along to the tape player. Then a shrapnel fragment hit the speaker and the music died.

Another fragment hit Shahid in the chest. So Islam took his wounded brother in his arms and dragged him to hospital but the hospital had been bombed too, and no one could provide Shahid with medical assistance. Shahid bled to death in his brother's arms. The wing of the house lost its roof, just as its inhabitant had lost his marbles long before, and now Elder Brother spent more and more time sitting about the yard mumbling. Islam and Movsar just kept quiet, barely speaking even to their parents.

One morning they went into town and came home in khaki uniforms adorned with weapons. They announced curtly that they had joined the guerrillas. Their parents – greyed from the death of their youngest child – could do nothing to stop them. Their mother begged them to stay and wailed at the top of her voice; their father moodily bit his lip and smoked.

Elder Brother didn't take up his weapon. He just muttered: 'Blood . . . oil's like blood . . . black blood, red blood . . . blood begets blood . . .'

Throughout the first war Movsar and Islam didn't put down their assault rifles. We saw little of each other. I was studying law at St Petersburg and only made brief visits home. Islam dropped in once and explained the principal teachings of the Wahhabis and said that I too should embrace the true faith. I listened without interrupting. Only then did I ask:

'But what about rock and roll, man? Don't you listen to rock any more?'

'Well you know, we're not supposed to. But so long as no one's the wiser, there are some songs which . . . Well, they're about the same thing. *We are buying a stairway to heaven . . .*'

After the first war Islam left the warrior's trade, he got married and started a family. Movsar, however, remained in his armed gang serving as Salman Raduev's[35] brother-in-arms and one of the movement's most prominent propagandists and ideologists. And even when it was clear that the outcome of the second war was already a foregone conclusion, he still remained in hiding, in the forests. That's what they say – in the forests. Don't take it literally. Nobody hides in the forests, or in the mountains.

What forests and mountains? You'd think it was the Cordillera! All our forests and mountains can be swept through by a single battalion in a couple of days.

It's a strange war, everyone says so. The frontline runs along every street, and there is no rear zone. A war of silence. Everyone knows everything, but no one will speak. Omertà.

They needed to find Movsar and liquidate him but this was more or less impossible. He left tracks here and there but always shook off his pursuers.

And that's when they took Islam, who was living peaceably at home. They simply let it be known that if Movsar didn't come of his own accord then his brother would disappear into Chernokozovo,[36] like thousands of others before him. They just let it be known. Whoever's keeping shtum would hear it and pass it on.

Movsar came. Two days later he came and asked them to release his brother.

They shot the two of them, with their hands tied behind their backs, against the blood-drenched wall in the basement of the commandant's headquarters. That night they smuggled the bodies out to bury them beyond the village, on the bank of the shallow brook.

'Are you okay? . . .'

The girl sitting opposite me at the table in the café was genuinely concerned. What girl? Oh yes, she's seventeen, tall and blonde. We've just made friends, right here, and her name is . . . Yana, maybe? She likes rock music.

The reason for her concern was obvious. I had been sitting there for half an hour not answering her, contributing nothing to the conversation, just staring blankly through the café's glass front at the neon-drenched Nevsky Prospekt.

I started to talk. Fast, scattily, cramming my words in as if I had something to prove:

'You know, recently I read that – and this really surprised me – I read that we're living in the third Ice Age. Yes, the third Ice Age. From the perspective of geophysics. The first one was ages ago, before the dinosaurs died out, then there was the second one, and now we're in the third. I can't remember the dates, they're all very big numbers. We're somewhere around the middle of the third Ice Age, it's already on the wane. But anyway, that's why we have permafrost, and the Antarctic, and icebergs – like the one that sank the Titanic, you must have seen the film. But at one time everything was different. The Earth didn't have any kind of axial tilt in relation to the sun. And there were no changing seasons, the whole

Earth had an even, warm climate. Summer. There was plenty of food, enough for everyone. And there was no need at all to use clothes – well, it was warm. And if you have food and don't need clothes, why bother travelling about all the time? What need is there for oil and petrol? But then the Earth was hit by a huge meteorite: WHAM! And the angle of the Earth's axis went askew. It's all because of that. The north became too cold, and the south too hot. Vegetation died out. The giant fern – it died out and rotted, and became oil. And there wasn't much to eat. People began killing animals, eating their meat and wearing their skins. At first there was anarchy. Then the most powerful, sly, evil people thought up government, claiming that now they alone had the right to kill, to share out the meat and skins, and they called this 'government' and 'the law'. Then people learnt to make lots of food and clothing, and there would have been enough for everyone but by this time the government had thought up coloured paper and began printing it in limited quantities, to make sure that there definitely wouldn't be enough for everyone. They called this "money" and you had to exchange the coloured paper for food. And the food started to rot, but people carried on dying from hunger. And they also needed oil, lots of oil. But oil runs out, and that type of fern doesn't grow any more. It's all because the Earth's axis went askew. That's the reason people kill, brother kills brother, friend kills friend. It's all because of the Ice Age – this cold, this glaciation, it's to blame for everything. See, the door's open, d'you feel that wind? It smells of arctic ice and permafrost. But it's not our fault. And you know what else I found out? Scientists have calculated the changes in the Earth's tilt and they say it's starting to even out! The Ice Age is going to end quite soon, in maybe another couple of million years. It'll be warm again everywhere, summer, eternal summer, and there'll be plenty of food, and nobody will need oil. And there'll be no reason to kill. And we won't kill, honestly, we won't kill anyone then!'

The girl looked at me in astonishment and incomprehension. There was a pause. She glanced at her watch and got up nervously.

'I'd better be going. It's late already. It's dark now. And . . . you know, I can't visit you at the weekend. I've just remembered, I've got something to do . . .'

'Goodbye.'

'Goodbye, sorry. It was really interesting talking with you. Maybe I'll call. You're so clever and . . . different. Bye.'

She hurried towards the exit.

I continued to look through the window. There are so many pictures which we would prefer not to revisit, but memory is a film which cannot be stopped. In the dark operator's booth sits . . . I don't even want to think about who's sitting there, but it's pointless asking him to stop the show or change the film.

Then I sat in the commandant's headquarters. On the simple wooden table lay a pistol, still warm from the shots. And I saw it again . . .

I went into the basement. They were on their knees, their hands tied behind their backs, against the wall. Islam cried noiselessly. Having turned round at the clank of the unlatching bolt, Movsar saw me and, moving his mashed, bloodied lips heavily, spoke:

'Oh, it's you. Hi.'

Behind me stood three St Petersburg OMON paramilitary fighters. Movsar nodded his head towards them.

'You see, man. You got your rock band together. Only there's no vocalist. Nothing but drummers.'

And hoarsely, at the top of his voice, he sang: 'Balls to the wall! . . . Ooo-ooo-ooo! Balls to the wall!'

I shot them very humanely, I swear. Each got a bullet to the head. Without any of that barbarity which the cops and soldiers go in for. Their heads bobbed, hit the concrete wall like balls and their bodies sank to the floor.

Two hours later I went home. Found a tape, turned on the old cassette player and, staring at the ceiling, listened.

'Shine on you crazy diamond.'

Come on and shine, crazy diamond, shine. Through the torrents of red and black blood, through the navy uniforms and the khaki uniforms, shine. Through the coloured paper lanterns . . .

A month later I was transferred back to the St Petersburg public prosecutor's office.

The café was closing. Between the tables flitted a young guy with a mop. Probably moonlighting after classes, I thought to myself.

Too many stories start in cafés. And some end there too. I felt as if today, here in this café, the story of my rock and roll had ended. Today, in this café, and not in the corridors of the law faculty, not in the basement of the commandant's office, not in the two-roomed apartment with my wife and child.

On Nevsky Prospekt my face was hit by a cold wind smelling of arctic ice and permafrost. I turned up the collar of my coat and strode towards my cave. Summer was a long way off.

The Pioneer Leader

I still have her photograph. I came across it almost by chance among a pile of old papers in my father's apartment. It is an old photo, in sepia tones. She stands in her school dress against a background of idiotically green fir trees, holds her hands behind her back and gazes. Defiantly, as she knew how to gaze. Signed simply on the back: 'Remember me. Aynet.' And I remember it all.

Aynet was the unofficial leader of the class, and Marya Ilinichna found her a force to be reckoned with. That day she approached her Class Mistress with a whole delegation of girls.

'Marya Ilinichna!'

'Yes, Aynet?'

'Our class is making poor progress.'

'Eh?'

'We often skip lessons.'

'Eh?'

'There's absolutely no discipline at all!'

'Eh?'

'And do you want to know why?'

'Why, Aynet?'

Marya Ilinichna already smelt a rat.

'Well, I'll tell you. We still have no Pioneer Leader! So there's no one for us to look up to, there's no one to set us an example!'

'All right, girls. I'll speak to the Deputy Head, we'll search for a good Leader for you. I'm glad you want to improve the discipline in your class.'

'Marya Ilinichna, there's no need to look for anyone.'

'Eh?'

'We've already found someone.'

Of course, I was surprised when the Deputy Head Teacher asked me to run Class 7C's detachment. It was the end of the eighties, when the Young Pioneer organisation was in decay; every link in the chain betrayed a system in crisis. And besides, I couldn't make sense of the ambiguous smile accompanying the request.

You could count on one hand the months left until the end of my final year at school. I was like a soldier a week before demob, only going to lessons occasionally, and here I was about to become Pioneer Leader! But I turned up for my meeting with 7C. Perhaps I'd begun to take an interest.

When I saw her brown eyes gazing defiantly at mine, all became clear.

That was how I became Pioneer Leader. Leadership proved an easy and pleasant burden. Out of the whole detachment, I ran only a bunch of six girls, led by Aynet. They were the class elite, pretty and clever. It turned out the rest of the pioneer detachment played no part in public life. As soon as lessons ended, they ran home to help with the chores, busying themselves with the animals, the rural work taught here from an early age.

Nor were Aynet and her girlfriends troubled by any special desire to introduce their classmates to our company. I remember how they dreamed up the idea to set off on a trip one Sunday, to an empty tourist camp beside a clear mountain stream in the forested hills. 'Let's go and tell the boys, they're bound to be interested too,' I suggested.

The girls kept quiet, then someone piped up, 'To hell with them, they're boring and stupid.'

And so we set off on our expedition, just the seven of us. We made our way there on a passing bus, we set out a picnic in the glade, lit a bonfire. We climbed through a window into a wooden cabin and sat there until evening, talking about this and that.

When darkness fell, we spread the blanket we'd brought with us on the grass and lay down on it together, facing up to look at the sky. Each of the girls pressed closer to me, but the best place, at my left shoulder, went of course to Aynet. We pointed out shooting stars to each other, jabbing our fingers at the sky, quibbling over who'd spotted them first, and then all of a sudden fell quiet, subdued by the beauty of the night. Cicadas chirred; the river roared over the white stones; the scents of the youthful bodies of the girls clinging to me gently giddied me.

An unshaven man who hasn't unpacked his travelling bag for months on end, living in trains and planes, dulled by a daily diet of cheap wine and dropping off to sleep with hotel prostitutes, will later dream time and again of this eternal moment, though it's hard for me to understand why he should remember and dream about something that could never have happened to him.

We also went for walks. At weekends and on weekdays, skipping our lessons, we roamed through the centre of the sleepy neighbourhood, drank *kvas*[37] and fizzy drinks from vending machines, ate our fill of rich ice cream till our throats turned numb, held hands and squinted at the spring sun in parks filled with bare poplars.

We locked ourselves in empty classrooms and danced slow dances to The Scorpions and Sting from a cassette player we brought. And we kissed, together and in turn, lips smelling of mint chewing gum, necks coated in their first tan, and breasts white with pink nipples. We kissed as you can only kiss in March, when the lilac is in bloom, and in April, when the cherry trees burst into drunken blossom, and in May, when the acacias throw their petals beneath the feet of passers-by on the dusty pavements.

It was a genuine sexual revolution in an ethnic province where if you held a girl's hand you had to marry her, where weddings are arranged by parents, where girls get married straight after school and even the boys save their virginity until their wedding night – not out of any desire to, but simply because there's no one to lose it with. Where contraceptives are unknown and they multiply the planet's population, bearing chaste children, with hot and unfulfilled eyes, one after another, who love and kill because they see no difference, rather blood smells as fragrant to them whether it's on a white sheet or beneath the green shirt of a soldier.

But we felt we were beyond the rules, outside the castes, we were untouchable – though also inviolable. It was our revolution, our tender terrorism, and we could save this earth, only we could save it. But we were too late. Because it was May. May had already arrived, and our time had run out. And then came summer, unexpectedly, like a tank regiment breaching the line of defence. And it became hot. Later it became very hot indeed.

The last bell, school-leaving certificates, medals, graduation balls. Everything was sorted out. I was applying to Leningrad University and I would get a place of course, and that meant I wouldn't be coming back. But they would be staying here for three more years, or perhaps longer, perhaps all their lives, perhaps beyond their lives. Our final evenings were sad.

We got together in the geography classroom. We didn't joke as we had before, didn't discuss teachers and school, we didn't even talk about the holidays, as we probably should have. We said nothing, all lost in our own thoughts. I sat on the teacher's desk and spun the globe. It must have been Aynet who suggested: 'Why don't we make little notes, why not write down our innermost thoughts – what we truly think about, straight out – and hide them in the globe?' The idea was good and we all perked up. Then I added, 'In ten years' time, on this same day, in this same place, we'll meet up, cut open the globe, and pull out our dreams from the bowels of the blue planet, to compare them with whatever's become of our lives, to find out how true we've been to ourselves, outshine our own expectations.' 'Hurray,' everyone shouted, cheering up. A future had appeared. The girls ran off to the corners of the room and scratched down a few lines each on sheets torn from a school exercise book. I wrote: 'Girls, I love all of you. May you all find success in your lives! I want always to be surrounded by such loyal friends and tender sweethearts! Aynet, you and I, that's what matters most, what we had in our spring. And we shall never forget it. Forever your Pioneer Leader!' Then I took the globe off its axis, stuffed the notes into the hole at the North Pole, and triumphantly hoisted the Earth into the cupboard.

I didn't return to the scenes of my childhood until many years later, in the interim between the first and second wars. Many houses had been destroyed, there were bomb craters wherever you looked and unexploded shells littered the place. I was about to go into town when my uncle shoved a heavy Makarov into my belt: for a man to show himself in public without a weapon was considered indecent.

I set off on a walk. Mountain dwellers briefly drunk on their hard-won freedom and independence sauntered the streets. Each had an assault rifle or pistol, some even had machine guns or grenade launchers slung over their shoulders, though they had perhaps just gone out for a smoke and a chat with the neighbours. Some greeted me politely and inquired after my family's health. I could hardly remember anyone and was surprised that they recognised me. But I stopped and talked. I too asked how so-and-so was, and how so-and-so was, and more often than not learnt that they were no more. One classmate had been shot by a sniper, another was killed by a cluster bomb, a third had gone missing, probably captured. Neighbours, distant relatives, mere acquaintances were dead, wounded, crippled. But people talked of this calmly. And each story ended with the national invocation, the blessing upon the dead: 'May the Almighty watch over him.' The name of the Almighty in these invocations was not the Arabic, not the Muslim, but the local name, a remnant from pagan times. And the meaning of the phrase was nearer to a wish for the departed to be accompanied to a field of happy hunting or a land of eternal spring.

Eternal spring . . . I asked after Aynet too. She and her brother had barely climbed into their car in a rush to escape the bombing when a shell fell straight on the vehicle. There was nothing to bury. Pieces of flesh mixed with ripped, mangled steel.

At the market they were selling watermelons, potatoes, cigarettes, carpets from Syria, cartridges for weapons of any kind, there were entire arsenals laid out on the tables, and nearby were mortars and even a small artillery piece. I approached School No. 8 slowly. The school stood empty; the holidays had already begun, though by all appearances it had seen little life before the holidays. Combat had blown out many window frames and only the odd pane was intact. The red brick walls were pitted all over by bullets and shrapnel.

I walked through the open door and started wandering about

the building, going into classrooms and laboratories. The geography classroom didn't spring to mind immediately, but when it did I found myself wanting to find the globe.

And I found it, to my surprise I found it. By some miracle it was there. The Earth was torn from its axis and lay in a corner behind the ramshackle cupboard. I stuck my pocket knife into the Atlantic Ocean, the planet ripped apart, and from its bowels fell little notes on yellowed paper torn from a lined exercise book.

They were ours. I read them, each in turn. The girls had written about how they dreamed of leaving here, of going to study in Moscow or Leningrad and staying to live in the big city. Of marrying for love and bearing their husbands' children. One wanted to be an actress, another a doctor. They revealed other little secrets. And they wrote to me, too. 'We'll miss you, Artur.' 'Thank you for teaching me to kiss.' 'You have delicious lips. I want my husband to have lips as delicious as yours.'

Her sheet was in there too. 'Artur, I love you, and I'll always love you. Come back and take me away, or stay with me no matter where I am, when you read this letter. I know you have to come back, and we'll be together. We should be together. For ever. Your Aynet.'

My throat felt strangled and I froze, staring through the smashed window at the empty schoolyard, ploughed up with craters. Into my palm fell the calm, cold steel of the pistol.

I've come back, Aynet. I've come.

Post No. 1

A sombre, grey sky, shrouded in scudding clouds and the ragged edges of weather fronts. The icy, erratic wind eddies around the yards like a hungry dog. From time to time a vile downpour falls, soaking the unwashed sheet of tarmac which swathes the ailing city with cold sweat.

My wife bellows to our daughter who is messing around in the hall: 'Put your jacket on! You'd think that summer's just around the corner.'

The little girl takes her hooded jacket from the hanger and puts it on in silence. It's no use arguing with Mama, it'll only make matters worse. She'll fly into a rage and not let her out at all. Although what Mama said was not true, the calendar shows that summer is indeed just around the corner. The girl knows the exact date, it's 9 May, she has her own little calendar in her school satchel with pictures from the cartoon *Ice Age*.

I don't split hairs, don't bother correcting my wife. Summer may be coming, okay, but it really is cold. Let her dress up warmly. And the child's wish to go out in such weather – amazing how much energy kids have!

The television is on, they are broadcasting the celebrations from Red Square. I lounge about on the sofa in front of the TV while my wife runs around the kitchen preparing breakfast, simultaneously nattering with someone on the phone.

The troops parade across Red Square. I watch half-heartedly. From time to time I close my eyes and doze off lazily on this weekend morning. Then I open them again to see the infantry marching. Something's not quite right . . . What is it?

Their uniforms. The detachment in this festive parade is marching in camouflage: baggy trousers, lace-up boots, NATO-style. It feels as if any moment now they'll break into a trot and start yelling boot camp chants. The show is being put on for the distinguished guests who occupy the rostrum – leaders of countries large and small.

What a shame they can't see how it used to be: the columns of veterans, with their medals glinting, moving on foot and not in trucks; the guardsmen in their dark-green parade uniforms with gold aiguillettes; the tanks, the mobile missile launchers. A procession of people beneath red banners.

After the parade in Red Square a rock opera based on the Great Patriotic War[38] begins, with costumes, choreography, props. A celebration for consumption abroad.

There is no rain in Moscow, yet the sky does not gleam blue, it's not lit up by the sun's bright rays. The Moscow authorities have promised to tackle the clouds, the air force chase them away from Moscow, and the dark rainclouds head in our direction. They have already taken our money and now they want the whole sky for themselves, the whole sun, these earthly gods, these supermen.

The sun alone remains beyond their control. The sun shines equally upon metropolises and villages, it offers its rays to the rich and the poor, to presidents and commoners. Or else it sulks and hides from everyone. They still cannot buy the sun or co-opt it into their power hierarchy.

In the afternoon, the sky over Veliky Novgorod clears. My

daughter asks me to take her for a walk in the central park. I get off the sofa, tidy myself up, and we set out for the Kremlin. Another Kremlin, Novgorod's one, which pre-dates its Moscow twin. Kremlin means 'fortress'; according to the conventions of early medieval military architecture, fortress walls would be built in the heart of a town, surrounded by a rampart and moat, for defence against enemies. In times of conflict, all the town residents – traders and craftsmen settled near the Kremlin – would await the enemy's onslaught behind the walls of the fortress.

The fortress's most fortified area – the last line of defence – was the Detinets. The root of this word, an Old Russian equivalent of the concept of a citadel, some people explain simply: Detinets derives from the word *deti* – children – because the inner part of the fortress is concealed within the fortification's outer wall like an embryo in its mother's belly.

But I've read research arguing a more plausible, more terrible etymology: that it was the custom of ancient builders to sacrifice innocent babies at the site intended for the main edifice. The wealthier the client and the more important and significant the building being erected, the more children were killed at the construction site. The victims' remains were buried at the foot of the foundations. This was meant to bestow a mystical resilience on the building; nothing in this world can be sound if it is not built on bones and blood, if a sacrifice has not been offered.

So believed the Slavs, and even after adopting Christianity they secretly carried out the rites of their ancestors. Thus, the citadel of a Russian fortress is called the Detinets. If archaeologists were to carry out excavations directly beneath them, perhaps they would discover the traces of this gruesome custom.

Well, why bother with archaeologists? Novgorod, Moscow, St Petersburg, the Russian Empire, the Socialist Revolution, collectivisation, industrialisation, the victory in the Second World War, advanced Socialism, the destruction of advanced Socialism, reforms, privatisation, liberalisation – to this day, do we really know how to build on anything other than bones and blood?

The Detinets failed to save Novgorod from its enemies. The people of Novgorod themselves granted the Vikings power over them – not vanquished, not plundered like the rest of Russia; they accepted the dominion of the khan hordes. Yet they would not accept the regime of Tsar Ivan the Terrible, and the tsar drowned Novgorod in blood; the River Volkhov turned crimson, corpses damming up her estuary.

These days, beyond the Novgorod Kremlin fortress wall stands the 'Detinets', the name of the restaurant in the clock tower. Here they serve mead, no longer brewed anywhere else in Russia.

Near the Detinets are the obelisk and the Eternal Flame, which stand in memory of those who fell in the Great Patriotic War.

I take my daughter by the hand through the square outside the Kremlin, past the park, past the strolling throngs, past the café where loud music is playing, the helium bottles with balloons, through the gates and further, to the obelisk.

A guard of honour stands at the Eternal Flame: two teenage boys and a girl assistant sentinel in the camouflage uniform of the local military patriotic club. In their hands the boys hold heavy assault rifles. The guard of honour stares sternly over the heads of those gathered at the obelisk.

In the cobbled square in front of the Eternal Flame schoolboys and girls dramatically declare poems dedicated to the war, to the resilience of the victors and the heroism of the fallen. I lift my daughter on to the stone plinth for her to see and hear everything. She watches, blinking, almost without turning her head.

When the recital ends, I take my daughter down and hold her hand, and we walk around the Kremlin.

'Verochka, do you know what day it is today?'

'Yes, it's Victory Day!'

'That's right. But whose victory? Who won against whom? In which war?'

'Umm, it was . . . the one against the Germans?'

'Yes, it was the war against the German Fascists. Did they tell you anything about it at school?'

Verochka frowns and says nothing. Either they didn't tell her, or she doesn't remember. In any case, she isn't happy when the topic of school, lessons, homework and other such boring stuff comes up.

'The war began in 1941 and ended in 1945. At that time the Fascists were in power in Germany. The Fascists thought that only the Germans deserved to live on the earth and that all other nations should be wiped out or turned into slaves. They invaded the Soviet Union. There used to be a country called that, the Soviet Union, which included many other nations as well as the Russians. Those nations had their own republics and all together, along with Russia, they made up one big country. There were fifteen republics in all.'

I began to recall them.

'Russia, the Ukraine, Belorussia, Moldavia, Lithuania . . . no, the Baltic republics joined after the war, so before the war there would have been twelve republics. Georgia, Armenia, Azerbaijan, Kazakhstan, Kirghizia, Turkmenia . . . I can't seem to come up with twelve. Well, there you go, I've forgotten them myself. Anyway, all these republics were together at that time but now they've become separate states. You and Mama go for your summer holidays to the Black Sea.'

'To Sebastopol!'

'Well, Sebastopol's a city in the Ukraine. That's not Russia, it's a different country. All of this used to be the Soviet Union, the USSR. The Fascists invaded the USSR, they occupied many cities, they killed millions of people, they destroyed half the country. But all the nations of the USSR rose up in defence of their big motherland and they chased the Fascists away, then they liberated other countries in Europe and took Berlin, the capital of Germany. We were helped in the war by England and America, they were our allies. Together we won. But the ones who did the most to smash the Fascists were the nations of the Soviet Union. And today we're celebrating the day of this victory. You understand?'

'Uh huh.'

'The Fascists took Novgorod, they occupied it. When the Soviet troops approached the city and were about to free it, the Germans destroyed everything they could, out of spite. After they left, Novgorod was in complete ruins. They even planted explosives under the church of St Sofia in the Kremlin – they wanted to blow it up. The explosives went off, but the church didn't come down. It was very strong.'

'That's the church there, yeah?'

'That's right. Your great-grandfather died in that war, Grandma Vera's father. He was called Pavel, he wrote letters from the front. I read them when I was a child. His last letter came in 1943, then he was killed. We don't know where he's buried, only which village he died near. It was in southern Russia, they were attacking the German positions, and a bullet hit him, or maybe it was shrapnel from a mine or a shell. And your other great-grandfather and great-grandmother also lived through that war. Some people fought at the front, and some worked for the army in the rear.'

I want to show my daughter the link between the story of that war, infinitely distant to her, and all of us living here and now. It seems to have worked: the little girl is quiet and listens with rapt interest.

We walk through the Kremlin along the inner perimeter, come out by the opposite gates and cross the bridge to the marketplace. There is a concert stage, with a children's dance ensemble performing. Vera pulls excitedly at my hand:

'Papa, I was in that group, in the House of Culture! Sofya Pavlovna was our dance teacher.'

My daughter used to go to dance classes. Then she stopped. They didn't give her a part in some dance concert and she was very upset. Personally I didn't like her classes at all: they used the tiniest children for small parts simply to melt the audience's hearts. They didn't teach them proper rhythm or flexibility.

When the dance ensembles finish, a folk choir takes to the stage with a wartime repertoire. I take my daughter to a nearby café and order a kebab. We sit at the table. The fresh air and the walk have fired my daughter's appetite and she eats her portion eagerly. At home we can't get her to eat a proper lunch.

I listen to the songs, chain-smoke, and think. I remember. Remember Sentry Post No. 1. The post at the Eternal Flame. Only this was another post, in another time, another place, another country.

A country called the Soviet Union.

That country had a small province, an autonomous republic in the Russian Soviet Federative Socialist Republic: the Chechen-Ingush

ASSR. The capital of the province was Grozny and in Grozny was the provincial committee of the Communist Party of the USSR. That's what it was called – the provincial committee. Because despite the official abbreviation of ASSR – Autonomous Soviet Socialist Republic – Chechen-Ingushetia was neither autonomous nor a republic. It was a province, an ethnic outpost of Soviet Russia.

Twenty miles south of Grozny lay the district centre of Shali. I was born in this village, grew up there, studied at School No. 8, located right on the central square, behind the buildings of the district executive committee and the Communist Party district committee.

On the other side of the square, across the road, was a memorial to those who fell in the Great Patriotic War; in front of the memorial, inside the iron flower of a five-point star, burned the Eternal Flame.

The monument was erected late, in the eighties, within my memory. In 1944 the Chechens and Ingush were exiled to the Kazakh steppe for assisting the Fascist invaders. In 1957 the repression was decreed unlawful, the nations were exonerated and were allowed to return. But information was carefully edited out of Soviet history about the Chechens and Ingush who participated in the Great Patriotic War, about their contribution to the victory. Archive evidence was destroyed. According to Stalin they were a traitor-nation, a betrayer-nation; they could have no heroes.

After the exoneration the truth still wouldn't come out. The facts about the Chechens who fought the Fascists, the war veterans, were kept under a secret seal of silence.

During the nineties, however, historians began reporting that an entire detachment of Chechens and Ingush had been in the garrison of the Brest fortress; they all fought to the end, all died, not one was taken prisoner. Throughout the Great Patriotic War not a single Chechen was taken prisoner. Chechens have never been taken alive.

Later, during the Soviet Union's military escapade in Afghanistan, Chechen soldiers also battled fearlessly against the mujahideen, their brothers in faith. Every Chechen village is home to the families of men killed in Afghanistan; none went over to the side of the Islamists, none surrendered into captivity. Chechens simply don't know how to surrender.

Everyone knows this, but no one writes about it, even now, because the historical truth conflicts with the social imperatives. The Russian ideology needs the image of the Chechen as an enemy of Russia in order to justify two grisly wars. The ideologists of the separatists – of 'independent Ichkeria' – proclaimed the evidence of Chechen heroism in the Great Patriotic War and the Afghan war a national shame, the mistake of mindless apostates fooled by Soviet propaganda. In their opinion, Chechens shouldn't have spilt their blood for Russia – they should have battled against Russia, even if that meant joining Hitler. And they certainly shouldn't have fought the mujahideen in Afghanistan. They too need the image of the Chechen as an entrenched enemy of Russia.

Amazingly, it turns out that the aims of the opposite sides' propaganda machines coincided. And that in actual fact the truth is quite different – so much the worse for the truth.

In the eighties, the central authorities finally permitted a memorial to be erected to the Chechens killed in the Great Patriotic War, and the names of the natives of Shali district who fell in the ranks of the Soviet Army took up two wide marble plaques. Probably as many as from any Russian village.

★ ★ ★

Only the crème de la crème, the brightest students in the district schools, were accorded the honour of standing sentry at Post No. 1, the Eternal Flame and obelisk to the fallen.

I was the crème de la crème. I was always the crème de la crème. There were many of us: straight-A students, political activists, in our white shirts, with our top honours. We memorised classical poems by the hundredweight, we knew astronomy, chemistry and physics, we pored over Hegel and Feuerbach while in the ninth form.[39] And we even believed in Socialist ideas.

We were too clever, we took everything seriously and this life should never be taken seriously. It is not real.

One morning we woke up in another country. Has anyone ever written about this? Even if they have, I mean something different. If everything here was real, then how could it have happened?

When they exiled the Chechens to the Kazakh steppe, they took them far from the motherland, they brought long trains with windowless wagons, encircled each village with a ring of machine-gunners, then carried them a long distance, groaning in the cramped conditions, dying of disease, hunger and thirst.

When they exiled all of us in a flash from our mother country, there were no trains, no machine guns. Or did we just not notice them? Perhaps we just didn't notice them.

Perhaps on the TV, during the news, they gave a secret hypnotic codeword and we were all plunged into a deep trance. Then they loaded us into freight trains while we slept, loaded us into forty-foot containers and took us far away, beyond the tall mountains, the vast steppe, perhaps even to a place beyond the ocean.

They prepared for this operation for a long time. They prepared thoroughly. Far away, in some foreign and desolate land, they built perfect replicas of our towns and villages, planted poplars and firs, even laid roads just like the ones we'd had before – covered in potholes and bumps. Only this was not our land any more, it was their land, and everything here was foreign to us.

But they knew the codeword, they woke us up with the morning news. Good morning, slaves. You are now our slaves, and you no longer have any hope of happiness, any faith in equality and justice. Thus we awoke one morning in another land.

This is easier to believe, it's a better explanation. How else could we suddenly have found ourselves here? A fantasy, it's some kind of grim, pessimistic fantasy. But I don't write fantasy, I am the last of the classical realists. Therefore we were loaded into wagons and brought here. It has happened once before, and as I say it's more plausible.

That first time we came back. It wasn't particularly difficult. So this time they took us very far away, so we wouldn't be able to find our way home. We were expelled without any right of return.

And what about our motherland? She was left behind, bereft and grieving, like a cat whose kittens have been taken during the night, every last one. The little black one with the white star on its forehead, the funny little fluffy one, the ginger tabby, and the smoky one with blue eyes. They were put into a polythene bag, which was sealed with tape and thrown down a manhole. The smothered squeaks soon stopped in the resonant concrete well shaft. But she walks around lost, looks up at her owners, engrossed in their affairs, and meows, bewildered and plaintive.

Our motherland.

No, I think somebody stayed behind. After all, not everyone watched the news. Some would have been too drunk to turn on the TV, others didn't even watch it at all.

I once knew a girl who didn't watch television. God, how long ago it was! She never watched television, she spent her evenings reciting Goethe in the original. She knew all of Alexander Blok's poems by heart and used to recite them to me when we were alone in her apartment on Sadovaya Street, overlooking Nikolsky Cathedral. She would recite Alexander Blok to me and I would recite Nikolai Gumilev. I knew all of Gumilev's poems by heart.

Good God, how long ago! So long ago that I don't remember a single line.

I knew someone else who didn't watch TV. He went to forestry school, because he wanted to live alone in the forest, in a forester's hut, with his books, a battery-operated tape recorder and some Pink Floyd cassettes.

They probably stayed behind. They must still live there now, hiding in the cold, unheated Soviet apartments, burning furniture in homemade stoves, reading Igor Severyanin.[40] But others, with dogs as angry as machine guns, and machine guns barking like dogs, hunt them down and kill them in the resonant shafts of empty space between the buildings.

It's easier for those who stayed in the forests. Sometimes they come out when their batteries are dead. They walk down the empty streets, shrug their shoulders: It was always going to end up like this. And they return to the forests.

No, it wasn't the best of countries. The world has many countries which are better. There are countries where it is warm, where the tender sea gently laps the soft shores. And there are countries where all the roads are level, with a rough surface providing reliable traction for the tyres of the shining automobiles.

Our country was great and poor. Great in poverty and poor in its grandeur.

No, I don't like the new one. You can accomplish anything here, so many roads have been opened to us. You can take the road to the left and lay down your tempestuous life. You can take the road to the right and lose your horse. Or you can go straight ahead, and nobody knows what awaits you. We are all walking straight ahead.

It is a very good country. As for me, I can't stand it when domestic refugees moan. My friend and I were once at a literary event and we left before the programme had ended. We walked a good mile in silence, then, speaking for us both, I said: 'What a bunch of miserable losers.'

A man should buckle down to work. And this is a great country for people who do. It's just that . . . the motherland. You only get one motherland.

And that ailing country was our motherland. It was where we came into the world, where we first fell in love, first learnt to fight. That's why – it is just nostalgia for our youth, you understand.

Did those four guys from Liverpool realise, when they composed another lively rock and roll song in the plane cabin on their flight to Tokyo which touched down for a couple of hours in Moscow, that they had written a hymn, an evening prayer, a secret mantra for an entire generation of a land unknown to them? 'Back in the USSR'.

It was spring, the youth of the world. Everything was young and fresh, like leaves of lilac not yet coated in grey dust from the road.

We stood at the obelisk, in our uniforms, with heavy assault rifles across our chests. We didn't use replicas from the military training classroom but genuine Kalashnikovs, the legendary weapon of all revolutions and people's liberation warriors in the second half of the twentieth century. It was just that the magazines were empty.

Youth always means war. It has always been that way and always will be. So there we stood in military uniform, pressing genuine heavy assault rifles to our chests.

Yet youth also means love.

Pure, fair, like a silk blouse and lovely to the touch, like an ironed Pioneer tie, the colour of first blood.

She was the assistant sentinel on our watch. Slender tanned legs with round knees emerged from under her short khaki skirt. Anzor and I stood in a pair. Anzor liked to grip the assault rifle in his hands, his brown eyes alight with exhilaration.

My eyes fell on her round knees. When the shift is over, we'll get changed in the store room. She'll put on her dress, a long one, as is our custom. Well, she's already nearly grown up. She's fourteen years old. In two years' time she'll get married, as is also our custom.

I looked at her naked legs. I have always been a poet, a songbird of love. I was never a songbird of war. So why am I now singing of war?

She was the crème de la crème too. Nobody knows about this. I hope nobody ever finds out. I could have dreamed it all. I could have fantasised about it, thought it up one night in my bed, with half-closed eyes, slowly and clumsily masturbating with my left hand.

We stayed behind, we were the last to leave. There was nobody left in the store room when she came up to me and stroked my head. Looking straight into my eyes, she took my hand and placed it on her thigh, a little above her knee. I felt her skin, tender as the summer night, covered in soft down, like an unripe quince. She brought her face close to me and I inhaled the aroma of her hair, the scent of sweet apricot.

We would probably have kissed, if only we had known how. But we didn't.

We did, however, know how to take apart and reassemble a Kalashnikov. They did teach us that at the military training lessons. It is true Chechens love weapons. More than they love women. Look at the face of a Chechen who has been given a weapon. What brilliant joy lights him up, what tenderness glazes over his eyes. Why did they have to give us heavy assault rifles?

Once you have given a Chechen a weapon, you will never get it back from him. Even in death his hands will continue to grip it, to embrace it like a bride on their wedding night.

Every Chechen also knows from birth how to shoot and how to see in the dark like a cat. He has no need for night vision goggles: on the darkest of nights, when the moon and stars are hidden by thick clouds, he will strike his target as though seeing everything in infrared light.

Perhaps Darwin was right about natural selection. All the other Chechens simply died out, the centuries of incessant wars creating the conditions for such selection. Those Chechens who didn't know how to shoot simply died without leaving descendants.

A year ago I was in Minsk on a business trip. A friend was seeing me off, a blonde girl descended from Polish aristocracy. We had two hours before the train departed, and we strolled through the town park. At a loose end, we went into the shooting range. I picked up an air rifle, gently stroked my hand along the barrel, pressed the stock to my shoulder. A sweet stupor arose inside me, as if I were dancing with a girl at a graduation ball.

Within a few minutes I had easily knocked out all the targets. 'You must have served as a sniper?' an elderly man standing nearby who had come to the shooting range with his grandson asked deferentially. 'No, he's just from Chechnya,' my friend answered for me.

I didn't serve as a sniper. I didn't serve in the army at all. We all just know how to shoot. We know how and we were taught to as well, at the school shooting range. We were taught how to shoot, to dismantle and reassemble a Kalashnikov assault rifle, how to throw a hand grenade.

But no one taught us how to kiss. They should have taught us how to kiss. We didn't know how.

So I let my hand fall from her thigh. I know what to do when an assault rifle is in my hands. I feel it.

But I don't know what to do when a young girl is in my arms. I don't feel it.

I probably look stupid when I ask, 'What do you want me to do?' People don't ask that. But I don't know, I don't feel anything!

And they never climax with me.

If it was an assault rifle in my hands, I would know what to do – it would choke with orgasms. It is hot and affectionate, it has a sweet smell of gunpowder. Women smell of fish, I know that much.

But we – we weren't created for love. We were created for war. That's how the gods created our tribe.

However, people don't multiply through war. They multiply through love, so my tribe will die out.

My tribe will perish in this war. In this war without end.

And I am to blame for this. Because I didn't kiss the girl I loved.

And also because I am writing this book, and on each page war signs its name. No matter what I write about, I write about the war, the war I wasn't in. That's why my books are the best. The best books on war are those written by deserters.

See, I wanted to write about love. About how I kissed the girl who smelt of quince and apricots. How afterwards I walked her home and broke off a sprig of lilac to give her: lilac, the sky, the stars, the earth, orchards and clear rivers, the entire world, and even more – my self.

But I didn't kiss her. And I walked home not with her but with Anzor. Along the way, another boy from our watch joined us – Aslan.

Aslan had a dream, a dream of the sky. No, he didn't yearn for paradise, he didn't even take drugs. He just wanted to be a pilot.

And Aslan had many questions, all of them addressed to me. To be honest, I found this hard going. For some reason Aslan thought that I must know everything, seeing as I was so clever at school. Perhaps I did know more poems than anyone else, read popular physics and academic translations of the Rig Veda. But how was I to know about the mechanics of aeroplanes?

I had to read through several articles on aerodynamics specially for Aslan. Yet I still didn't know, had no way of knowing, the answer to the big question which troubled Aslan: Would he get into flight school?

Aslan had defective vision. Not bad, he wasn't terribly short-sighted or far-sighted, but all the same he was just below the norm. The flight school medical commission might not let him pass.

Aslan spent hours asking me if there was anything he could do. Could he train his vision? Maybe yoga would help him? I didn't know. Maybe it would.

Or maybe it wouldn't. Aslan was just born that way. He was the only one out of the entire school to fail target practice. His vision was good enough to read books, watch television, look at pretty girls. But not good enough to shoot straight. Or to fly a plane.

* * *

I take my daughter's hand and head home. It's time for us to go.

I think about her, this tiny being, the dearest thing on earth, a little part of me. No, the best there is of me. And it is what I leave you people. I leave you my very best. Take good care of her.

At home, in the heap of old photographs, is a chart with my family's lineage written out carefully by the elders: Borz begat Lechi, Lechi begat Magomet, Magomet begat Turpal, Turpal begat Akhmad, Akhmad begat Lom-Ali, Lom-Ali begat Umar . . . And right at the end they begat me. I ought to beget a son and hand him down this chart. This thread joining us to the deepest past.

I can't give it to my daughter. My daughter will enter another family, she'll take the surname of another lineage, she'll bear children who will take up entirely different threads.

Who was the woman in whose belly Borz begat Lechi? Was she Chechen, Russian, Tartar or Greek? Did Akhmad have daughters? Whom did they marry – a Georgian prince, a European merchant, a blacksmith from the neighbouring *teip*? The elders wrote nothing about this.

My mother was Russian. My grandmother was Russian. The mother of my daughter is Russian too. My daughter has a Russian first name. What remains in her of our tribe? Only the surname. Which she'll change when she marries.

Thousands of years end with me. In my last will and testament I ask not to be buried in the earth, according to the custom of my ancestors. Let my body be burnt in a crematorium. And burn the genealogical chart along with it.

Let everything come to an end. This has gone on too long. I feel the burden of the centuries, unpaid debts, too much bloodshed. Blood flows through the centuries, blood spilt by my ancestors for one purpose alone: to beget me. How many of them there were, those who were poor shots and failed to leave offspring!

My daughter won't shoot though. She will love, she will be loved, she will bear a child – and no one need be killed for this to happen.

I'm thinking about that country again, our lost motherland. After the return to Chechnya life gradually began to improve. We lived a whole thirty years without war. Maybe the reality didn't always correspond to the proclamations, but equality, friendship, the cultural advancement of each nation existed at least on paper. Internationalism wasn't just a long word. If that had been the case young Chechens wouldn't have gone to die in the faraway Afghan mountains, doing their internationalist duty. They knew all about duty. Accepted into the family as equals, they knew that it was now their duty to die for their vast country.

All the same, that wasn't real war. Compared to the gore-filled past centuries, it was peace. A whole thirty years of peace! We had never gone so long without war. How avidly we embraced our earth! Now we wouldn't have to leave for the mountains, we could simply work the earth. Boys like Aslan began to appear, poor-sighted and unable to shoot, who dreamed of the sky.

We once again became foreigners in our new land. We were declared the enemy. And we returned to our most beloved, truest, sweetest brides. Hello, weapons!

Aslan didn't get into flight school. He became a mechanic servicing aeroplanes. At least he could touch the sky that way.

In 1994 at the training aerodrome, Aslan was the first to spot the Russian aeroplanes, the first to realise it was a bombing raid.

All the planes were on the ground, there wasn't a pilot in sight. So he took to the cockpit.

He had been training all along, in secret. He had studied the theory, practised on simulators. How badly I want to believe that he escaped! That he made it, that the fuel tanks were full, he taxied out on to the runway, lifted off and faded like a silver bird into the blue sky, hiding from death in the white clouds.

But I know that's not what happened. Not a single aeroplane managed to get airborne, which means Aslan didn't make it. He burnt to death in a trainer plane on the runway.

But it couldn't have happened! All my knowledge wouldn't be worth tuppence. Aslan and his aeroplane simply shed their skins and it was their skins that burnt on the runway. Aeroplanes – like magical flying snakes – escape from traps, they cheat death, leave their skins on the ground to explode with their fuel tanks full. They are flying now above our heads, in the blue sky, beyond the white clouds.

I saw Anzor once on the television. I hadn't seen him since back then and thought I'd never see him again. In this new country people think that your life has been in vain if you haven't appeared on television at least once. Those who haven't made it as politicians or celebrities get on to shows, they take part in quizzes. That is how immortality is now understood. Well, nobody wants to die and once a man has been transmitted over the airwaves, he will never die. He will fly through space, for ever encoded in radio waves. So television is a religion, and the television set a household altar.

Anzor was shown on television, although maybe it was too late for him to achieve immortality.

The news programme reported that in the village of Avtura a

group of defiant rebels led by Emir Anzor Musaev had been surrounded and eliminated. They even talked briefly about him, to emphasise the importance of the operation and the significance of its success. It turned out that Anzor was a major figure in the resistance. I don't know, I'm not in the habit of believing such claims. Every week the Russian media report the elimination of 'major figures'. Every rebel killed turns out to be a 'well-known field commander', although for some reason no one had heard of him while he was alive, or he's a 'Brigadier General', and wherever do all these brigades come from, or at any rate he's someone's 'right-hand man'. These right hands are in quite a muddle. After hearing several such stories, I have begun to imagine the rebel leaders as multi-armed Indian gods with nothing but right arms.

The motives for such a tactic in the information wars are clear: they need to assure the viewers that this time everything really will turn out all right, that the Resistance is headless and even its arms have been chopped off. That's all well and good, but what they would do well to learn now is how to cauterise the wounds, as they do in fairytales, to stop the heads and arms growing back.

So they showed Anzor on the television, or rather they showed his corpse, lying in a pile among the corpses of some other rebels. At this point I ought to tell you that I recognised him straightaway but that would be utter drivel. How could I have recognised him? A few identical corpses in dirty, tattered clothing. One of them was Anzor.

The weapons lay nearby, the victors had proudly piled them in a heap not far from the dead bodies. Parted from their bridegrooms.

So it was that Aslan remained in the sky, and Anzor flew still further, into space. Though dead already, it's true. He didn't achieve immortality. He was buried in the cosmic beyond, his body encoded in the radio waves hurtling through the universe.

The girl from our watch was killed by shrapnel during a mortar attack on the village. She wasn't shown on TV. She didn't burn and ascend smokily towards the sky. They buried her, which means she simply returned to the earth.

Now I am left alone at this post. At Post No. 1.

I don't know how to end this story.

I am tired, my arms have gone numb, the strap of my assault rifle is chafing my shoulder. How much longer do I have to wait? When will someone relieve me?

Victory Day

Old people don't sleep much. When you're young, time feels like a magic rouble, while an elderly person's time is copper pennies. Wrinkled hands thriftily stack up the minutes upon minutes, hours upon hours, days upon days: how much longer is left? Each night is coveted.

He awoke at half past five. There was no need to rise so early. Had he not risen from his bed at all – which was bound to happen, sooner or later – nobody would have noticed. He could have simply not got up, let alone so early. For the last few years, he longed more and more for the day when he wouldn't awake. But not today. Today was special.

Alexei Pavlovich Rodin rose from his old, creaky bed in his studio flat on ___ Street in old Tallinn, went to the toilet, relieved his bladder. In the bathroom he began to tidy himself up. He washed, brushed his teeth and spent a long time scraping stubble from his chin and cheeks with a razor which had seen better days. Then he washed once more, rinsing away the remains of the foam, and refreshed his face with aftershave.

Rodin entered the room and stood before the wardrobe with the cracked mirror. The mirror reflected his haggard body, covered in old scars and clothed in faded pants and a vest. Rodin opened the wardrobe and changed his underwear. For a couple of minutes he looked at his parade jacket with its orders and medals, then pulled out a shirt ironed the night before and donned his uniform.

All at once twenty years slipped from his shoulders. In the dim light of the ceiling lamp, dulled with time, his captain's epaulettes glowed brightly.

At eight o'clock Rodin met another veteran, Vakha Sultanovich Aslanov, at the entrance to his building. He and Vakha had spent much of the war together, in the same reconnaissance unit on the First Belorussian Front. By 1944, Vakha was already a senior sergeant, he had a Medal for Bravery. When news came through of the deportation of the Chechens, Vakha was lying wounded in hospital. He was transferred directly from the hospital to a penal battalion, for no other fault than his ethnic status. Rodin, then a senior lieutenant, approached the company command and asked them to bring Vakha back. The intercession was to no avail. Vakha ended the war in a penal battalion and straight after demobilisation was deported to Kazakhstan.

Rodin was demobilised in 1946 with the rank of captain, and was sent to serve in Tallinn as an ideological instructor on the municipal committee of the Party.

At that time this city had only one 'n' in its name, but my computer's spell-check is a new one; I'll write Tallinn with two 'l's and two 'n's so it won't rail at me and underline this word with its wavy red line.

After the Chechens were exonerated in 1957, Rodin tracked down his old comrade. He made inquiries, utilising his position – by this time Rodin was already the head of a department. Rodin managed not just to find Vakha, he even secured his relocation to Tallinn, found him a job, helped him get a flat and residential registration. Vakha arrived. When he began his efforts, Rodin worried that Vakha would not want to abandon his homeland so he saw to it that Vakha could come with his family.

But Vakha came alone. He had no one to bring with him. His wife and child had died during the deportation, contracting typhus in the freight cars, and passed away soon after. His parents had died in Kazakhstan. Vakha had no close relatives left. That is probably why he found it easy to leave Chechnya.

Then began . . . life, bringing good times and bad. That's right, an entire lifetime. Well, sixty years had gone by. An entire sixty years since the end of that war.

It was indeed a special day. The sixtieth anniversary of victory.

Sixty years – an entire lifetime. More, even. For those who did not return from the war, for those whose age stood still at twenty, it would be three lifetimes. Rodin felt he was living these lives for the men who never returned. But this was no mere metaphor. Sometimes he thought: These twenty years I'm living for Sergeant Savelev who was blown up by a mine. The next twenty I'll live for Private Talgatov, who fell in the first battle. Then he thought: No, that way I won't have enough time. Better stick to ten years. Well, to live to thirty isn't so bad. Then I'll have time to live for three more fallen fighters.

Oh, sixty years is plenty! One whole lifetime, or six makeweights for the abbreviated lives of dead soldiers.

And yet . . . it has to be equal to, or perhaps less than, four years of war.

I don't know how to explain this; others before me have explained it much better. A man lives for four years of war, or six months of Arctic winter, or a year in a Buddhist monastery. Then he'll live a long time, an entire life, but that slice of time will remain for him the longest, the most important. Perhaps it is because of the emotional intensity, because of the simplicity and vividness of sensations, perhaps it goes by some other name. Perhaps our life is measured not in time, but in stirrings of the heart.

But he will always remember, always compare his present with that time which for him will never become the past. And the comrades with him then will always remain his closest, truest ones.

Not because he will stop coming across good people. It's just that those people – those others – there's so much they will never be able to understand, no matter how you explain it. Whereas with your own comrades – with them you can even just sit in silence.

With Vakha, for example. Sometimes Rodin and Vakha drank together, sometimes they disagreed and even quarrelled, sometimes they just sat in silence. Life was varied, indeed.

Rodin had married and lived twelve years in wedlock. His wife divorced him and left for Sverdlovsk, to her parents. Rodin had no children, whereas Vakha, no doubt, had many. He himself didn't know how many. But Vakha never bothered marrying, Vakha was still the same old philanderer.

Neither of them had built high-flying careers. But in Soviet times they had retired with decent pensions as respectable individuals. They stayed in Tallinn. Where else were they to go?

Then everything began to change. Rodin did not like to think about it. Everything simply changed. And he found himself in a foreign land, where the wearing of Soviet orders and medals was prohibited, where men who had watered the earth with their blood from Brest to Moscow and back to Berlin were called occupiers.

They weren't occupiers. Rodin knew better than most about all the wrongs that took place in that country which had sunk into oblivion. But back then, for those four years . . . no, they hadn't been occupiers. Rodin couldn't understand the rage of well-off

Estonians who even under Soviet power had enjoyed better lives than Russian people out in the Urals.

Take Vakha. After the deportation, after the monstrous injustice, the tragedy of his people, Rodin was prepared for Vakha to start hating the Soviet Union, and Russians in particular. But it wasn't like that. Vakha had seen too much: the overcrowded camps, the prisons, Russian officers in the penal battalion who'd heroically escaped from captivity and had been stripped of their rank as a result.

Once Rodin asked Vakha bluntly whether he blamed the Russians for what had happened. Vakha replied that the Russians had suffered worse through all this than any other nation. Stalin had been a Georgian, after all, though what did that matter.

Vakha also said that not only had they been together in the camps, they had also conquered the Fascists together; they had sent a man into space; they had built Socialism in their down-and-out, impoverished country. All this they had done together, and all this – not just the camps – was called the Soviet Union.

So today they put on their medals and awards from the battlefield. Today was their day. They even went into a bar and had a hundred grammes of vodka, frontline style, that's right. And there, in the bar, youngsters in fashionable military wear with SS-style armbands called them Russian pigs, drunken old bums, and ripped off their medals. They called Vakha a Russian pig too. The knife was just lying on the bar, the barman probably used it for cracking ice.

Vakha thrust it with precision between the ribs of the Estonian youth.

There was a phone on the bar too, and Rodin flung its cable in a noose around the neck of another. His hands no longer had the same power, but power wasn't needed, every move of the veteran scout was a well-honed reflex. The puny kid wheezed and collapsed on to the floor.

They returned to real time. Once more they became Soviet scouts, surrounded by the enemy. And all was right and simple.

For five minutes they were young again. Five minutes while they were kicked to death on the wooden floor.

They added another five minutes to those four years of real life. And this was worth more than the several years they might have lived had they not gone out in their orders and medals on Victory Day.

And I don't pity them a bit. I just cannot belittle them with my pity.

Snuff

We woke up in New Orleans – a ghost town – up to our necks in water. And, of course, jazz was playing. It was Duke Ellington's orchestra, and 'Sun Valley Serenade' carried over the flood water like a drifting spirit. I closed my eyes and saw it – the sunny valley, fringed with a blue necklace of distant mountains.

Remember when we wrote on the gates: 'Don't shoot! People live here'. Well, here the walls of the houses bear almost the same signs, only in English. The signs are almost the same, meaning they are completely different: 'People live here. We'll shoot!' No, you don't see and you don't remember. You weren't there and you aren't here. Nor am I.

We woke up in New Orleans, amid overturned, broken furniture, in a room where damp wallpaper helplessly and blissfully peeled off like a drunken tramp's rags on to the swollen parquetry. You're lying by the wall with the faded white drawing, curled up on your side with your hand under your head, like you always did when we slept together.

Perhaps I'm still not awake and everything is too odd for me to understand. Look, it's you, Katrine. You burst into my life like a hurricane, wrenching out trees, overturning cars, toppling houses as if they were made of cards. Now you sleep calmly by the wall with the faded white drawing and breathe quietly, are you back with me? And how did we find ourselves in New Orleans when we fell asleep in another city, one also surrounded by water?

Or did we fall asleep in the sunny valley?

And where is the music playing? Who is playing the saxophone solo, if everyone is dead?

I turn to face you, you're lying curled up so invitingly, sticking your buttocks towards me, you're wearing nothing but skimpy panties, no need to take them off, I can just pull them aside and enter you from behind, like I've always wanted to. I squeeze your hips, I nuzzle up to you. You breathe deeply in your sleep.

I can't. I can't get it up, Katrine! I even try masturbating, but it doesn't help. You wake up, you look at me. I tell you I can't get it up! You raise your eyebrows in surprise.

I show you my limp penis, you dreamily touch it with your slender fingers. Then you laugh silently for a long while, you kiss my forehead and get dressed.

I can't get it up, Katrine! You have ripped up, wrenched out, ruptured everything that was in my heart, in my soul, in my pituitary gland! I don't want you any more, Katrine.

It is strange for me to think such a thing, strange to understand how it could have happened. It's you, Katrine, you here with me. But I don't want you any more. It's hard to believe. Well, no harder than believing that we woke up in New Orleans and that jazz is drifting out of nowhere.

Looters are terrorising the city. They ransack houses, they search the corpses. Sometimes they find people alive.

We bought this cassette in a little shop of erotic videos on Nekrasov Street. The pretty salesgirl came up to us, throwing a bored glance at the garish covers. She said she's got something really interesting for us. An illegal video with real scenes. We'd like it. It's the best stuff, from New Orleans.

The tape was called *Katrine*. Just *Katrine*. That's why we bought it. The scenes were real.

A group of looters break into the first floor of a half-submerged house and slaughter the terrified family. All but the teenage girl. They overpower the girl and drag her on to the roof, where they start raping her to the backdrop of weird and wonderful views of the submerged city. The soundtrack reproduces genuine screams filled with pain and terror. Having screwed her both together and in turn, having shown the rape from all the best angles, the characters decide to end with a dramatic finale. A muscular man climaxes in the girl while his partner slowly strangles her, squeezing his hands tighter and tighter around her slim white neck. The girl wheezes and convulses in spasms that look like a multiple orgasm. When the body has stopped moving, they push her off the roof, and the camera follows as she drifts and sinks in the murky water.

I throw up. You look at the screen entranced, with dilated pupils, barely blinking your long black eyelashes.

Why do you love violence so, Katrine?

Death is sex, you say.

Sex is death, I think.

I don't want you any more.

It was a snuff film – real shots of barbarity and crime. You want to go back to that little shop and ask if they've got more of this snuff. I shrug my shoulders. Why waste your money? Just switch on your TV set, baby. Watch the news, or wait for a special report.

New York, Nazran, Beslan, Nalchik – shootouts, smouldering

buildings, corpses, corpses, more corpses. Real corpses. When they killed Aslan Maskhadov and showed the whole world the body disfigured by barotrauma, what was that? Snuff. Our media leads the world, for many years they've been professional snuff film makers.

They've got the whole country hooked. Without owning up to it, people crave gruesome news stories. People start pining when there's nothing happening. They greet each new release of serial snuff with baited breath, pressing up hungrily to their TV screens, to the monitors of their computers, they grab fresh newspapers with trembling hands. And afterwards, when they've had their fill of broadcast blood, they paw their sexual partners' bodies. Why, without regular doses of snuff they wouldn't be able to make children. But with snuff they can. Only what kind of children?

'They? Who are "they"? You're always talking about "them",' you say. 'They got us hooked, they show us snuff, they start the wars. They're the cause of all our troubles. Where are they, who are they? They don't exist, you invented them, like in the film *Conspiracy Theory*. There's no "they", there's only "we", and that's the plain truth.'

I stay silent.

In *Conspiracy Theory* it turned out the conspiracy was real. But you're right. After all, you're one of them.

The day is as tortured as a stripper's smile. Katrine isn't coming this evening. Maybe she'll never come back. I don't need any more of this. No more wars, no more hurricanes. No more snuff.

Katrine phoned me on Saturday. Katrine, whom I loved madly. Katrine, who dumped me and married someone else. Katrine, whom I hadn't seen for six months. We met, we walked through the city, we bought a video. In the evening we watched snuff at my place. On Sunday we woke up in New Orleans. She got dressed and left. The next day I went to work as usual.

How lucky we are to have jobs. Whatever would we do if we couldn't forget ourselves from dawn to dusk, absorbed in other people's problems? How could we survive if we spent too much time all alone.

After work I went home on the metro. One of those new pedlars, a wandering salesman, got on the train. What a godforsaken job. He was selling pens.

'Spy pens, write with one end and erase with the other. You can erase all your mistakes!'

How I need such a pen! That's exactly what I need. More than anything in the world I need just such a pen!

I have made so many mistakes. There's so much I want to erase. To tell the truth, I would rewrite my entire life from scratch. And in the new edition there would be no Katrine, no war, no snuff.

I would stay in the sunny valley.

I probably idealise this land. If I had spent my whole life in the sunny valley, started a family and filled a house with junk, gone to work and drunk with friends in the kebab house, I wouldn't have felt – wouldn't have known – its wondrousness.

Perhaps that's why I was exiled, was thrown out into the world, in order to discover how wondrous my motherland is.

And how odd, how surprising and painful for me to see her, my beloved, in the magic looking glass, in the crooked window of the television screen, when everything that they show about her is snuff – barbarous, dirty snuff!

But, no! She's not like that. You have no idea.

★ ★ ★

Now I'll say it, this terrible, coarse, obscene word: Chechnya. Sounds like *khuynya* – fucking bollocks – only with blood.

My motherland, the land of my dreams, promised land of my childhood – she can't have a name like that.

I'll think up another name for you, my sweetheart.

And I'll tell you about her: she is quiet fields, balmy air, blue skies, she is mulberry groves and poplar avenues, all the things which I cannot carry on writing about, because I . . . because I'm . . . it's like . . . no.

I won't tell you that name.

But everything you knew before was snuff.

And it has nothing to do with New Orleans or Katrine.

This tale will have no spectacular denouement, nothing to bring the story full circle.

Heaven's Door

When you write about real people, you ought at least to change their names. I once narrowly escaped a beating when the entire alternative readership of the Russian internet read a short story about the love lives of my friends. Of course, I had used their real names.

The idea of writing about real events is worse still. You shouldn't write about them at all. Yesterday I was looking through some dusty old copies of *Inostrannaya literatura*[41] from the seventies. They were left by the people who used to live in this flat. By people who are obviously already dead. There's nothing strange about this. I've lived like that for ages – in two worlds, on two sides – straddling the other world and this one.

Only I don't know which of the two worlds is on this side.

Too much remains in that other world. I am rooted in death, I feed off its mineral fertiliser. I'll probably find it easy to die.

So yesterday I was looking through dusty old copies of *Inostrannaya literatura*, that's right. What kind of style is that, jumping from one topic to another!

In one of the magazines I found a piece by Ernest Hemingway, 'On Writing'. In it the author writes little about writing. Most of the text is taken up with a tale about fishing. It's often the way with Hemingway.

But in that small section devoted specifically to writing, he wrote about exactly this. About how one should not write about oneself, or about other real people. Nor about real events which happened to those real people.

Probably, if you're no good at making things up, you could combine observation with imagination. Take real people for example and think up the action which happens to them. The result will be a modern novel, or a detective story even. Or the opposite, study real events, preferably from the distant past – for only the past is genuinely real – and invent your characters. That will give you a historical novel.

But if you write about what actually took place and your life doesn't happen to fall into any decent story line, you have only one genre left, the least noble of all – the diaries of a madman. Well, there's no plot to life. As soon as anything starts up, the thread is lost. And everything always ends at completely the wrong time.

At any rate some try to stick to one style but how is it possible? Today you'll be as tragic as a funeral pyre, tomorrow you'll be as mundane as a microwave oven. No, art is something else entirely. Perhaps a writer's imagination exposes – it alone can expose the depths of reality. When you document life's absurdities, you always remain on the surface.

And if you simply can't make it up, you must disguise reality. At least change people's names.

But my cousin was called Marat. I can't call him anything else. They were born in March, he and his twin sister. He was called Marat and she was called Mareta. If they had been born in Düsseldorf perhaps she would have been called Martha, which would have been more beautiful and logical, but they were born in Gudermes. Girls in Gudermes aren't called Martha, they're called Mareta, a common name. I don't know where it comes from or what it means. Most likely it is yet another version of the biblical name Miriam.

I never hear anything but the root in these names – Mara. Which, of course, means death in the most ancient of Indo-European languages, Sanskrit. It is where we get the words *mor* – pestilence – and 'mortal' from. But it's a good name. Death likes that name. Well, Mareta survived.

In the end, we all die. All of us, even the non-smokers who spend their weekends in the gym, who drive carefully, observe the highway code, or perhaps prefer travelling by underground. People who don't travel by plane and people who have good jobs die too. People die regardless, even those born in Düsseldorf and not Gudermes.

It is not true that I only know how to write about the dead. See, I'm writing about the time when they were alive. I don't actually describe the corpses. Which means I write about the living.

I had many cousins. My father's line was long and many-branched.

My grandpa on my father's side – whom I never met, he passed away before I was born – returned from Kazakhstan with a new family. When they deported the Chechens they left his first wife at home with her infant children. She was called Tonya, she was Russian, that is why they left her at home. She would have accompanied her husband but she was afraid for her infant children and she was right to worry. In the windowless wagons, without food and water, amid diseases brought on by grief and overcrowding, the children would have been the first to die.

In Kazakhstan, Grandpa got married again, this time to a Chechen. He returned home with a new wife and four new children to add to the three left behind in the motherland.

At first they all settled in one house. Then Grandpa built a second house in the same yard. That's how they lived thereafter, as one big family. They argued and quarrelled constantly, but in the usual domestic way, and no one ever paid any attention to whose child was whose. The wives didn't tear Grandpa in half.

Grandma Tonya embraced Islam, she learnt the Chechen language and Chechen customs. She became more Chechen than the Chechens. Two wives, one family, and no one batted an eyelid. As for Grandpa, he continued curing other men's young wives of infertility until the day he died at a venerable age. Using folk medicine methods, especially when the fault lay with the man, who would refuse to admit it. That's why I shall never know just how many half-cousins bearing different surnames I have.

Grandpa died like a saint, on the auspicious holiday marking the end of the great fast of Ramadan. When faint stars appeared in the evening sky, showing the faithful that they could break their fast after the day's abstinence, Grandpa consumed a mountain of mutton and died of abdominal bloating.

The holy sheikhs said that he had doubtless entered paradise. Assuming there was no mix-up in heaven, he would have gone to the paradise prescribed for him. I expect the fourteen-year-old houris were greatly appreciated by Granddad.

As it was, I had more than enough officially recognised cousins. I am ashamed to admit that I didn't know them all by name. Sometimes they were born too thick and fast! Almost all my father's brothers and sisters married and had children, with one exception. The only one to remain childless was my uncle, Im Ali, known more simply as Emelya. That's what he was called by the Russians with whom he grew up.

Three times Papa tried marrying off Uncle Emelya, but the marriages didn't last. The first two wives, both Chechen, Uncle chased out of the house. The third – a beautiful and crazy Russian *Komsomol* member – left of her own accord. One morning Uncle Emelya found a note on the kitchen table: 'Bye bye, honey! I've left for the Baikal Amur Mainline.' Im Ali never married again.

The Sadulaev family were prolific enough as it was.

My father's half-sister – a pure Chechen with the Russian name Lyusya – married an Avar and moved to Gudermes. That is where Marat was born, along with his sister Mareta.

Another aunt of mine also married a Dagestani, and he carried off his bride to a distant mountain village. Her youngest daughter, my poor little cousin, only started speaking at six, unsure which language to choose to avoid causing offence either to her mother's line or to her father's abundant family. In Dagestan each mountain village is inhabited by its own tribe, speaking their own language. At six the girl finally began to talk. Straight off in five languages – Russian, Chechen and three Dagestani ones.

After Marat and Mareta, Auntie Lyusya had another boy, Aslan. All three considered themselves Chechen, even though their father was Avar. Chechen blood is stronger. Their father didn't mind. He was called Allaudi, a placid and well-spoken railway engineer. In all the time I knew him, he only spoke Russian.

Allaudi had a record collection with the complete works of Vladimir Vysotsky and a library filled with rare books. Two or three of them I never returned, having taken them to read before my next visit. Uncle Allaudi tactfully failed to mention it, though I am sure he could not have forgotten.

Well, how could I return books like those? The illustrated history of all the famous battles in the history of the world alone was priceless! What's more, by reading it every day, I had well and truly thumbed the lavish edition to bits and was simply too scared to show my fastidious uncle what had become of the gem of his collection.

I wouldn't say that Marat and I saw a lot of each other. We lived in different towns, and our families were absorbed in their own lives. My father, however, the eldest brother of the large Sadulaev family, always tried hard to unite our ties of kinship. No less than once a month, Papa would sit us in the car and drive us to visit Auntie Lyusya.

One summer he managed to get hold of much sought-after vouchers for the Pioneer camp near Serzhen-Yurt for me, my cousin Marat and cousin Bislan, who lived in Shali. Bislan fell homesick in the camp and ran home after only a week, whereas Marat stayed with me for the whole period.

Don't be deceived by my use of the past tense. It's just that I'm describing the past. I don't want to tempt fate. Papa still tries to bring our entire family together now, and Bislan still lives in Shali.

If only all the Sadulaevs would stick together, as my papa had wanted them to, what a mighty clan we'd make. With all our uncles and aunts, nephews and nieces, boy cousins and girl cousins, grandsons and granddaughters, we could fill a small town or make up an important diaspora in some capital city. But we are scattered across the face of the earth like seeds over tarmac.

That time, at the camp, our beds stood close and we chattered through the nights. In the daytime, after breakfast, we'd run up the mountains together to collect white slate, from which we each built a tower.

I fell in love, of course. The girl was called Maya, she was probably born in May. Maya had travelled to our camp from Belorussia.

We recited poems together at the formal assemblies. Marat was the first and last person in whom I confided my heart's secret.

My cousin immediately proposed decisive action, and offered to sort the affair out himself. After tea, he went to find Maya, called her aside and told her that a certain boy liked her very much and wanted to make friends with her.

In the evening we met in the block for our detachment. Marat shrugged his shoulders: 'Nothing will come of it, cousin! She said that she's already fallen for another boy. And she doesn't want to make friends with anyone else.'

I fell despondent, mumbling only: 'Who's the lucky guy? Come on, let's smash his face in.'

'Let's!' Marat responded, getting ready.

'How will we find him?' I pondered.

Marat furrowed his brow and answered: 'Maya said that he's tall, good-looking and very clever. They recite poems together at assemblies. But she doesn't know his name, because she's too shy to speak to him.'

I clutched my stomach and collapsed on the bed, in hysterics.

'What is it?' asked Marat, puzzled, somewhat hurt even.

Holding back my laughter with difficulty, I replied: 'You can tell Maya that the boy is called German. And do come and listen to us reciting poetry at assembly some time.'

Marat always shirked official occasions, seizing any excuse he could. Usually he'd have a sudden attack of stomach ache. Under firm pressure from the group leaders, he would say, 'But what if I soil myself right in the middle of the assembly? That would shame the entire detachment.' And they'd leave him alone.

I no longer remember how it all ended with the girl. Probably we danced a couple of times at the evening disco. For me, with my chaste upbringing, that was already plenty. There were no kisses, of course. Let alone vice. I remember the sheet from the exercise book where she wrote her address in Belorussia before she left. But I don't think we wrote to each other. Oh, so much of life has passed me by. There are so many lives I haven't lived. One of them is the one in which I wrote Maya a letter and got one back from her.

The life we did live has turned out odd, wrong.

There was a series of Pioneer camps along the river Bass; they were at Serzhen-Yurt, where the river is still pure, clear, and the mountain water runs over stones. Below, on the plain in Shali, washing the clay soils, the river turns dirty yellow. Our camp was called 'Smena'.[42] There were also 'Svetlyachok',[43] 'Zarnitsa'[44] and some others which I can't remember any more.

After the first Chechen war the rebels built their bases in the Pioneer camps. Here they were trained in shooting all types of weapons and in skills for sabotage operations. Day and night, from the direction of Serzhen-Yurt, could be heard the crackle of assault-rifle fire and the boom of shells.

During the second Chechen war they pounded the camps from the air and ground, then took the ploughed-up mountains by storm.

Recently, I filled out an application form for a new job. I had a long wait for the interview. Bored, I amused myself as best I could. In the section on Further Training, I wrote: 'Attended a course at the sabotage training camp near Serzhen-Yurt.' Well, I really did attend camp there, just at a different time.

After that summer in the camp, Marat and I drifted apart. We seldom met, we had little time. During my last year of school I was studying hard for university entrance. And I got in, in 1989 I got a place to read law in Leningrad. Marat also got a place a year later, at Grozny Oil Institute.

We were busy studying, we had plans for our lives. No one thought that everything would turn out so differently. We had plans for earthly life, but on top of that we had other aspirations too.

Now I'm going to start grumbling, probably because I am very old. Age is not always measured in calendar years. I am very old, and old men always grumble, they rail that the new generation are utterly unrecognisable.

'Yes, there were men in our time, not like the present generation . . .'[45]

But it really is true. It's not that we were better. Maybe the reverse. But we were different, it really is like that. I'll try to explain. I'll do my best.

In a sentence: we were drawn to the sky.

New people, they don't raise their eyes to the sky, they feel at home on the earth. They believe genuinely in everything earthly. Believe earnestly. In money, for example. And what they wear is terribly important. What type of car they drive matters particularly. And they are going to live for ever, live here eternally. On earth.

Whereas we didn't believe all that much. We sensed – what's the best word for it – the fragility, that's probably it, the fragility of everything earthly. The thinness of the earth's crust, beneath which lie hundreds of miles of raging magma, and above which are the fathomless depths of the sky.

And we knocked on heaven's door.

Everything is like in Bob Dylan's song. The seismic wave reached us thirty years late. We knocked on heaven's door, we put up any old ladder against the walls of ruined buildings if we thought it could be a stairway to heaven.

But not the new people. They don't need the sky any more. And quite right, sky gazers go mad. Here, down below, we have work and homes but up there you'll find nothing but glacial blueness. Just looking at the ceiling is terrifying enough – what if you find a hole in it? Those who have seen the sky find it hard to live on the earth.

That's why they don't look. Only a small number have found a short cut, or think they've found a short cut – they'll travel to the sky along the white lines of cocaine and heroin, they'll get in through the back door.

We wanted to ascend.

Everyone saw the sky and the road there in his own way. Aslan just wanted to be a pilot. He wanted to fly through the white clouds in a silver aeroplane, high above the earth. When you soar over the earth, everything becomes small at first, then you can't see it at all. Just ribbons of rivers and unknown cities glimmering at night like precious gems. That is how the angels see the earth, and Aslan wanted to become one of them.

He became an angel, burnt to death in his trainer plane on the take-off strip when the Grozny aerodrome was bombed by unmarked aircraft.

I first ascended into the sky in 1989. On an Aeroflot plane, a Grozny-Leningrad flight. I remember looking through the window at the cotton-wool blanket of clouds, through whose holes I could see the earth, so distant and small.

Childhood is paganism. In childhood we talk with the trees and the grass, we know the soul of the wind and see the face of the rain. My paganism knew its gods by name: in my room, on the table where I did my schoolwork, lay thick academic editions of the Aryan myths.

Looking through the cabin window, I almost saw the gods. Shadows scudding across the clouds were not just shadows: it was Indra travelling with his retinue of Gandharvas and Apsaras, heavenly musicians and dancers.

Against the solar disc shone the figures of the Ashwini divine twins. And, of course, here was the sun itself. I knew its 108 names: Surya, Aryaman, Bhaga, Tvashtri, Pushan, Arka, Savitr, Ravi . . . I still remember them.

Yet ascending into the sky on Lufthansa and Emirate Airlines aeroplanes, I don't see them these days. The sky has become empty. No one lives there any more. Now the sky is like a vacated communal apartment, awaiting new owners who will knock down the walls, refurbish it in Western style and fit uPVC double-glazing.

I studied at university, went to lectures, sat exams. But after lectures I went to the library on Mendeleevskaya Liniya and read a pre-Revolutionary edition of *Life of the Buddha* in Konstantin Balmont's translation.

I read translations of the Upanishad. I remember that evening well: I was travelling on the tram, crossing Dvortsovy Bridge. I read that we are sparks which have flown far from the fire. That's why we find it so dark and cold. And everything around is alien. Yes, that's how things are, I realised that was how things are. I have always felt the darkness and cold.

We have to return. To the fire, to the blue sky, eternally aflame with luminescent fire.

That year I dropped out of university, left the girl I wanted to marry, shaved my head and took austere vows. A year later I flew to India, on an Aeroflot plane, a Moscow – New Delhi flight.

That's a long story, another story. But this tale isn't about me. I simply wanted to say that we tried to get to heaven, and that each of us saw the road in his own way.

Marat lived in Gudermes. I don't know what happened to his studies in Grozny – perhaps in independent Ichkeria they closed all the institutes, perhaps there was no point studying in them any more. So, Marat never finished his studies at the oil institute, just like I never finished studying to be a lawyer. Though Marat did start studying something else.

Preachers had appeared in Gudermes, offering instruction in how to become a genuine Muslim. This new Islam differed from the free faith to which the Chechens had been accustomed for hundreds of years. Earlier, Chechens had followed Sufism: religious life was built around the community of believers, headed by the sheikhs, the saints. There were no strict rules or hierarchies. Everyday life was regulated by *adat* – local custom. Such was the way accepted in traditional Islam.

The new preachers did not respect *adat*. Instead of the familiar freedom there were austere and harsh rules of conduct, self-control, regular prayers, submission and discipline.

Marat became a strict Muslim. He grew a beard, prayed regularly, didn't watch television, wouldn't read books or newspapers, didn't drink, didn't smoke, didn't even look at girls.

All this worried Aunty Lyusya terribly. She railed vociferously, shouting herself hoarse, calling the newcomers all kinds of names and banning Marat from the sect's gatherings.

Marat smiled in silence and looked at his mother with his clear blue eyes. Then he pressed her to his breast and said: 'Mama, I love you very much. But this way lies the road to paradise. And there is no other path. I want to return to Allah. Don't you cry. Allah promises that each of His faithful servants will be able to take all his relatives to paradise. I'll take you with me to heaven, Mama.'

Faithful servants of Allah must take part in jihad, in holy war. After teaching the theory of the creed, they began preparing the neophytes for religion in practice. Marat was trained on the sabotage course.

When the Federal troops were approaching Gudermes, Auntie Lyusya shut Marat up in the summer kitchen. She put out a camp bed for her son, locked the door from the outside and went to bed but in the morning Marat was gone. He had escaped his house arrest through the narrow ventilation window. The sabotage training had not been in vain.

That little window was to become his gate to paradise. And he was carried to paradise in a battered old truck. He and many others like him, the sabotage group given the task of mining the approach to Gudermes.

They didn't know that the rebels had already made a deal with the Federals to surrender the city without a fight. That they had been offered in sacrifice.

The truck contained explosives and mines, but not a single assault rifle.

On the early morning road the Federals awaited them. They allowed the truck through then encircled it.

There was little beauty or heroism in their deaths. To die like that is neither beautiful nor heroic: to tumble out of a truck, run in different directions along the roadside and fall face down after single shots fired by OMON paramilitaries with cigarettes hanging out of their mouths.

The corpses were loaded into the same truck, driven to Gudermes and turned out in the central square. Auntie Lyusya collected Marat and buried him.

Well, Allaudi had died in a bomb raid. Aslan had died of heart trauma. Out of the whole family only Mareta and Auntie Lyusya were left. They buried Marat.

Nine days later, however, Auntie Lyusya saw Marat alive once more, for the last time.

She awoke in the middle of the night, for no reason, not to relieve herself, not because of any loud noise. She just opened her eyes, then realised what had awoken her. It was that gaze, the gaze of those clear blue eyes. Marat sat on the chair by his mother's bed, looking at her.

He was dressed in dusty camouflage, with a tear at the breast, stains from the caked blood. He looked . . . tired, very tired.

He said:

Forgive me for leaving you, Mama.

Auntie Lyusya started crying and asked: 'My son, how are you?'

He said nothing and didn't even smile in reply.

Then he said:

Soon I'll have to leave for good. I came to say goodbye to you.

Auntie Lyusya asked: 'What's that, my son, are you flying off to paradise? Now you're a shahid, like those preachers taught you, they promised that you'd go to heaven. You wanted to go to heaven so badly, you even ran away from your own mother, through the window. Will you get into your heaven now?'

He averted his eyes and said:

It's not that simple, Mama . . . it's not that simple.

And he was gone.

* * *

This tale is about how we searched for the road to heaven. You probably wanted to find out about the war. You probably wanted to hear of heroism and cowardice, of the tragic deaths of the main characters, you wanted some battles and, of course, a bit of snuff. Perhaps you wanted to read once again about the depravity of leaders and politicians, about the sordidness of those who profit from others' suffering.

You'll find all that without my help, in newspapers and books. You'll see it in films. There'll be plenty of others willing to write about that.

My concerns are elsewhere. There, at the top of the social ladder, you'll find other people who divided up the money and oil, who privatised the country one piece at a time, who fought over power. But we looked for the road to heaven, we knocked on heaven's door. Perhaps we no longer believed that we could find decency and justice here, decided that we wouldn't be deceived again. That's why we wanted so fervently to ascend. With prayer beads or assault rifles in our hands, on the straight path.

And we were deceived again.

This time we were deceived by the sky, and no one reached paradise. We knocked on heaven's door, we had no key, no picklock, we didn't know the entry code. We knocked, Lord it was us knocking on heaven's door! But You didn't let us in. Perhaps You were busy, asleep, or You just weren't home.

That's what I sometimes think, when remembering those years, years which lasted longer than the whole of the rest of my life.

But as I get older, I generally think of things differently. Perhaps we deceived ourselves. We desperately wanted to be deceived. And the truth is that if there is a Heaven, then there is no short cut.

You have to walk a long way, bearing all your troubles patiently, helping your neighbours, preserving love in your heart and not allowing hate in. You have to do good and fight injustice here, on this earth, given to us by God for our life. To become a better person, perfect ourselves, change the world for the better. And if need be, to fight for this.

It is a long road, but we cannot cut corners or jump the red lights, sirens wailing. Each of us, individually and collectively, persons and nations, we have to walk this path. We have to conquer evil, to rise above hatred.

This world will never be perfect. Once we've done our very best, however, we'll be able at least to leave it with a clean conscience.

And then the doors will open. The doors of heaven.

Notes

1. International Women's Day.
2. Russian school grades range from one to five (five being the highest).
3. Russian for 'fluff'.
4. Russian for 'cannon'.
5. The Turkic name for Chechnya adopted upon secession from the USSR. Ichkeria was originally the poetic name for the mid-highland region.
6. 'Federal' refers throughout to the armed forces of the Russian Federation.
7. The Chechen goddess of fertility.
8. From the Bhagavad Gita.
9. Son of the poets Nikolai Gumilev and Anna Akhmatova, a Russian historian who developed theories on ethnogenesis and founded the Neo-Eurasianist movement. Many of his works were banned under Communism.
10. Meaning the vital energy of an ethnos, subject to phases of growth and decline.
11. As proposed in Lev Gumilev's theories.
12. Russia's Federal Security Service, successor to the KGB.
13. Caucasian sheepskin hat.
14. Russian for 'sunrise'.
15. Russian for 'swallow'.

16. From a song by Vladimir Vysotsky (1938–90).
17. From Kabardino-Balkaria, in the North Caucasus.
18. These were the cards predicted to win a fortune for the protagonist in *The Queen of Spades*, Pushkin's supernatural tale.
19. Joseph Stalin's nickname.
20. From a Young Pioneer song.
21. Mighty heroes in Russian folklore.
22. Medieval Russia.
23. Translations by Mohammed Marmaduke Pickthall.
24. An austere outlaw warrior, 'noble bandit' of the highlands.
25. A wild and skilful horseman of the Caucasus.
26. In contemporary Russian *nemtsy* means 'Germans'.
27. Aged twelve or thirteen.
28. Aged fourteen or fifteen.
29. Awarded to a nationally ranked player.
30. Typical Caucasian first names.
31. Vladimir Putin.
32. Mufti Talgat Tadzhuddin, head of the Central Spiritual Board of Muslims of Russia.
33. This verse refers to the miraculous victory at the Battle of Badr. The Muslims were heavily outnumbered – 313 Muslims to over 900 pagans. Yet thousands of angels swelled their ranks and they won.
34. Pope Innocent III.
35. One of the most important field commanders of the Chechen resistance (nicknamed Lone Wolf).
36. A 'filtration camp' notorious for the brutal torture and abuse of its detainees.
37. A soft drink made from fermented bread.
38. The Soviet term for the Second World War (or, more specifically, the Eastern Front).

39. Aged sixteen.
40. A decadent poet, founder of the Ego-Futurist literary movement (1887–1941).
41. 'Foreign literature', a Soviet magazine.
42. 'Changeover'.
43. 'Glowworm'.
44. 'Sheet Lightning'.
45. Mikhail Lermontov, 'Borodino'.

Translator's Acknowledgements

This translation is dedicated to the memory of Ilya Kormiltsev, publisher, poet, friend. Without Ilya Kormiltsev's courage and vision, *I am a Chechen!* would never have been published.

My heartfelt thanks to Robert Chandler, Stuart Williams at Harvill Secker, Oliver Ready, Miriam Frank, Clive Perrett, Emma Craigie, Evelyn Frank and Philippa Rees. Above all, I am deeply indebted to my husband Alexander for all his invaluable help.

www.vintage-books.co.uk